SIERRA DELMAR
Katharine Branham

Your Divine Birthright Publishers

Published by Your Divine Birthright Publishers

www.ydbpublishers.com

Copyright © 2024 Katharine Branham

All rights reserved.

First Edition

No part of this book may be reproduced, stored in a retrieval system, or transmitted by any means, electronic, mechanical, photocopying, recording or otherwise without written permission from the author.

Editorial:

Ray Thompson

Sabrina Galindo

Cover Art:

Consuelo Parra Perez

Cover/Interior Design

YDB Publishers

ISBN'S:

eBook- 978-1-956925-17-3

Paperback-978-1-956925-25-8

Hardcover-978-1-956925-49-4

Your Divine Birthright® is a registered trademark with the United States Patent and Trademark office.

Contents

Dedication	V
Introduction	VI
Author's Note	VIII
1. Retaining	1
2. Coming for Cole	32
3. Foot Fetish	62
4. No-Child Policy	90
5. Kissing Homeless	115
6. A Slap of Confidence	132
7. Out of Balance	159
8. Tripping Relief	182
9. Last Night	216
10. True Confession	243
11. Spiritual Crossroad	279
About the author	296

Also by Katharine Branham

Dedication

To the real Sierra Delmar.
Thank you for finding *ME*.

Introduction

I felt a deeply profound kindness in Sierra's energy field the first time I spoke with her. The energy field is the light around any living thing, referred to as the aura. The aura allows a better way of seeing a being's true essence. You usually don't see it on the surface of a person, like the way they dress or their mannerism. An aura or energy field gives details of certain aspects of that being (i.e., illness, kindness, trauma, and love). I knew Sierra's career was no indication of the soul inside her.

She thought those claiming to live a daily spiritual life would consider her broken. Sierra explained that well-known spiritual gurus would call her names when she tried to seek their guidance.

Even professionals often discarded Sierra, except for a psychiatrist named Dr. Vasquez, who referred Sierra to me. The year I met Sierra was a time of some significant spiritual leaps. She confided in me, and I held a safe space for her. We began to change each other the moment our lives crossed paths. There were moments when, even in the eye of danger, I learned the spiritual dynamic of why we met.

This journey was about getting to know the person's heart, not what they do for a living. I have learned so much from the spirit world while reading for clients over the years. Many things I knew I would not have thought to ask or wouldn't have seen if it were not for them. Most of the time, I don't get the opportunity to meet my clients in person. Those who I have met in person have been highlights of my career. A deeper spiritual bond for us may not be apparent through those unique connections. But I now understand that meeting them in person and being in the same space can be life-changing on both the spiritual and physical levels.

A desperate call from Sierra's sister, Marisol, changed how I view my client connections. Sometimes, I would get emergency calls in the middle of the night to visit a rehab or hospital to meet with a client. Those were all discussed and agreed upon before the meeting. In the case of Sierra, it was more than an agreement between us. It became a journey.

The journey was more than a *request*. It became a *quest.*

Author's Note

This book is based on true events. It reflects the author's present recollections of experiences over time.

Some names and characteristics have been changed, some events have been compressed or added, and some dialogue has been recreated.

Chapter 1

Retaining

Google has educated us all in some way. Many people have different opinions about Google. But for someone like me who doesn't spend much time researching, it's much simpler to *google* the answer. As you'll soon learn, this quick research tool became very useful in understanding the vocation of a future client—Sierra Delmar.

I had recently received an email request from Dr. Francine Vasquez. She is a psychiatrist in Chicago, for whom I had previously done psychic readings. Dr. Vasquez has been a great source of new client referrals. She only refers someone to speak with me if they want to understand their spiritual walk more. I understood that this must be the case with this newest referral—Sierra Delmar. My spirit guides urged me to answer her back and accept the request. Sierra was delighted when I replied that I could have a session with her later that afternoon.

Accepting that day's session came with some homework: to *google* what a dominatrix was because I had no prior understanding and she insisted that I quickly learn. I knew that whoever Sierra Delmar was, she had already researched me well. I had set our appointment for 2:00 p.m. While *googling* the definition of dominatrix, my love and manager, Butchie, stopped by and came into the office to drop off a file on my desk.

Now, to help you understand about Butchie better: I gave him that nickname because he is far from anything *Butch*. He is the *anti-butch*, if that's a thing: masculine looking on the outside but kindhearted on the inside. Don't bother spellchecking Butchie or waste your time *googling* the word Butchie. The rabbit hole you will fall into is much deeper than anyone ever wants to go. I went down that hole myself, admittedly.

Butchie glanced at the computer screen, noticing what was in the Google search bar and the information it produced. He seemed shocked and began to read in a very automated voice, "Dictionary states dominatrix—noun—a woman who takes the dominating role in BDSM sexual activities." He sat on the stool next to the desk, stretched his legs, and crossed his arms. A smirk began forming on his mouth as he curiously shook his head.

I laughed and said, "I have a new client who requested that I understand what she does for a living before our session."

Butchie uncrossed his arms, repositioned himself on the stool, and picked up the lint roller to clear the debris on his shirt. "She surely doesn't understand how much you can already see about her!" he exclaimed.

I turned my chair to face him and explained, "If she asked me to look it up, it wasn't for my benefit. It was for hers."

"What do you mean?" he asked.

I explained, "She wanted to ensure I was not condemnatory. I understand her feelings. Come on, Butchie, think about when we've been out, and someone strikes up a conversation with me, asking what I do for a living. I don't always tell them about my profession. First, I look at their energy psychically, and then if I know they cannot mentally comprehend my work, I will say, 'I do yard work.'"

Butchie's eyes widened as the answer tickled his funny bone.

"It's not a lie. I do yardwork, housework, and other things," I protested.

Butchie reverently nodded in agreement, rubbed his shin, and laughed, recalling a few nights before when I kicked him under the table to stop talking about my work.

Anytime the question "What do you do?" is asked, it's always open to interpretation. I could say I hula hoop, tap dance, and play the drums, but that could require more conversation than I'm willing to give. It's amusing sometimes when I look at the color in their energy field and see judgment, noticing how their eyes shift when I answer.

Butchie stood up and glanced down at the stack of papers on my desk while he made a list of the errands he needed to run. "I have lots to do today," he explained— "dry cleaners, get cat food, and go to the mall for a dress shirt." He glanced at my outfit and offered, "Do you want to come with me? We could have lunch, and I'll help you find an outfit for your Tuesday interview."

He laughed, "You can help me find the right shin protection to wear when I am around you."

I stood behind the desk and said, "Yes, to lunch and the mall, but no to the other since I need to be back before two o'clock for a call with this new client."

As Butchie and I pulled into the mall parking lot, we noticed a large sign, 'Grand Opening,' hanging over what looked to be a new, cool-looking flower shop. It was a few shops down from the vegan burger joint where we planned to have lunch.

Neither can pass up a new shop, so we just had to stop in.

Upon entering, I noticed a counter in the back with the most beautiful arrangements. The woman who greeted us had a unique green energy field around her. I was delighted by the uncomplicated swirls in her energy field.

There was also a gift shop side, and I noticed Butchie was already making new friends. As I approached, he held up a small shopping basket with a handful of purse alarms, typically marketed to women for extra protection to feel safe.

Butchie showed me his basket. "Pick out which color you want", he suggested. "I am getting you and Breezy both one. This way, I can feel better knowing you have it when I'm not with you."

I selected a pink one for my daughter, Breezy, and a blue one for myself.

After lunch and the mall visit, Butchie dropped me at home and drove off to finish his errands. I skipped to the community mailbox, just a rock throw from the front door.

I opened the box and found a small package marked overnight delivery. A beautiful perfume-like scent emerged from the box; my guides told me it was from my new client. I was in such a great mood that I didn't stop to think about the box's contents—sometimes, clients send personal items falsely thinking it will help me with the reading. I just skipped back to the house, singing joyfully, unaware of the mail dropping everywhere!

When I did manage to get the mail stack in order, I took everything up to the office and plopped down in the chair. I set the mail down and reached for my phone to check for new messages. There was a mysterious text from my new client, Sierra Delmar, that read:

> Confirmation shows you received the box. Please open it now.

I sifted through the mail, dropping most of it in the recycle bin – except for my son Zach's Chess magazine and the box from Sierra.

The box was well sealed. A stack of money and a tiny note card slid out when I sliced the end open. It read: *Here is Twenty-five Thousand dollars, which should be enough to retain you for a year.* The amount of cash in the box was exactly the yearly amount I charge a client for my special access promotion. It allows them to call or text me a quick question anytime, day or night. The promotion worked well for medical or legal clients who needed to contact me by calling or texting at odd hours but didn't need full one-hour sessions with me.

The phone rang at exactly two o'clock.

I answered, "Hi, Sierra."

"Hello, Katharine. I'm thrilled to talk with you today. I have friends who have had readings with you." She sounded happy.

I sensed her energy was good. She seemed to have a beautiful heart.

"Sierra, I, too, am grateful to read for you. I did not imagine you would want more than a few sessions. The twenty-five thousand dollars is a yearly fee for those who don't want long sessions but would like to access me by text, phone call, or Facetime for fifteen to twenty-minute visits at a moment's notice."

I could hear her shuffling a few things around and I knew she must have been pulling items out of shopping bags. Sierra had the phone on speaker. I was remote viewing her and caught a glimpse from her line of view of the bags she was removing items from. I noticed the items were from high-end stores.

Sierra explained, "My psychologist, Dr. Francine Vasquez, is one of the friends I mentioned who had a session with you. It was Dr. Francine who suggested I book an appointment. When I heard you offer this VIP package session that allows me to call or text you anytime, I knew that would be better for me. Are you okay with taking me on as a VIP client?" she asked.

I noticed my spirit guides, who were now in the room. With a positive confirmation, they motioned for me to work with Sierra.

"Yes, of course," I stated. "Why do you feel you need to have readily access to calls and texts? That is usually for people in the legal or medical field."

There was a long pause before she spoke.

"Most professionals don't seem to agree with what I do for a living," she said. "I need to be as transparent as possible before any sessions because I have had people refuse to work with me. But I knew you could psychically look into my life and energy field. I was curious if you'd allow me to book a session. Francine had a sister who wanted to read with you, but you told her she should find someone else, that you didn't feel you would be the psychic she needed to talk to."

My spirit guides shared that Sierra knew why I had turned away Francine's sister, but I was being tested for some reason.

I explained to Sierra, "Sometimes when someone wants to book a session with me, I go to write it in my schedule, and my spirit guides or *their* spirit guides say: *This client is not ready for what you need to tell them.* So, I end up canceling and referring them out."

There are a couple of reasons for this. Sometimes, they are not ready to hear what they need to do or how to take steps to change their current mindset. Secondly, they need a few more hard lessons to get there. Lastly, there's the case with Dr. Francine Vasquez's sister—I saw her death coming soon.

Francine learned soon enough why I refused her sister—she was killed a few months later in an automobile crash.

If someone does not know they are going to die soon, and I have a session with them, one of their questions may be: "What do you see for me next year?" And knowing they are not ready to hear me tell them to get their affairs in order, I tend to refuse the reading.

Francine knew something was coming when I refused to have a session with her sister. Although, she didn't ask.

I could feel that Sierra already knew the information I just shared. Suddenly the bags Sierra had been rustling with became silent.

"It was worth twenty-five thousand just to see if you would have a session with me!" Sierra exclaimed. "I, too, get strong intuitions at times, and I have been worried about a job recently offered to me. Francine had told me that you refunded people and refused a reading when you knew you couldn't help them or you knew they would be leaving Earth soon. I was relieved that you chose to read for *me*."

She paused for a minute. Her voice changed as her energy began to shift.

"The two of us chatting now is confirmation that it would be fine for me to accept the four-week job offer up north," she said excitedly.

I scanned her body psychically and could see her living several years into the future. So, I understood this to mean she would be here on Earth well beyond the job she is referring to.

I answered, "Well, I did check for any unforeseen departures before our call. Your life force looked good for the next several years."

Sierra blurted out, "You're the best! That's what I was hoping to hear."

I paused for a few seconds, knowing there was more to why our paths had crossed. Immediately, I felt a wave of energy and anxiousness run through me.

This feeling only occurs in cases of personal growth. I noticed my spirit guides were standing next to me in protective mode. I began to realize this may be part of *my* spiritual development. I could sense there were spiritual lessons ahead for both Sierra and myself.

"Sierra, the fact you will live through this job may not be what we need to examine," I explained. "Maybe the focus should be on the decisions you're making with this job and how it is effecting your spiritual path."

Sierra's murky orange energy field indicated she was scared about something ahead. Still, she didn't want to stop because it was her primary source of income. I felt an overwhelming sensation that her decision was careless.

We continued talking for forty-five minutes. During our conversation, I realized Sierra was a romantic at heart despite the tough girl persona she showed the world. I could see the room she called me from was her bedroom.

The closet door was open. Sierra had dolls lining the top few shelves, usually used for handbags. My spirit guides motioned for me to look at the books stacked near her nightstand. One of them had a handwritten note on it.

The books were from a mystery suspense writer who turned several of his stories into blockbuster movies. When my spirit guides highlighted the author's name for me to notice, I realized the books themselves were not my main focus.

When something is energetically highlighted, spirit is informing me to remember it. *This must be something important for me to know*, I thought. I decided not to tell her I saw the book or the author's name since she would have already told me if she wanted me to know.

When the session ended, she professed, "I feel that I can trust you and trust you'll never divulge this to anyone unless I tell you it's okay."

I smiled and said, "I would never tell anyone."

After the call ended, I got up to walk outside and release some of the energy I felt during our conversation. I walked down the street to the bus stop since I knew Zach's bus would drop him off in ten minutes. A big, affectionate cat was rolling around in the driveway in front of the bus stop. I noticed the thread of energy from the cat to the house next door, which showed me he lived there.

I squatted down next to him and lightly petted *Loverboy's* belly. I knew *Loverboy* was not his name, but it seemed to suit him better than Henry, which is on the name tags hanging from his collar. He loved rolling in his neighbor's driveway. Somehow, I didn't notice the sound of the bus pulling up to the kid's drop off as I had become so engrossed in this sweet cat.

Zach jumped off the bus while flinging his backpack over one shoulder, overjoyed to see me.

"Mom!" he exclaimed. "I'm surprised you walked down here. I didn't know you ventured this far from the house."

I smiled, "I have been working on walking farther and farther each day. I have to keep telling myself I am very close to home, and if I need to get back, I can do it."

While we walked and talked about his day, he proudly added, "I did my homework on the bus coming home."

As we turned onto our street, Breezy had just made it home and stood in the driveway. "Wow, Mom, where did you go? I got home, looked for you, and started to panic when I couldn't find you," she said.

"I walked down to the bus stop and visited with Henry until Zach's bus arrived," I explained.

I saw Breezy and Zach look at each other in surprise because I don't normally walk off our street, much less down the main street to the bus stop. I can't blame them for their shock. For about ten years, I didn't leave the yard of our house on foot, and I didn't drive more than five miles in any direction.

Breezy moved next to me. "I'm proud of you for walking and trying to push your limits," she said.

I knew Zach was happy, too, but he was busy dribbling the basketball and working on his best Michael Jordon shot.

While watching Zach, I zoned out, thinking about my earlier call with Sierra. I thought about her acceptance of being restrained or tied up by her clients. It wasn't an experience that I would ever like.

Sierra's call made me think about an evening out with friends when I was twenty-two...

The location was a karaoke club in Houston. I was apprehensive about going because spirits had tried to warn me, but I didn't want to let my friends down, so I went anyway.

It was forty minutes from my home on Westheimer Road, so I rode with a trusted friend. The place was packed, and there turned out to be ten in our group. The MC was walking around, inviting people onto the stage to sing.

My friend Stephanie had a fantastic voice. She would take song requests, mainly from me. I loved hearing her sing two songs: *Sitting at the Dock of the Bay* by Otis Redding and Delta Dawn by Tanya Tucker. The MC kept coming over and talking to me.

He made me so nervous that my hands were sweating, although my hands don't usually do that. Some other girls at the table were flirting with him and thought he was cute and made comments that they'd like to fuck him.

I didn't trust him, and he seemed so pushy. Most everyone at the table was drinking except for four of us. Two of the four who were not drinking were Stephanie and me.

By now, the table had grown massive, with people I didn't know joining. Stephanie had been singing on stage off and on several times that evening. No one was paying attention to drinks.

Whenever they'd finished singing, they'd return, sip their drink, and look for another song.

Stephanie said she was not feeling right and brushed it off as being tired. I was exhausted, too, and mentioned a local diner to get her some coffee so we could drive home.

The energy around her body didn't look normal. We asked the other girls if they wanted to go to the diner next door, and they said no. Everyone had decided to go to the MC's apartment.

He lived next to the club, and some people who joined the table mentioned they had gone after the club closed to keep the party going. Stephanie and I got into her car to drive to the diner and pick up coffee.

She said, "Let's just sit here for a few minutes, and then I'll be fine."

I didn't believe that, but I was too tired to argue.

We must have both fallen asleep at the same time.

I woke up with my wrists bound together and tied to an ornate queen-sized bed. My purse was on the floor, I had a crick in my neck, and my shoes were gone. I was fully dressed and wearing black tights with seams up the back.

I would have known if somebody had undressed me because it's difficult enough for me to line-up those seams much less someone else.

I had the smell of bourbon on me. Stephanie was nowhere in sight, and it was daylight.

I could hear music lightly playing from the other room. I tried to work my wrist out from the rope. The MC entered the room smiling. He was wearing boxers lowered on his waist and no shirt.

"I hope you're not sore with me," he said while running his fingers through his hair.

He sat down next to me, touching my inner leg, and began kissing my neck. I then realized where the bourbon smell came from; he reeked of it.

I heard the spirit guides say, *he will let you go if he thinks you will see him again. It's the only way out.*

He put his hand on my leg and tried to kiss me.

I played along.

"I didn't realize you liked me," I stated. "My friend Raeann is in love with you."

"I like you, though," he said.

I nervously replied, "I think I'm gonna be late for work, but how about I come over after I get off?"

"No, I want you now *and* later," he urged while kissing me.

I reluctantly kissed him back, thinking this was my only way out.

I said, "I have to go to work. Then I can come back to play with you."

He was eager to get me untied, thinking I wouldn't resist and maybe give in.

There was no way I was going to do anything with him.

When I emerged from the bedroom, I tried to stay calm and reminded him I didn't want to lose my job. His place looked like a major party had taken place. A guy was sleeping on the floor, and a woman had been passed out on the table.

He picked up the phone while smiling at me and ordered a cab.

I held his hand, guided him to the front door, and opened it. I asked if he would wait with me until the cab showed up.

He was looking at me, excited that I was going to come back. He stayed with me until the cab pulled up, and I faked liking him until I got in the cab.

Well, of course, I didn't go back, but I did call the police when I got to work. Stephanie never mentioned what happened to her, but I knew it was horrible. She moved to Oklahoma shortly after that night.

That night is only one example of why I learned not to ignore guidance from the universe.

I did respect Sierra's life path, but I knew she would have a turning point and realize the danger is not worth the money.

The phone lit up with a text from a local client, Shannon, requesting a call. Shannon was one of the wealthiest women in Houston. I met her while doing a psychic reading at a party. Since that party, I have read for her and most of her friends.

She was a sweetheart to me, but seemed to get under the skin of others.

I had an instant admiration for her due to her tireless efforts in fundraising for homeless pets.

The problem i had was that she lived in the Memorial area of Houston, and the traffic was more than I could handle driving. My anxiety can often kick in at any moment. I get stressed when I become engrossed in a deeper-dimensional view, and spirits begin to show me things they think I need to know.

When I notice these random spirits, I habitually see what happened to them. Often, I don't realize I'm still in the present moment. It feels like I am there, where and when they lived, and then suddenly, I am here again at my present location and time.

When I don't recognize I am here in the present moment while peering into another dimension, I immediately begin to have a panic attack. Breezy and Zach have learned to recognize the onset of these events, and they know keywords that can calm me down.

The most calming words are *you are here,* and *you are safe.*

I often had Breezy drive me when I needed to go places until Butchie introduced me to a guy named Carter Adams. Butchie knew Carter during his Army times. They worked closely together in several classified missions and both retired as Major's.

Major Carter lived close by and now owned an executive limousine service that catered to the elites of Texas. The elites used the service because the drivers received special training in emergency situations.

Carter looked tough but had a heart of gold and was incredibly honest. He was married to his high school sweetheart, Marilyn, and they had an adorable son named Ramsey.

Butchie, Carter, and Marilyn first met at Fort Campbell and then deployed to Germany the same year.

As a result, all three of them speak fluent German.

Marilyn was not enlisted in the Army, but married Carter the day after he signed up.

Before I met him, Butchie told me about some of Carter's special training and how skilled he was at just about everything you could imagine. His car service was also the only one Butchie trusted to drive me anywhere if he or Breezy were unavailable.

Carter was a very calm person, and that always helped, too. He had seen me in full panic mode and knew the words and phrases to get me back to this world. It's hard to explain to those who cannot imagine it, but when I look into a space, I can see and feel what is happening now and what happened in the past. I see the people and events from the past taking place as though they are in the now. This can be physically crippling at times, to the point I can't even walk and need assistance to stand.

I knew if Butchie trusted Carter, then I would, too.

By the color and beauty of his energy field, I knew he was a good person.

It's interesting how a couple can be different yet simultaneously similar. Carter's wife, Marilyn, was a hoot. She was the life of the party, while Carter was quiet and observed everything and everyone. He didn't creepily do this; it was performed more in a military Special Ops kind of way.

Marilyn's maiden name was Monroe, and her parents thought it sounded good together.

She looked like a Black Marilyn Monroe and was very beautiful.

She once told me she took on more of that persona in her teens when she heard about Hollywood's Marilyn. She was in drama classes and always landed the lead role, as no one could compete with her.

I could definitely see that.

She would wear her hair like a blonde Marilyn, too; not so much the color of her hair but the style, and she always looked like a million bucks.

Carter and Marilyn knew that in the past, I couldn't travel beyond the confines of my house, and this lasted for many years. Some of the progress I had made just going into a grocery store was monumental.

It isn't the store's space that freaks me out so much as stepping into another dimension. It intrigues me so much that after experiencing it, I realize I have forgotten where I am in that moment, and I go into full panic, thinking I am far from where I believe I'm safe.

Sadly, the only real place I feel safe is my house. When I remote-view, I merely think about the location or person and see what is around them.

This was something I could always do, but now I am at a point where I can just think on it and I will see it instantly.

My business was booming. It had gone from a solid medical intuitive practice, looking into a person's medical issues by viewing their energy field, to remote viewing the personal life of an individual that my client was interested in.

I conducted two distinctive types of readings. Usually, medical field workers inquired about a patient, or a doctor referred someone to me who refused some type of medical test. This is where I would look into their energy field and see what was medically wrong. Of course, I was their last resort, but if the patient refused any tests, the doctor would say they knew a lady who could see into the body.

Then they would share my background about how I have helped others.

The doctors would ask, "If she says you need a test, would you at least do that?"

The patient would be open to talking to me versus doing nothing.

The other type of readings, callers primarily from the psychic hotline, are with people who do not care about anything other than getting details at that pressing moment.

Those callers do not care about expanding their gifts or developing a spiritual life. The majority only care about what is needed in their 3D experience for temporary satisfaction. They maintain a facade to impress others but never attain spiritual growth.

Some people laugh at me and my choice of outfits—some days, I look like I got dressed in the dark. When you get down to it, I am not focused much on how I dress. My only focus is work, but I do enjoy having lunch with the kids, Butchie, and friends.

I will force myself to stop for lunch and not let people book a session during my break time. Even when the kids were at school, I would go to lunch alone or with a friend. I don't get panicked as much because I have all my favorite places to eat within a two-mile radius.

My absolute favorite place is a nearby deli because of the friendly employees and the sweet tea, which is my only addiction. I volunteered for five years with a group on a feeding route for county cats spayed or neutered and then released. My responsibility was to leave fresh water and food.

It's a *Meals on Wheels* for cats.

I help the county control the cat population by feeding, trapping, fixing, and re-releasing them. I am proud to say that I have found homes for all the cats I have trapped. This has become a secret passion of mine.

The only people who knew I did this were the employees of the places where I'd trap the cats at. They would see me bring food and water in the early hours.

There were a few days I was sick and couldn't go, so I sent Breezy and Zach to put food down. There was no way I would have felt good about eating if I knew the cats were hungry.

I told Butchie about the cat experiences; everything from trapping them to their forever homes, and he loves to help me, too. Sometimes, he finds a puppy or cat that needs help and takes them to a vet and pays for it himself.

That is just one of the many reasons to love Butchie.

He does have a kind heart. And he will do anything for me. I would call him for support in the morning while dropping food off for the cats because it was still dark, and I felt unsafe.

He would insist that I wait until daylight, but I tend to have early appointments and need to feed the cats first. I have everything I need for my cat trips in the back of my car. The typical items are extra blankets, paper food bowls, jugs of water, food for cats and dogs, and a cage in case I need to trap a new cat.

We have three cats and two dogs of our own, which is enough for us. However, I often think I have too many cats, especially when it's time to clean litter boxes. Our cats are housed inside a patio, where the litter boxes stay. The two dogs are housed inside, under the stairwell, and are let outside for exercise and potty breaks.

We keep this arrangement for the pets mainly because our street is backed up to a busy road, and I have seen too many dead cats along the roadside. The other reason for not leaving the dogs outside is that our neighbor behind us, Ms. Gibson, harbors raccoons. This sheltering has the potential to lead to a serious and dangerous situation.

I am not talking about one or two raccoons, but three generations.

I know it is three generations because she proudly boasted how the females bring their young to meet the humans when they are ready.

They have infested her home.

It started with her feeding them in the attic after the raccoons had broken in, but then it became entertainment for her as she had cameras installed to watch them while she was at work.

Ms. Gibson works at the funeral home in town as a makeup artist for the deceased. She is a seventy-three-year-old sweet and stylish woman. Lately, she has been coloring her hair pink. Surprisingly, she wears it well, not in an 'oh no, my hair is pink' way. You have to admit it can be charming on older ladies.

She sent me photos of raccoons dining on top of her table, which made me cringe because of the possible diseases they could transmit. Ms. Gibson would text me periodically about random things, but never about a psychic question. The bottom line is that she is a lady who keeps to herself.

But sometimes it's crazy scary living near her and reminds me of the movie: *The Sandlot.* Zach and his friends have lost various toys over the fence and would not even dare each other to go and retrieve them.

They were afraid that Ms. Gibson's raccoon army would get them.

After dinner, a few evenings later, I checked the status on the psychic hotline. Four people were in line waiting to talk to me, so I sat down and pressed 1 on my phone to accept the first caller.

I waited for the hotline to connect me.

I had been reading for some clients for several years on the hotline. They only seemed to have a couple of questions each time. It wasn't enough to warrant an hour call, so I was happy to maintain my listing for this site.

I had never asked a client from the hotline to call me on my private professional site. That particular site is for those who want to awaken or make a spiritual change, and that's not the usual hotline crowd.

I answered, "Hi, this is Katharine. How may I help you?"

She hesitated, "Hi...um...well, my name is Roxy, and I want to ask about Craig. Do you see him ever marrying me?"

Roxy's spirit guides moved forward, opening a spiritual window to Craig. They showed me that Roxy had been a caregiver for Craig's wife, who was an invalid. They also told me Craig would never leave his wife.

It was Roxy who only wanted to torment his wife.

I must've paused too long because Roxy began to get irritated and asked, "Hey, are you getting anything?"

I was startled by her voice and responded, "Yes. I'm sorry, Roxy. Your spirit guides told me that the guy you're asking about is very much married. And that *you* have enjoyed the thrill of tormenting his wife."

I continued, "When I asked your spirit guides if he would ever marry you, they said no. They continued saying that Craig will give you a ring but never follow through with an actual marriage ceremony. You can expect the ring soon, even though he'll never get a divorce from his current wife. He believes the ring will keep you happy for the time."

Roxy's energy shifted to anger, and she bellowed, "I told him if he doesn't file for divorce and ask me to marry him soon, I'm out of here."

She paused and then asked, "Do I mean anything to him? Can you at least take a look at the situation?"

Her spirit guides opened a window and showed me that his wife, Emily, had made all the money in the relationship.

Craig lacked the motivation to be successful on his own. He had known all along that he would be set financially if they married. When Emily was diagnosed with multiple sclerosis, she had to be monitored by a home healthcare professional. Roxy had been hired as an in-home care person for Emily.

When his wife became bedridden and unable to speak, Craig had cameras installed all over the house. Even though Emily could not move her head by herself, she could see the monitor screen and knew he was not far away. Emily could see him wash the car when he was in the driveway, giving her peace.

When Roxy's spirit guides opened a giant portal before me, they showed me that Roxy had started a relationship with Craig. Roxy always made sure that they were in the view of the camera when they were having intercourse.

This was her way of ensuring that Emily knew.

During the times that she was unsure if Emily saw or not, she would just blatantly tell her. Poor Emily wasn't able to do anything about it.

I was being shown that it wasn't Craig who started the relationship as much as it was Roxy. She always made sure to whisper in Emily's ears what she was doing with Craig.

I recognized that this was a challenging situation and explained to Roxy what I was being shown.

Roxy laughed, "That's right! That's exactly what's going on. Emily is such a bitch! I don't like her. She was rude to me long before I was hired to be her daily care provider. Craig didn't realize I had encountered Emily previously while working at a local restaurant."

She continued, "I never said anything. So, when I was hired for this full-time position, I thought it was a perfect way to get to know Craig. I knew right away Craig liked me. He would text me even when I wasn't stopping by to check on Emily, back when I just came by twice a week. He was nice to me."

Roxy continued spilling her guts, "We engaged in conversation, and there were a few times when he acknowledged it was my birthday or Christmas with a gift. He bought me the things I cherished the most."

Roxy began to get angry and raised her voice.

"He can't possibly stay married to Emily! She can't do anything for him. She can't fuck him." Roxy laughed and calmly stated "She can't even get up and take care of herself. I'm the one changing her diapers."

Suddenly, she shifted, "Do you ever feel like he's going to marry me?"

"Listen, Roxy," I said. "I've already told you that he has no intent of going through a marriage ceremony with you. There's nothing I can do about it. I can see the beginning to the end of someone's life. I see the spiritual contracts they have and the true intentions of their heart. His intent with you is to keep you around at this moment, but he will never divorce Emily because of the money."

"That's fucking wrong!" she yelled. "I believe the future can change. I know he's going to recognize the fact I will not stick around and wait for him. Besides, I've had other psychics read for me and tell me the future can change. And they said that Craig will marry me. So, what do you think about that?"

I began in a sympathetic voice, "Roxy, I don't have an emotional attachment to what I'm getting for you. I'm only telling you what your spirit guides are saying. It doesn't matter what other people tell you. Sometimes, they believe telling the customer what they want to hear will keep them coming back. That's just not my way. I'm not going to give you false hope."

I continued, "I will only tell you the truth, so later, whatever you decide to do, you can look back on it and say, *Katharine was honest with me.* Your connection to Craig is as good as it's ever going to get. He will give you a ring, continue to give you extra money, and continue to buy you pretty things. But it will never lead to marriage."

I became even more stern, "Even if he were not married to Emily, he would not marry you. He would find somebody with money to support him and possibly keep someone like you on the side. I'm not a genie. I'm a psychic. I don't change the future. I tell you what your spirit guides are showing or telling me, not what you want to hear."

I could feel her getting irritated, but I knew she understood I was telling her the truth.

"It is up to you to determine if this is a good use of your time or if you could put your time into someone who would be putting time into you," I said. "Someone who you could have a wonderful connection with that's not just using you."

I heard something shatter in the background before Roxy exclaimed, "So much for that stupid Baccarat crystal rabbit he bought me for Easter!"

I glanced by *remote viewing* Roxy and saw she had thrown a crystal rabbit into a full-length mirror, breaking both.

I said calmly, "Roxy, please look at the situation for what it is and make the best decision for you. Is there anything else you would like me to look at?"

I felt Roxy begin to cry, but she didn't let on. She exclaimed, "I will make him pay for everything I want! I know you're right, but I was hoping for something different. Thank you, anyway."

The phone line disconnected, and I was alerted with a prompt from the recorded operator to press 1 for the next caller.

The time seemed to fly, and I noticed two hours had passed. When I finished with the fourth call, the phone alerted another caller. It was Roxy. I started to feel anxious.

She sounded relieved, saying, "Good, I am glad you're still online. So... when I got off the phone with you, I swept the glass under the bed and called Craig. I thought about what you told me and decided to take your advice.

I was nervously thinking, *what advice is she talking about?*

She said, "I will just continue to enjoy this connection as much as possible, but I will find a way to use him!"

She took a breath and continued, "I sent him a text letting him know I needed to go shopping for some clothes and that he needed to meet me at the store. I encouraged him to sneak away from Emily for a few hours but couldn't get him to meet me. He *did* say he would put some money in my account and asked me how much I would need. I told him five thousand dollars. I had never asked him for money before, but the gamble paid off, and he gave it to me."

She stated, "I'm gonna go out tonight and buy something expensive with the money. I'll just keep asking him for more and continue fucking him in front of the cameras so Emily can see *just how much* Craig loves her."

Roxy laughed so proudly as if she had just solved a world problem.

What I was trying to convey and what Roxy heard were two different things. Of course, this is typical for most callers, who only hear what they want.

I calmly replied, "Roxy, I'm afraid you missed the point I was trying to convey when I said, 'Make the best decision for yourself.' I was hoping you would understand and take the high road, finding someone who could put time into you rather than staying with someone who is only using you. When you turn it around by using *him*, it doesn't bring *you* long-term happiness. It is only short-lived and packed with bitterness."

Roxy laughed, "High Road? Nope, I am going backroads. Then I will put it in Emily's face!"

Contemplating her next move, she ended the conversation abruptly by saying, "You have helped me a lot. Thank you, Kat."

The phone disconnected.

I heard the attic ladder being pulled down and wondered what was happening down the hallway. Butchie was talking to Zach. I got up and moved to the office doorway while keeping an eye on Butchie.

He gestured a wave and said, "Are you still working for the day? I came by to see if I could borrow the luggage bag Breezy had used when she went to Germany."

I laughed when I imagined Butchie rolling Breezy's luggage through the airport.

"Sure, but *you* have nicer luggage," I stated.

"Yes, but mine tends to get lost," he said. There are thousands of black bags at the airport. The last time I flew, the luggage didn't arrive on time, and I had to wait a few days for it."

"So, you want to use Breezy's so you can spot it easier?" I laughed.

Unashamed, he remarked, "Absolutely."

I snickered as I watched him examine the big purple bag.

He laughed, "It's hard to miss this thing with the giant unicorn plastered to the side. Who'd wanna steal that luggage?"

"I see your point," I said. "Of course, you can borrow it. Where are you going?"

He answered, "LA. I'm working on a new movie project. I'll be leaving in a week, and I must get everything lined up and packed. My friend TJ is gonna meet me there before filming begins. It's his birthday week, so I got VIP tickets to a Dodgers game. I'm planning to visit some friends and do some shopping."

He paused and said, "TJ will fly back after a week, and I will be on the movie set the following week. I'll be gone for two months, so please take care of Sprinkles for me."

"Wow!" I exclaimed. "I'll miss you. And, of course, I will take care of your kitty-cat."

Later that night, I laid in bed trying to quiet my mind by relaxing into God's light. I tend to have a strange feeling before significant change happens. It's a feeling of being disconnected from everything. It's as if everything is slowly happening before me, with critical points being spotlighted. This usually happens before significant spiritual leaps.

Chapter 2
Coming for Cole

Breezy screamed, "Zach, you're going to be late!" I awoke and kept trying to open my eyes. During that time, it sounded like Breezy was conducting a demolition project in the bathroom.

I finally got my eyes open and made my way out of the bedroom. I saw the door open to the kid's bathroom, and Breezy emerged fully dressed, with hair styled and makeup on. She ran down the stairs, screaming that Zach had missed the bus.

I am not surprised, I thought.

Zach and I were up until midnight watching TV. Sometimes, it feels like Breezy is the adult in the house. She warns us when we lose track of time and are up past bedtime.

I peered into Zach's room. "You need to get up. You know I can't drive you to school!" I exclaimed. "It's out of my driving radius. I'll have to call Carter and see if he has someone to pick you up."

Zach appeared disappointed in missing the bus and suggested, "Mom, you should call a taxi. It would be cheaper."

I smiled at his thoughtful idea and said, "I'm not upset. Besides, I should've been more mindful of our late-night TV watching. You are important to me, and I only trust Carter's transportation service since all his drivers have had a background check and are safe. I'm not comfortable with random taxi drivers."

Zach grabbed his clothes and made his way to the restroom. When he reached the doorway, he gazed at me and said, "Mom, how can you see all these other things psychically, yet you can't see if I'd be safe in a random taxi?"

I answered, "I can't see *everything* psychically, but I have psychically seen a lot of horrible things happen in random taxi cabs. My spirit guides told me you would be safe with Carter's service. You are part of my experience here on Earth. I, like everyone else, am experiencing an earthly life. I'm not *always* privy to what will happen on *my* spiritual path. And you're part of my spiritual path. I don't want to take a chance with my special boy."

I winked at him, and he winked back.

He seemed to understand and continued getting ready while I called Carter's service.

The dispatcher told me Hammad was en route from an airport drop-off and would arrive in fifteen minutes. Hammad was one of Carter's best drivers and was the most requested among businesspeople.

His energy field was a beautiful green, which showed he was a natural healer and a lover of the Earth.

Zach pulled himself together and made a sunflower butter and jelly sandwich while waiting. He stood with his face in the front door window while eating.

I noticed Hammad's black limousine pull swiftly around the cul-de-sac.

Zach yelled, "Hammad is here!" while swinging the door open in his excitement to see him. I waved from the upstairs window, noticing an odd handshake exchange between them.

What is that? I wondered.

At that moment, my spirit guides said, *it is a handshake that Carter taught Zach to identify safe drivers. Carter had told them if a driver does not do the handshake, don't get in the car.*

That's very Carter, I thought as I watched them drive away.

After opening my planner, I noticed that I had four appointments for the day, one of which was Sierra. The phone rang promptly at 2:00 p.m. She had a myriad of questions ready, just like I had asked.

I explained in our last conversation, we could move through quickly with questions and get a lot done if she had the questions ready.

She seemed somewhat hopeful and excited about the session by her tone of voice. She started with her first question about another client and wanted to know if she would be safe accepting the job. After she stated the person's name, I peered into their energy. She wanted me to tell her if I heard 'yes, she would be safe' after each name she gave.

She continued down the list before taking a long pause. I, too, paused to look at her energy, which happened to be a murky red.

I told her to tap her chest like her doctor, Dr. Vasquez, had taught her. Tapping is a technique most commonly known as EFT, which stands for Emotional Freedom Technique. It helps open the flow of energy in the meridians of our body. The method has been very successful for Veterans suffering from PTSD.

"Sierra," I said calmly. "Please put both feet flat on the floor and run your eyes down that list again."

She began repeating the list as I looked for the name that would trigger her energy.

"Okay, stop," I interrupted. I noticed that Sierra began tapping again.

She tried to ignore talking about the trigger by interjecting, "I don't see how this is going to help me."

I peacefully explained, "Doing this helps me to see what happened in the past with you and this person during this lifetime or in a past lifetime. This helps me to see what *will* happen between you and them."

I could tell Sierra didn't want me to look because I noticed the color of her energy field turned to a light grey. Then she said, "Well, it seems a bit creepy since my relationship with all of these guys is sexual."

I explained, "Your sexual connection to someone may not give all the answers, but your spiritual contract could explain why your energy shifted when you stated that name."

I started some energy work on her while explaining how I see and feel things.

Sierra's energy significantly shifted to a dirty orange, and she said, "I know you can see things, but how can you see me now at a distance?"

I knew she'd be surprised because she was unaware I could see a subject like I did.

I told her, "I can see the space surrounding a person, place, or energy as if I am there. I can also see from the subject's viewpoint. This means that I can see what *they* see and feel from their perspective. I use this technique when I read for law enforcement or clients that want to check on their spouses."

Sierra stuttered, "So...um...um... you can see... my place?"

"Yes," I answered. "I saw the bags from the places you shopped at today, the dolls that line the top of your closet, and the hair salon that is ten paces to your right from the front door of your high-rise. I also noticed a small scar on the right foot on top of your big toe along the natural line of the metatarsophalangeal joint. You touch it with your thumb periodically while you are on the phone."

I paused for a moment, then continued, "You seem to use it often as a soothing technique when you are distressed."

Sierra laughed as if she had been entertained by me pulling a coin out from behind her ear. Her energy shifted again while focusing on new questions.

"Why didn't you mention seeing me do all that in the first call?" she asked.

"It was not important for what we discussed," I replied.

I could see Sierra sitting on the edge of her tub while remote viewing her.

She eagerly stated, "Ok, so let me just say what I think I understand: if needed, you can see through my eyes where I am."

I explained that it can be strange for most people to understand this.

"Yes, that is right," I said. "I can see now that you are sitting on the edge of the tub, and there is a small bottle of glitter spilled on your white marble floor. There is a tampon wrapper next to the toilet."

I could tell by her exaggerated breath that she was shocked.

The timer I use to keep track of calls chimed, indicating it was time for my next appointment. Sierra respected the time and didn't push to extend our session. After each session, I clear the intense energy from my body by walking outside to *ground* if the weather permits. Sometimes, I walk around the cul-de-sac in front of my house.

I usually set another timer for fifteen minutes, so when I step outside to avoid getting distracted. This helps me stay on track, so I can start the next session on time.

I returned to the house to prepare for a client named Bailey Sharma.

She contacted me last night asking for an emergency appointment. As I tore the sheet of paper from the notebook from the previous session of my automatic writing, I had a vision of a healthy dead horse. I often get visions before a reading that foretells the storyline. Bailey had insisted on a phone session. I didn't feel she gave me the right last name, though. But I understood she had never read with me and wanted to keep as much privacy as possible.

The phone rang.

I answered, "Hi, this is Katharine. How may I help you?"

The energy was very intense, and a young woman began to speak. "Hi Katharine, I'm Bailey... My father has many thoroughbred horses and a veterinarian team that cares for them. The team makes routine weekly visits, so we all know them well. I have fallen in love with Cole, one of the group's junior veterinarians."

She continued, "We have kept our passion for each other a secret because he is from a different culture and class. A week ago, a senior vet requested a blood vial from each of the four horses. Cole came alone to draw the blood. There was no one else around. Everyone was busy working, and my father had been away traveling for two weeks. It was the perfect time to be alone, and we took the opportunity to have sex in the stables. Cole seemed scared and a bit unusual after we got dressed."

She took a deep breath and continued, "He hurried to draw the blood and left without saying anything to me. Do you feel Cole will be in trouble for anything that happened that day?"

I immediately sensed that a short explanation would not be enough to clarify the deeper spiritual reason for the call. My spirit guides came in and told me that all four horses had been put down because the blood results showed they were infected. But the truth was that only one of the horses was infected, and the other three were healthy.

They continued to explain that Cole took four vials of blood from only the sick horse, and the veterinarian's office put down all four horses, thinking he took a separate vial of blood from each horse individually.

My spirit guides showed me the cameras at the top of the rafters of the stables, letting me know Bailey's father had already seen the video footage. Then they showed me the sick horse again and then three healthy ones. I knew there was something important that they were trying to convey to me. They also showed me a rafter high up in the stables and two other cameras. Now, I began to understand.

I must have paused too long for her comfort because Bailey blurted out nervously, "Hey! Are you still there?"

I felt Bailey's anxiousness, and with a quick sigh, I said, "Walk out to the stables where you and Cole made love. Go do it now!"

Bailey couldn't calm down and asked with great concern, "Is everything going to be okay? I am panicking, and I feel dizzy?"

I knew she would freak out if I told her what I was seeing, but I also knew she had to see it for herself.

"I want you to ride the golf cart out to the stables," I encouraged. "I think it will help calm you down more than walking will. You're going to be fine."

I heard the wind whipping through the phone. The cart began to beep as she backed up. I heard her put the cart in gear and take off. A few minutes into the ride, her spirit guides warned me she needed to stop quickly.

"Bailey, stop!" I exclaimed.

"Wait, what? I am not even close to the door," she answered.

I replied, "I understand, but your spirit guides are asking me to tell you to stop and look up to the right corner at the very edge of the stable."

Bailey answered, "OK, but I'm not seeing anything."

Desperately, she asked, "What am I supposed to be looking for?"

"Your spirit guides said the black round thing at the top corner is a camera," I answered. "They want you to remember what it looks like. Go ahead and proceed into the stables."

I heard the cart stop as she pressed the brake to the floor. It clicked in place, and she hurriedly stepped off. She quickly entered the stable and began walking through it.

"I wish you would just tell me without having me return to the stables!" she exclaimed.

I knew she was about to freak out, but the only way I could get her to understand it was to see it with her own eyes.

"OK, I'm standing exactly where Cole and I were when we started kissing," she said.

I began to direct her, "Bailey, now I want you to go to the place where you ended up making love."

I heard her boots clicking on the ground as she walked to the location.

I continued, "Bailey, I want you to look up to the ceiling of the rafter to the right."

She answered, "OK, I'm standing in the same spot. And I'm looking up to the right. I don't see anything!"

Suddenly, she gasped, "Oh no, there's one of those cameras, the same kind on the outside of the stable."

She began breathing hard and started crying.

Trying to calm her down, I said, "Bailey, it will be okay because your guides are saying the thing your father hates the most is when he feels he is being lied to. And, if you didn't know the cameras were there, you would have carried on with a lie. That would have made things worse. Now, I want you to return to where you were standing when you first greeted Cole. He came in holding some papers."

She closed her eyes and visualized that moment.

I continued, "If you look up, there is a camera above your head on the rafter over the doorway."

"What?" she was confused. "When did my father get all these cameras? I never even knew there were cameras out here. What do I do?"

Bailey's spirit guides showed me the horse again—the sick one and then the three healthy ones.

"Bailey," I began. "When we got on the phone, your spirit guides showed me one sick horse and three healthy ones. They said the four blood vials Cole had drawn all came from one horse, the sick horse. Although Cole did not intentionally want to harm the horses, your father would consider it an egregious act. And this is why he would never forgive Cole."

I continued, "When we started the call, you didn't want to admit you knew what Cole did. You wanted to see if your father would discover the outcome."

She began to speak through the tears and sobbing, "Yes, I thought if you didn't say anything about my father finding out, Cole wouldn't lose his job."

I explained, "I'm sorry, but Cole's going to lose his job and will have difficulty getting hired on at any veterinarian's office ever again. There will be physical repercussions for Cole as I see him getting in an altercation with some of the people who work for your father. Deep down, your father knew you and Cole liked each other but that wouldn't have been an issue.

I continued, "What he's going to be angry about is the needless killing of his healthy horses. The veterinary clinic will be held responsible for Cole's negligence. Your spirit guides told me that some men are coming for Cole."

Still crying, she said, "I know he's gonna be severely angry. Those horses were costly. My dad loved them. I know he loved them more than me!"

I knew there was nothing more I could do for her; the rest she would have to make peace with herself.

As Bailey continued crying, I asked, "Is there anything else you would like me to look at?"

Trying to calm herself down, she said, "No, but I'll be in touch after my father returns."

I was having a tough time shaking off visualizing a bloody Cole. I knew from my spiritual understanding that the beating he would take from the men hired by Bailey's dad wouldn't come close to the harsh experience Cole's Higher Self was going to put him through when he returned to the spirit side.

I get asked about hell and heaven often. And while there is no hell, some may confuse it with an *intense life review* that we all encounter at the end of our physical life experience. Our Higher Self is connected to the creator, who continues to guide us and works toward reconnecting us to be whole again. In a life review, our Higher Self takes us through every experience of pain, suffering, or torment we've ever put another being through. Also, we will have to experience the pain and suffering that 2nd and 3rd parties endured because of our actions. Many people misconceive this scenario as hell.

We experience it all. It is part of what our Higher Self forces us to learn so we know what not to do in the next life. It helps us to understand where we are and what it feels like to be that other being so we will never want to do that again. Some souls learn, while others will find themselves in the same experience doing the same thing or worse during another lifetime.

The toxins we take into our bodies and the altered experiences we perform in this human life keep us from knowing the true actual harm we have done. When the physical body dies, our Higher Self doesn't punish us. Instead, it teaches us. Love and teaching come from a viewpoint entirely different from anything on the human level.

I tried to keep that in mind as I repeatedly got visions of Cole's beating.

I got up from my desk and went outside to clear my energy. My eyes caught the time on the clock, and I realized Zach would be home soon.

I skipped to the bus stop with high expectations that the cat, Loverboy, would be rolling around in the driveway. When I approached Loverboy, a.k.a. Henry, he looked like he was waiting on me.

He seemed to have an internal clock set for when the kids gathered at the bus stop in the morning and when they were delivered back to the stop in the afternoon. Whatever the nirvana that Loverboy was experiencing by rolling in the driveway brightened his energy field. It seemed that there could be nothing more he could ask for. I squatted down and rubbed his belly.

The tranquil moment was interrupted by the screeching sound of the bus one block away. Loverboy was hypnotizing me with his peaceful energy field and loving nature.

I quickly snapped out of it when I heard Zach yell to his friend, Thomas, that he had dropped his book. Zach's aura was a beautiful yellow, which indicated that he was happy. He smiled at me, and we walked down the street towards home.

Then he finally turned to me and said, "I'm so glad you could make it down here again. Have you tried to walk any further?"

"Not as far as I'd like to," I answered. "I'm trying to go a bit further every day. Some days are better than others."

I realized we were alone on this road, and very few people were within eyesight. Suddenly, I noticed a little girl's ghost spirit down the street about fifty feet. I mentioned it to Zach. I knew she wanted to talk to me, but I didn't like going that far yet.

Zach's curiosity kicked in gear and he asked, "Mom, how did the little girl die?"

I immediately went into psychic mode and said, "It looks like she died from neglect. I knew when I saw her, she hadn't been treated for an illness and died from a seizure that a high fever had induced. The people who live in the home now don't know about her. I have driven by there a few times.

I continued, "The little girl's spirit was not out. She usually does not come out until around six o'clock, and I didn't want to call her from in front of the house, so I kept driving."

We continued into the evening by talking about ghosts we had seen, followed by some TV time. I was super tired and didn't realize how fast I fell asleep. I woke up to what sounded like an iron door shutting.

The TV was still on. When I opened my eyes, I realized the door I had heard was from the spirit world, not in my current space-time. My contemplation faded away as I began to stretch my arms upward. The sunshine filled the room, and I felt like I had slept hard.

Zach looked at me with a disappointment and let me know he had missed the bus again.

Are you serious? I thought.

Then I heard my guides say, *It's Saturday; Zach is just trying to be funny.*

I carried on with the game and told him, "You better start walking then." I couldn't keep a straight face and started laughing. He started laughing as well.

We jumped out of bed, woke up Breezy, and got ready for the day.

Later, I received a text from Marilyn letting me know she and Ramsey were running late. We were going to take the kids to the Art show in town. Twenty minutes had passed, and Marilyn finally arrived. Zach swung the front door open and ran to her van. Breezy slowly followed.

The snack bag I had packed was hanging on the stairs. As I went to grab it, I quickly got a flash of Cole lying near Bailey's property. He appeared to be alive, bloody from the beating, and I knew he had some broken ribs and a punctured lung.

I walked out of the house and stepped into Marilyn's van. Zach closed the door from the back seat.

Marilyn looked at me and said, "Whatever that look is from, shake it off, and let's have fun today."

I shook my head, smiled, and said, "Okay, let's have fun."

I looked down at my phone and turned it off. I realized that if I didn't turn it off, I would catch a glimpse of it later and feel obligated to answer anyone who messaged me about work.

I was feeling good and excited about the day. The weather was great, and the kids were happy. I turned to the back and noticed Zack and Ramsey filling their backpack with water balloons.

"Wait a minute, you, guys!" I exclaimed. "You can't take those into the art show."

Marilyn stopped the van for a moment, turned her head to the back, and said, "Well, it is an *outdoor* art show, and I'm sure they're not planning to throw them at other people. Just each other. Right boys?"

Ramsey and Zach answered simultaneously, "Yeah."

Ramsey added, "We just brought them to play with in case we get bored. It could get boiling hot out there."

While we were walking around, I kept getting visions of various clients for whom I had been reading for. Some of the images I just couldn't shake from my mind. I had been constantly having trouble staying in the present moment.

After the art show, we were all exhausted. I had to wake Zach up from the back when Marilyn pulled up to our driveway.

Once we got inside, I rallied the kids in the bathroom to brush their teeth. After several minutes, I finally got them in bed. I turned on my phone and tossed it on the bed while brushing my teeth. I took a quick shower and jumped in bed.

I looked at my phone as I tried to get comfortable. I started to notice dozens of text messages, all from various people; half of the texts were from Bailey, and four were from Sierra. I answered every one of the text messages as quickly as I could.

I threw my head back on the pillow and lay there for a few minutes, looking at the ceiling. There was a piece of paper on the ceiling in Zach's writing, which read, 'I'm safe everywhere I go.' I knew this was Zach's attempt to help me go outside of my limited boundaries. He and Breezy had taken it upon themselves to research various techniques to help me overcome my fears of travel.

I was overwhelmed thinking about what their life had been like having me as a mom. The panic attacks brought on by spiritual energies hindered me from doing some activities with the kids that other parents had no trouble doing.

I was startled by the sudden ringing of the phone.

It was Sierra.

I answered as I walked outside onto the bedroom balcony.

Excitedly I said, "Hello!"

Sierra spoke quietly, "Hi, Katharine. I need to talk to you later tonight. Do you take calls after hours?"

I smirked and stated, "After hours? There are no after-hours for those on the retainer. You can call anytime you're ready."

While on the balcony, I looked at the sky and noticed the moon was full and bright. I thought about the full-moon craziness that some people experience. Then I suddenly remembered that I needed to text Bailey. She had just sent a few texts before I answered Sierra.

As I began texting, I got an alert that someone booked an appointment through the website.

I realized it was Bailey.

I watched another text from her pop up on my phone:

> I just booked an appointment for Friday but need to talk to you now.

I knew she was panicking, so I immediately called her back.

I explained that I don't normally do this unless it's an emergency.

"It *is* an emergency, Katharine!" she cried out. "Cole has been missing all day. The veterinary office that he works at told me he quit yesterday."

She was breathing heavily and crying.

"Bailey, calm down and get your breathing under control," I encouraged. "Cole is alive and lying in a field near a road by your place." I had already remote-viewed this.

Bailey seemed relieved as her breathing seemed to be getting normal. "Do you know where he is?" she asked.

I replied, "Yes, while I can't recognize the name of the street, I do see a sign near him that reads, *Royal Tomatoes*."

Bailey seemed satisfied and responded, "That's great, and that makes sense to me. I know where that is. I'll head there now."

I objected, "Wait a minute, Bailey! You can't lift him by yourself. You need someone to help you or an emergency crew to pick him up."

"Ambulances don't come out to the country!" she exclaimed. "Anyone that needs to go to the hospital just calls for the helicopter or gets driven to town. I can't get the helicopter pilot this late without questions."

I realized she was in shock and not thinking clearly. So, I tried to reason with her.

I said, "Bailey, find someone who can help you, but don't go alone and please be careful. He has a few broken ribs, a punctured lung, and a bad head injury."

Bailey was hurrying to get off the phone to get Cole.

Before she hung up, I explained, "Wait a minute, Cole didn't quit his job. The veterinary office lied to you. After finding out what he did with the blood order mix-up, the office told everyone. He didn't even make it work."

After the call, I looked at the time and realized she had paid for a one-hour session and only used thirty-two minutes. So, I texted her that she had twenty-eight minutes on the books for another call if she wished.

A few minutes later, the phone rang, and it was Butchie.

I sure missed him, and we talked for a while. Suddenly, I noticed Sierra calling in and told Butchie I had to take a call. He respected the importance of my work and consented to an incoming call without hesitation.

I was able to answer it on the second ring.

Immediately, I heard Sierra whisper, "Did you get the photo I sent you?"

I had noticed texts come up during my call with Bailey and Butchie, but I had yet to open them.

I tapped my phone and opened the text. There was a photo of a man and woman.

As I reached over to the nightstand pouring a glass of water, I answered:

> Yes, I see a photo of a couple.

Immediately, I heard Sierra's spirit guides say there would be no problems.

"Katharine, do you see any problems for me from this guy?" she asked. "I accidentally dislocated his shoulder during our evening together. When we finished, I helped him get dressed, and he hurried to the hospital to look at it."

She continued, "He seemed to be in pain, but it didn't stop him from making new plans to see me for next week. Are you sure there will be no problems for me associated with him?"

I psychically inquired into all the times that Sierra had spent with her client.

I confidently answered, "No, there won't be any problems at all. I can see the entire connection, and you will continue working with this client after tonight."

"You don't even know who that guy is, do you?" she tittered.

I felt she was testing me. So, I cautiously answered, "I don't look to see anyone's identity unless it's crucial to know. But now that your attention is on it, your spirit guides are telling me that he is an elected official."

She erupted in a hysterical laugh, "Bingo!"

She slowly calmed down and breathed out the last bit of laughter. Then I heard her call out to someone, "A dirty martini, please."

She began to confide, "He is an excellent client, and I don't want him or me to be in any trouble. I've been seeing him for a while."

"He has endured many nights of my talents and keeps returning." She giggled.

"Most importantly, he's sweet and pays very well," she boasted.

There was an awkward stillness.

Finally, I broke the silence and said, "There are some clients with whom we align, and there are some with whom we don't feel a connection to at all."

I heard her take a sip from her drink, and then, with a sobering declaration, she said, "I feel that with you. I trust you as I know you are a good person."

I heard a man's voice close to her ask if she was ready. Sierra purred out to him, "I'll be up shortly. Get prepared."

She focused back on the phone and declared, "I have to go. Thank you for checking on that for me."

A sudden hush filled the air and the phone went dead.

The next night, I absolutely couldn't go to sleep after talking to Butchie. I couldn't turn off my mind and relax. Zach was next to me and fell asleep almost immediately. He was flat on his back and worn out from chasing and being chased in an all-out Nerf war earlier. I rolled to my side and faced him, just staring at his sweet face. I realized, I needed to do better not only for myself but for my children. I don't want them to remember me as never really living and experiencing life.

They need to see me get out more and experience more places. I started forcing myself to be around more people and not be so consumed by the spirit world. I'm grateful for my work and where I live, but I need to expand and focus on *this* life.

I've worked hard on clearing the hurt and anger I had toward my mom for locking me in that tiny closet when I was a child. For most of my adult life I've had difficulty overcoming the fear of being trapped in small spaces and unable to escape. The torment still appears when faced with current experiences that trigger those old wounds.

Finally, I focused on the TV show I had planned to watch. After a few minutes, I became alarmed by a strange sound that seemed to be coming from the rooftop. As I focused on the noise, I fumbled for the remote to mute the TV, but it got pushed somewhere under the blanket. When I finally found the remote and muted the TV, the noise became so loud that I thought someone was tap dancing on the roof.

I began to hear the siding being ripped off from the house. I called out to my Spirit Guides and asked what was going on? The Spirit of the Land, an elemental spirit that governs the territory and its residents, told me that it was an adolescent raccoon from Ms. Gibson's who was looking to move in my attic to prepare a space for a mate.

I heard the raccoon slide in between the siding and the interior sheetrock.

I screeched, "Oh no!"

Zach momentarily opened his eyes.

I gestured in the direction of the sound and exclaimed to Zach, "A raccoon is in between the wall and exterior siding!" Zach didn't even flinch and had already closed his eyes when I looked back at him.

I lay there watching the wall where the raccoon seemed to have entered. I could see his energy field beam through the sheetrock. The Spirit of the Land came back in and said, *The Raccoon will not go through the sheetrock; you're completely safe.*

The raccoon left as fast as it came in, and its beautiful green energy trailed off. I must have fallen asleep right after the Spirit of the Land left, and I slept like a rock.

I woke up worried and realized I needed to call someone about the raccoon. I didn't want the raccoon to be killed. I just wanted it trapped and taken off to an area where it could live happily. A safe place, anywhere far away from my house.

The wild animal expert came to my house and checked the opening where the raccoon got in. He set up a no-kill trap and told me it was a live trap. When they take the raccoon out to release it, they video the process so you can see the raccoon run off to its new habitat.

The company's owner had a twenty-five-acre property out in Willis, Texas. It had a pond stocked with fish and lots of trees. This is where they release raccoons, opossum, and other animals that they capture. I felt like that was a much better place for him than trying to set up a home between the walls of our house.

Suddenly, I had a strange thought, *I wonder if Ms. Gibson will realize one of her raccoons is missing once he has been trapped and living in Willis?*

I drove past the front of Ms. Gibson's on my way out of the neighborhood and noticed the back door of her car was open.

I decided to stop and tell her about the raccoon and check on her health and welfare.

I didn't know if she had anyone who checks on her. I would get occasional text messages from her about things going on in the neighborhood, but I didn't know if she ever text anybody other than me.

When I approached the open car door, I noticed a large bag of dog food hanging halfway out of the backseat. I walked up to the door and saw many animal spirits around the house's front left. There were several different types of animals, including several cats and a few dogs.

I was shocked at the massive number of raccoon spirits. I watched them run through the yard, and off to the left in front of her house. There was a small pet cemetery to the side of the house, equipped with headstones and animal statuary and guarded by massive concrete angels. All of them looked like products from the place she worked for.

It was quite interesting but very out of place for where we lived; we don't live in a rural area. I had heard many rumors that the Homeowners Association had been on to Ms. Gibson for years about cleaning up her front yard. It was a terrible mess.

It looked like one unfinished project after another. The years took a toll on that yard. She finally had a yard guy come out and clean everything up. But the massive number of raccoon spirits continues to intrigue me as I pass by.

Ms. Gibson finally emerged from the front door and greeted me with a smile.

I told her about the raccoon, and she sadly replied, "It's unfortunate. They're just looking for a handout."

"I understand, Ms. Gibson," I sighed. "But I don't want them living in *my* house. They go to the bathroom wherever they want and that can affect someone's health."

I paused for a moment, and then, attempting to lighten the subject, I asked, "By the way, would you like me to help you get that bag out of your car?"

Ms. Gibson brushed off her discontent and said, "Sure. That would be helpful."

"What's the dog food for?" I inquired.

"It's for the raccoons," she boasted. "They love the dog food. I've got four more bags in the back."

Puzzled, I said, "Four more bags. How much dog food are you feeding them?"

"I feed them a fifty-pound bag every other week," she said.

Amazed, I asked, "Wow! So, you put food out every day?"

"Yes," she proudly stated. "I'd initially open the bag and just let them feast. They were much smaller bags and a much smaller group. But my family has grown."

I was trying not to upset her, especially since I had just told her that one of her raccoon family members was gone now. I said, "I understand. I can see you've had quite a few over the years. I was looking at your cemetery."

She gushed, "Yes, I like to keep them close, and a real pet cemetery is so far from here. It's nice to come out here, sit in a chair, and talk with them."

I knew I had to get a point across to her, so I spoke with conviction and said, "Ms. Gibson, you know you don't need to have them buried near you to be able to talk to them. You can talk to deceased animals and people at any time. As soon as you say their name, they come into the space. And you can talk with them. They hear everything you say. You talk to them like they're in the room with you."

The words seemed to wash over her as she started to wipe off some of the tombstones from the pine needles and leaves. I could tell she was brushing them off so I could see the names proudly displayed on each headstone.

She must've had a thing for food because some of the headstones had names such as: Chips, Relish, Fries, Apple, Cocoa, and Pickles.

It was charming how she had everything set-up. She even had some little angel figurines sitting on top of some of the graves. She pointed to the newest tombstone that read: *Pickles*.

As she began to talk about *Pickles*, I was unsure if it was one of the dogs, cats, or raccoons because there were now several spirits circling us; five spirits were laying at her feet.

Suddenly, a cat spirit stood out. The frequency became apparent, and it was indeed Pickles Gibson.

Ms. Gibson admitted, "The Racoon dynasty has done some damage to my own home over the years, but I enjoy having them come in to visit. It makes me feel like it's my family visiting."

I turned the conversation in a different direction and said, "Ms. Gibson, neighbors told me your son lives with you. What's his name?"

"Are you referring to James?" she asked.

She hesitated. It didn't appear that she wanted to talk about James much.

She finally answered, "James is not my son. He's my younger brother. I've just been the one to raise him. We were several years apart. Although, he might as well have been my son."

Her spirit guides added, *Ms. Gibson did have a baby, but it only lived a few days.*

I knew this was a touchy subject, so I didn't open up the discussion. But as soon as I had the thought, Ms. Gibson began telling me about a child she had been pregnant with and that it was born premature.

She mumbled, "They placed the baby in a shoe box and told me to take him home. I tried to care for him, but he didn't make it."

Everything got silent, and when that happens, it's usually the time spirits come in to speak.

"Ms. Gibson, whenever I see spirits, I hear exactly why they come in and the purpose of their incarnation," I explained. "Sometimes, spirits don't have everything lined up to fulfill their mission on Earth. So, rather than go through life, they return to the spirit world to reenter a new life. If this occurs, they could have a chance to return at a better time."

Ms. Gibson smiled and said, "I sure hope you're right. I occasionally think about holding that baby when I was able to. I couldn't feed it with a regular-size baby bottle, so I bought a kitten bottle from the feed store. Back then, they didn't have things for *preemies*. And the hospital knew the baby wasn't going to make it. The day I left the hospital, they put him in a small shoe box with no lid and a tiny cloth towel as a blanket."

I sat there in silence for so long waiting for my next cue from the spirit world.

Her spirit guides acknowledged that Ms. Gibson never named the baby and she needed to, so she doesn't continue referring to the baby as *It*.

The spirit guides urged me to ask Ms. Gibson what she named the baby.

So, I slowly leaned into her side and inquired, "What did you name your baby boy?"

Ms. Gibson looked up at me like I was a crazy woman and said, "Name him? I didn't name him. If I had given him a name, then his passing would have been more difficult."

I understood she felt to be in a resolved state, but I knew there was more that needed to be reconciled.

I needed to address the issue for her sake, so I asked, "Ms. Gibson, if you had to name a baby boy right now, what would you name him?"

She smiled sweetly and replied, "Benjamin Shawn Gibson."

I said, "Since you have a name that you like, let's give it to *your* baby."

She looked inquisitively toward the tombstones as if she could see Pickles Gibson sitting there. She had a content smile on her face as she let out a breath of relief and said, "Ok. His name is Benjamin."

I walked away feeling complete and climbed into the car. As I drove away, I was reminded that we are all doing the best we can with our experiences, even with the difficulties and trauma we endure each day.

I couldn't help but wonder if I was ever going to get beyond the trauma I had experienced as a child and the limitations it has caused me.

Maybe one day, I thought.

Chapter 3
Foot Fetish

As I approached the door of my favorite lunchtime restaurant, I noticed Maria, one of the daytime employees, power washing the outside patio.

She had worked there for many years and was such an amazing person. Everyone there was so friendly. I usually order only two things on the menu: a salad bar or veggie wrap—no cheese, of course, because I'm vegan.

They always remember what I like and how I like it. I eat there about four times a week, and it has a great atmosphere. I can also get in and out quickly on long workdays.

I placed my order and then asked about the elusive feral cat I had been feeding in preparation for trapping. Zach had already named him Luke, so he had that whole Jedi force with him.

I chatted with Maria while she moved tables around on the patio. I noticed another employee named Chris walking toward me with a tray when suddenly I heard my name being called. I glanced around but didn't recognize anyone right off.

Out of nowhere, a woman came up behind me and asked if she could join me at my table. I leaned forward to see where she came from, and it appeared she had been camped out a few tables over. Her table was anchored with a large Louis Vuitton weekender bag, laptop, half-eaten lunch, oversized rhinestone bowl, and a small dog whose leash had been wrapped around the legs of the chair.

Typically, there are only two reasons that a stranger asks if they can join your table when you're sitting alone. They either want to ask you out, or they secretly know who you are. In this case, I psychically knew my profession drew her in.

"My name is Gretchen, and I overheard you talking to the guy at the counter," she explained.

"You mean Daniel?" I asked.

"Yes, the friendly guy with brown hair. So, you're a psychic?" she queried.

I smiled, and as I nodded in confirmation, my spirit guides whispered that Gretchen wanted answers about her rocky relationship.

Still standing, Gretchen waited for my response. I replied, "Thank you so much for your interest, but I would prefer you not to join my table. I'm taking my lunch break, and I usually like to sit here and relax. I would love to read for you sometime, though. Here, I can give you my contact information."

As I began to pull out a business card from my bag, she persisted, "Okay, Katharine, I understand, but I only have one question. Do you know if my husband has cheated on me?"

I looked at her with a blank stare, realizing she was unprepared for what I was seeing psychically.

"Gretchen, you're not ready for what I see since you already know he has been cheating on you, and you've ignored it. You thought it was a one-time fling, and it wasn't. After all, you didn't get Chlamydia on your own; he brought it to you!" I exclaimed.

Gretchen looked at me, devastated. I felt sad for her and stood up, opening my arms to console her with a hug.

She embraced me and whispered, "What do you think I should do?"

Exasperated I replied, "I answered your one question and yet you have more. You need to be grateful that chlamydia is all you got from this man since he chases everything that moves."

Without paying more attention to Gretchen, I began wrapping my food and tucked my chair under the table. I briskly walked to my car, and I didn't look back. Sitting in the car, I took a deep breath and closed the door. I sat and grounded myself for a few minutes before pushing the start button and fading into the distance. Grounding is the only thing that helps me quickly clear myself of other people's erratic energies.

When I finally got home, the hotline notifications displayed on my phone that I had a customer waiting. I felt Roxy's energy before I left the house earlier, which indicated I would hear from her sometime today. Usually, when I'm in the flow with work, I will feel or see the client visually before they call later that day.

I finished my bagged lunch under the tree at the table in the back yard, which was pleasant. I noticed the little flowers that I planted a week ago beginning to the surface and some loosely abandoned watermelon seeds sprouting independently. We would often come out here to slice the watermelon, and the seeds would fall off into the dirt. They get watered whenever I quench the thirst of all the other plants in the yard, and now, they're sprouting.

I love to watch seeds naturally sprout from the earth without human manipulation. Eating things that have grown in my yard also feels so refreshing. I have yet to grow a watermelon, but I was hoping that would change soon.

I left the sanctuary of my backyard and walked to my office inside. I sat down at the desk and ground again before pressing on the phone to accept the call I had seen earlier. I realized a few other callers had gotten in line as well. The automated system went through two rounds of calls before it moved to the next customer in line. I moved through the calls quickly and noticed another caller had been added to the waiting list.

I answered the call with my usual greeting, "Hi, I'm Katharine. How may I help you?"

"Oh my God, girl, where have you been?" Roxy replied, as she let out a sigh.

I could feel her frustration and tried to mitigate the circumstances by speaking calmly.

"Hi, Roxy, how may I help you?"

She protested, "I was first in line waiting, but when the ring back came in, I was with Craig so that I couldn't answer the call. I waited an hour and a half for you to call me back. What the hell have you been doing?"

I wasn't surprised by Roxy's intimidating attitude—it comes from the environment she had been raised in.

I shot back, "I'm sorry about the wait, Roxy! I went out to lunch. The waitlist is for those who want to talk with me, with the understanding that I will call back."

Roxy argued, "Look, can you just give me your number? I don't want to wait in line like everybody else. I should just be able to call you!"

I knew that wasn't the craziest idea she had come up with, but I realized it would be disastrous for *me*.

I explained, "Roxy, that's not how I want to do things here. I don't move hotline callers to another method of communication. I believe in not biting the hand that feeds me, and this is the best way for you to get a quick call with me."

She took a deep breath and calmed down. "Ok. Well, listen," she said. "I've been thinking, especially about the last time we discussed Craig. You said, *I should do what's best for me. The highest and best for me.* And I believe Craig *is* the best and highest for me. I only get Craig's attention when he feels that I need some type of support. He must love it."

Roxy was acting weird and sinister, laughing at what seemed to be an inside joke. She carried on for several seconds, then finally stopped. She seemed to be struggling to fight off the urge to continue laughing. It wasn't infectious like a comedian's laugh; it was disturbing like a laugh from The Joker on Batman!

She regained her composure and began, "I mean, umm... you know, he's kept this vegetable wife around and has me taking care of her."

I intervened, "Roxy, you missed the point completely from the last time we spoke. I was hoping you'd lean more toward desiring someone who will be there for you physically *and* emotionally. Not someone who is just using you as their *toolbox*."

"Toolbox? What is that?" she quizzed.

"It's sometimes loosely used to reference a female used only for sex. She's referred to as a *toolbox*," I explained.

She insisted, "Okay, Katharine, I understand the concept of being a *toolbox*. But I'm *not* Craig's *toolbox*. He bought me a ring this week. He gave me money to go clothes shopping, and recently, I told him I wanted to have a baby this year."

I knew there was no way to calm her down, but perhaps my words needed to sit with her for a while.

I tried to reason with her, "Roxy, that would be the worst thing you could do. Your spirit guides have advised me that you should move on to someone else. Trust me, you don't want to experience more lessons from this karmic situation."

She refuted, "Katharine, you don't know what you're talking about. Karmic situation? I'm the one with all the gifts. I'm the one with the money. I'm the one sucking his dick! And that's what I told his wife when changing her diaper. She can't say anything. She can't even yell at me like she did before her illness progressed."

She continued to ramble, "Since I have been hired full-time, I have been whispering in her ear what I do to her husband and what he does to me. I turn their photo towards us when he's fucking me in the living room—the same place they used to sit and watch TV."

I realized I was taking more abuse by listening to this than what it was worth, although I couldn't say that directly to her.

I said, "Roxy, I don't feel I am the right psychic for you. There are a lot of psychics out there. You could find someone that is more aligned to the reading you want."

I knew she would probably find someone on the hotline who would keep encouraging her bad behavior to keep her as a customer. Some of the *so-called* psychics have told customers all sorts of things and encouraged horrible decisions to make a caller think they are doing the right thing. And this *feel-good tactic* entices them to call back again and again.

Roxy shouted, "Listen, Katharine! I know you know some shit, but you're the only one who can calm me down. I have read with a lot of psychics, but when I hear your voice, you calm me down and make me walk like a lady."

She made me laugh a little with that walk-like lady comment.

Smiling, I said, "Thank you, Roxy. Is there anything you want me to look at psychically, or did you just call to tell me about the sofa action?"

I giggled again, thinking about the walk-like-a-lady comment.

Roxy chirped, "Thanks, Katharine. I appreciate you. Now, what I want you to look at psychically is do you see me being able to have children?"

When I peered into Roxy's energy, I saw some souls waiting to come in for her. That means she would be a mother if she chose to.

I summarized, "Roxy, several souls are waiting to come in if you decide to bring them forward."

She questioned, "Umm, Katharine, can you ensure you're looking at the right thing? I've had several abortions, and so I was wondering, are those the souls of my *aborted* babies?"

I realized I needed to elaborate on this more because most people don't understand. So, I explained, "Roxy, if a baby is stillborn or if a woman has a miscarriage or an abortion, no soul is ever assigned to that body. Which means no soul dies."

I find it helpful to explain this to parents who have had miscarriages. They often believe that there was a baby soul that died, and they mourn for that baby. On the *other side,* souls know much more than we do; they won't enter a fetus unless they know it will go full term. It would simply be a wasted *trip* for them.

I continued explaining to Roxy, "It takes a bit of coordination for souls to plan their earthly lives. And so, when a baby is born, whether it's for a few days, months, or a whole lifetime, upon that baby's first breath of air, the soul enters the body. When the body dies, the soul exits through the mouth or the top of the head. I've seen them exit from the side, but it's usually under special circumstances."

I stated, "The waiting souls are willing to come in to be your children who have spirit contracts and lessons with you. That's if you choose to bring them in during this lifetime."

She refuted, "But before some of the abortions, I felt the baby move in the womb."

I explained, "There is so much happening when the baby is developing in the womb, like the nerves and muscles that react to sounds, movement, and touch just like someone touches *you*. It's almost like seeing or hearing a ghost."

Roxy asked, "Where are the souls that will come in?"

I continued my lesson, "They wait until the body takes its first breath and enters. Until then, they stay close to the parents before the time of entrance."

I could tell by Roxy's silence that she was in deep contemplation.

Solemnly, she stated, "I have read with another psychic who told me she saw a baby in my energy field. I told her I had had an abortion, and the psychic immediately said, 'Yep, that's the baby you aborted, and now it's in spirit.'"

Roxy's spirit guides began filling her energy field with light while transmitting the frequency of love and acceptance to her.

I pointed out, "Roxy, your guides are telling me that that psychic was just guessing, and when you said to her that you had an abortion, she jumped on board with the aborted baby routine. If someone is an actual seer, they know the spirit world can see whether a pregnancy will go to term. Only humans are clouded with guilt and greed."

I concluded, "I know you won't listen and will try to do it anyway. But having a child with Craig would not serve you as well as you think it will. I'm only telling you this so that you will know I tried to lessen the hardship when you look at this years later."

With great appreciation, she said, "Thanks, Katharine. I feel better and smarter after talking to you."

"Is there anything else you want me to look into?" I queried.

She said, "No. I'll talk to you later. I hope you have a great day."

I checked my cell phone and noticed a few texts from Butchie. I spoke into the phone, *Hey Siri, call Butchie.*

When he answered, he asked if we could meet this afternoon. I knew he wanted to review several things before his big trip. I agreed to meet at his office for a discussion.

This week, he has been working on finding the right bookkeeper to make things easier as we continue to focus on other things. Butchie has a massive whiteboard in his office where he draws out plans and strategizes business ideas.

I brought a notebook, a phone, and a small bowl of fruit left over from the lunch I picked up earlier. When Butchie entered the room, he nodded as I bit into a pineapple chuck. He sat down and looked at me with a soft smile.

He likes to speak in the third person during these meetings, which makes me laugh.

"Now Butchie has everything put together for you and full contacts of anyone you may need to reach while I am gone. I will also share my calendar to your iPhone, so you'll know my shoot times. If you need anything, just leave a message, and I'll handle it when we finish for the day."

He then handed me a presentation folder with information and project notes we had worked on together. He went into great detail and explained everything that's been happening. When he finished, he stood up, opened his arms, and gestured for a hug.

"You're gonna miss your Butchie, right?" he said.

I suddenly had a flashback of watching Tom Cruise sliding across the floor after realizing his parents were gone in the 1983 movie *Risky Business*. I didn't recall it because Tom Cruise was only wearing underwear and a shirt during that scene; I recalled it because of the sense of freedom he was celebrating. I was hoping for a few months of freedom for myself from the daily grind. But that idea was just a wishful thought, as I was not yet aware of the events soon to unfold.

I giggled and hugged Butchie while giving him a pop kiss. I said, "Of course, I will miss you. I appreciate all you do for me and know you do it with love. Nobody has ever helped me as much as you."

He kissed me and then gave me a bear hug.

I knew he was feeling down at the thought of being gone for so long, so I jokingly added, "The only thing I would change is how you refer to yourself in the third person. It creeps me out sometimes, depending on the topic you are referring to."

He laughed and playfully said, "C'mon, say Butchie's the best organizer I know," while prodding my ribs to the point of tickling.

He placed the presentation folder in my hand, threw his arm around my shoulder, and walked me toward the door. "I have a lot to get done before the trip next week," he said. "Now hug and kiss me, and off you go."

When I finally returned home to my desk, I noticed a few emails and text messages I needed to answer. One of the messages was from Sierra. She was requesting a thirty-minute call for tonight if possible.

Of course, it's possible, I thought.

I messaged her back quickly and asked what time she was looking to call so I could plan for it.

Then I added:

> If you're available now, I am, too. You can just call.

I psychically smelled freshly baked baguettes, and then the phone rang.

It was Sierra.

"Hi Katharine, thank you for making time for me," she said.

Smiling, I replied, "Of course, Sierra, I could smell fresh baguettes as I thought of you right before the phone rang."

"Really?" Sierra laughed. "That's interesting because I am sitting here at a wonderful French Bakery that is all vegan, and they've been baking baguettes for the last twenty minutes."

I wished I had a French Vegan place near me, I thought.

Sierra continued, "I spent some time educating myself on the treatment of animals, and now I understand why you are vegan. I was going to an appointment, and when I walked by this place, I thought of you and decided to stop in."

I responded, "Thank you, Sierra. I appreciate your open mind about this subject. What do you want to discuss today?"

Sierra paused for a moment and took in a deep breath. She exhaled and said, "Well, I have a job that could require an eight-week stay with a client. I have interacted with this client before, but not for the length of time he's requesting now."

Sierra seemed very anxious and took in another long, deep breath.

She continued, "After I sign the contract, the client will pay for everything up front."

Suddenly, Sierra's spirit guides showed me a quick glimpse of Sierra being tied up. I paused while looking at the scene.

"Katharine!" Sierra shouted. "Are you there?"

I took a deep breath and stretched. Then I answered, "Sierra, I got a flash of you tied up."

She didn't seem too concerned since she replied, "Well, don't worry about that. Suppose I'm tied to a bed, then fantastic. I don't put restrictions on my clients."

I didn't believe it was a good situation, but Sierra thought it was okay.

She changed the subject and said, "Katharine, I have been listening to recordings of you speaking while I sleep. I play them on a loop, and it makes me feel calm. It's nice to hear your voice, and it makes me feel safe. Is it okay if I tell you a story?"

"Sure." I agreed.

I heard Sierra's shopping bags crinkle as she gathered them. The chair made an annoying screeching sound as she pushed it to the high-top table.

Sierra instructed, "I will walk home from here and tell you a story on my way."

I said, "That's fine. I'll be listening."

She began, "I grew up in a small region of Spain, which is a popular tourist attraction. I would sit near the walkway railing on a small bridge and dangle my legs off the side. My mother would be hanging laundry while screaming at me, 'Sierra, stop that, you could fall off the ledge and die.'"

She stopped to ask, "Katharine, do you know why I'm sharing this with you?"

I paused to consider the question. My spirit guides' frequency came in and stood in front of me, sharing, *Sierra wants you to know that she's a risk taker and she will always choose that type of path.*

I answered Sierra, "You want me to know you will always take the risk."

Sierra approved, "That's very good. My reason for having our initial session was to find out if I was going to die. The session made me feel like I would live a good life this year."

Knowing it would not change her outlook, I replied, "I understand, but sometimes there is more to realize than if you are going to die or not. Most people want to know how to stay safe or avoid harm's way to live a more fulfilled life."

I heard her pressing the key code to the entrance of her building. Then I psychically saw the number 1119. Sierra's high-heeled shoes echoed as she walked across the marble floor.

I asked, "Sierra, is there anything else you want me to look at psychically for you?"

She replied, "Yes, I would like to work on removing the guilt of not getting my mother out of Spain. I have felt the guilt ever since I moved to the U.S. with my sister. I wish I could have convinced Mom to move here. I wish she could have had a better life."

Sierra started to cry softly as her mother's soul entered my view.

I revealed, "Hey, Sierra, your mother is here *now*. She conveys that she loved living *and* dying in Spain—it was her home. She says she made love with your father on the water's edge, which she watched daily from the front window. She loves the fact that you wear her rosary."

I heard the phone drop. Everything was silent except for some small background noises. I remote-viewed to see what Sierra was doing. I could see that she had moved herself to the floor and was kneeling in front of a large painting of her mother leaning against the wall.

She spoke softly while looking at the portrait, "I love you, Mom."

Her mom's spirit echoed, *I know you do, and I love you too. I have also seen you enjoy a fig cake like the one I used to make for you.*

I parroted every word to Sierra as her mother showed me the rosary Sierra kept. Her mother explained that she first wore it for Sierra's father at her wedding. She bragged that he was her only true love.

I knew that it was important for Sierra to hear this.

I excitedly informed her, "Your mother showed me the rosary you often wear. She told me she wore it wrapped around her wrist when she married your father."

She sniveled, "Thank you, Katharine. I needed this tonight. I have to say bye for now."

I held the phone to my ear until her voice faded into the ether.

Later that night, while sleeping, I heard a noise coming from the next street. I could barely open my eyes when I heard the spirits in my room say, *it's an ambulance with its siren and lights on.* I got up and walked to the window to see what was happening. I saw several emergency vehicles lined up the street. *I hope it's not Ms. Gibson*, I thought.

As soon as I thought about Ms. Gibson, I immediately got a message that it was the neighbor across the street, two doors down from Ms. Gibson. I sent Ms. Gibson a text anyway. It was 3:40 a.m. I figured when she got up, she'd text me back.

I texted:

> Hi, Ms. Gibson; I saw the lights and wanted to check on you to ensure you're okay.

> Let me know if you need anything.

I was deeply concerned for Ms. Gibson because I knew she wasn't taking care of herself like she should. I sat the phone down and laid back in bed. I was in the most comfortable position to fall asleep when my phone buzzed with a new text:

> Hi, Katharine. I'm glad I'm not the only one up at this hour. I have no idea what's going on down the street, but I'm doing great. I just got back from the hospital. I had to have my second to the end toe amputated. I had gotten a pedicure, and the girl who did it cut my skin. I guess I ignored it afterward, and it became infected. The doctor had to amputate it. But I'm doing better. I may not be able to hang ten, but I can still hang nine.

She finished the text with a foot and a surfing emoji. Although I was so tired, I about lost it laughing. I was impressed by her carefree attitude.

When I left for the lunch the following day, I exited the part of the neighborhood that took me past Ms. Gibson's. A yard guy was mowing the grass in front of her house. I was impressed with her efforts to maintain the landscape but thought letting raccoons live in her home was unsanitary.

Ms. Gibson managed to keep her life rolling. She was much more exuberant than those her age who gave up on life. She was standing in her yard looking around as if searching for a place to put a new cemetery statue. *What an inspiration she is. Without the raccoons, of course,* I thought.

Her pink hair, long eyelashes, and colorful makeup looked fantastic whenever I saw her. Come to think of it, she appeared to look like the typical carnival psychic who might invite you to join a séance. I realized I was lacking sleep when I laughed out loud at the thought of Ms. Gibson conducting a séance.

During lunch, I took a call from Andy, a guy I read for about relationship stuff.

"Hi Andy, what's going on?" I answered.

He seemed nervous as he began to explain, "There's this guy I met through an ad a few years ago. He buys the shoes from me that I no longer want. He was always great with the payments after I shipped him the shoes. I began to consider it weird when he started sending extra money for me to buy more expensive shoes for myself."

Andy paused then said, "I haven't heard from him in a while. I'm not so worried about him not paying me more, as I am about his well-being. His name is Mason."

I said, "As soon as you began talking, I saw Mason's energy. I didn't know what to look for at first, so I looked at his health. Your spirit guides showed me that he was fine. He's still alive. He's just been busy. It seems like he's been worried about work and office drama. He'll get back on track with you in the next week or two. He had been focused on other things.

Andy was eager to hear what I saw and how I saw him.

"What does he look like?" Andy queried.

"Oh, you have never seen him?" I asked.

"No. I answered his ad posted on a gay dating site for purchasing used shoes," Andy stated.

He continued, "We've only emailed each other but not very often. It's usually about the shoes. He likes talking to me about different types of shoes. I thought it was a little unusual when he offered to send extra money for me to buy better shoes. I mean, I have a good job and everything. I can buy nice shoes, but my money goes toward other things."

"I understand completely," I replied.

He continued his inquiry, "So, Katharine, what does he do? I mean, can you tell what he does for a living?"

I smiled and responded, "He's a doctor—an orthopedic surgeon. I don't think it's wise for you to contact him at his practice, though. He'll be in touch with you soon enough.

I asked, Andy, is there anything else you want me to look at?"

He continued questioning, "Since you know he's an orthopedic surgeon, can you tell me if he's married or single and if we will ever meet?"

I explained, "As soon as you asked if he's married, I heard no. But there is somebody in his life. It is someone who knows about his foot fetish."

There was a sudden silence, so I said, "I mean, you do understand that's what he has—a foot fetish, right?"

He stayed silent as I resumed answering his questions, "The person Mason has a relationship with is so in love with him that he puts up with a lot of crap just to please him. You asked if you would ever meet him. I'm sorry, but I heard no. He is very handsome. He has an average build and enjoys working out. Does that answer your questions?"

He said, "Yes. Thank you very much, Katharine."

Then he expressed, "I don't even know his last name."

I replied, "Interesting, Andy. As we were talking, I kept hearing *good water*. It seems like his last name is Goodwater, Mason Goodwater. As you spoke, my guides showed me clean drinking water and a person liked it. That makes it crystal clear. I hope all this helps you. But whatever you do, do not contact him at his practice. Just wait for him to contact you. He will."

Andy asked, "Do you know how long he'll keep wanting to buy my shoes and sending me money to buy more?"

I said, "It looks like it'll go on for another year. And then it will completely stop."

"Why does it stop?" he pleaded.

I stated, "He has purchased several hundred shoes over the years, and his partner demands they either marry or he is moving on."

Andy sighed, then asked, "So they marry?"

I responded, "They will not legally marry. I know you have some emotions connected to Mason, but you don't really know him. Just like anything else, when you have a partner who may be interested in one thing or another, they can't control themselves. It tends to wear on the relationship, just like with the man he's been in connection with. I have spoken to people who have been out with their spouses; they know when they are staring at someone else. They know their *tell,* and they know their fetishes. It begins to destroy the connection because it starts to destroy the partner's self-confidence. That's what it's been doing to their relationship."

Andy had one more question and asked, "All these guys I've been dating seem like they're not available. Katharine, do you ever feel like I will have a partner?"

I explained, "Andy, you subconsciously chose guys who were unavailable to protect yourself for as long as I've been reading for you. I noticed so many guys in and out of your energy field. It's time for you to decide what you really want. You need to focus on changing what you need to create the life you want."

He ended the call by saying, "Thank you, Katharine. You truly do care about me."

After finishing my lunch, I stopped at the store to pick up groceries and a few trash magazines with the latest celebrity gossip to help Ms. Gibson's recovery. When I turned into the driveway, I ran into the house to pee before walking to Ms. Gibson's. Zach, Ramsey, Breezy, Ruby, and a few other kids were resting under the tree in the front yard.

The boys were sweaty-looking, so they must have played for a while. They got excited when they saw me come home and jumped up to greet me, but I told them I'd be right back out.

When I came back outside, Breezy said, "It was a half day at school, so we all got out early. They usually hold us until after lunch before releasing us, but not today. They let us go before lunch, so we've been waiting for you to get home."

I exclaimed, "I wish they had let me know! I would have waited and taken you guys to lunch with me. How about I order some lunch to be delivered, and you guys can continue playing? I've got to take some things over to Miss Gibson, but I'll be right back."

Zach said, "That would be great, Mom. We can take the things to Ms. Gibson for you, though."

I handed the bags to Zach and explained, "She just had surgery, so she may not be able to get up and walk. Hopefully, her son will answer the door."

Zach assured, "We got this, Mom."

I went inside the house, and then noticed a text from Sierra. I let her know I could call her back in about thirty minutes. I wanted to order food for the kids and get them situated before I started working again.

Zach and his friends returned from the trip to Ms. Gibson's. He came inside the house to get the Monopoly game. Zach had been playing so hard that he smelled like he hadn't showered in days. Breezy loaded a tray of drinks and took them outside. I told Breezy's friend, Ruby, that I ordered the food and should arrive in thirty-five minutes.

I noticed a few more kids pull up on bikes and drop them in the driveway, joining the other kids at the table under the tree. I called back to the pizza place and ordered extra food. I told them to give the food to the group of kids out front when they got to the house.

Before I picked up the phone, my spirit guides told me that it would be a short call about Sierra's new customer. I texted Sierra and let her know I was ready for her to call me. The phone rang almost immediately. It was Sierra.

I answered, "Hi, Sierra. What would you like me to take a look at?"

She seemed in good spirits, "Hi, Katharine, I just got a job. It's for this weekend. Could you look at him for me?"

"Sure. What's your client's first name?" I asked.

She replied, "I'm unsure if this is his first or last name, but the name on the message is Kingston."

I felt she would be safe with him as soon as she said the name. And I sensed that she would actually have a good time.

I relayed the information and asked, "Do you have any idea where you are going?"

Sierra stated, "He told me not to bring dressy clothes. Only bring comfortable clothes. I've never had a request for that before."

Her spirit guides pointed to a window that showed a future vision of Sierra on a Yacht. She was laughing and having fun.

I said, "Sierra, it looks like you're going to have fun. They're showing it to me. You are laughing and having a good time on a yacht. I see you enjoying the weekend and wishing you had another one like it. Do you want me to look any further?"

She replied, "No, that's great. Whenever I ask you to look into a weekend rendezvous, I mainly want to know if I survive it."

I acknowledged, "Yes, I understand."

"Hey, Katharine, what does someone like *you* do? Day-to-day?" she queried.

"Well, I work every single day, seven days a week. But in between, I try to have fun with my kids. They were let out of school early today, so about thirteen kids came over to play."

"What are your kid's names?" she asked.

I informed her, "I have a daughter named Breezy, who is in high school, and a son named Zach, who is in middle school."

Sierra continued questioning, "Are you married?"

"No," I replied.

She asked, "Why are you working every day?"

"I want to give my kids a good life in a good school area," I confessed.

The conversation finally ended, and I walked out front to ground. The yard was filled with kids. Each had a positive glowing energy field, and all the beautiful colors made me smile.

Curious by the extra stack of pizzas, I queried, "There are more than I ordered. Where did the extra pizzas come from?"

Breezy looked up before she rolled the dice from the game she was playing and said, "The pizza guy said the extras are from an accidental order that came in at the same time. He said to tell you Trevor said hi."

"That's thoughtful of him," I said.

Glancing up, I noticed Butchie was parking his truck in the cul-de-sac.

He approached, admiring the bikes and all the kids from the neighborhood, and commented, "Nice party on a weekday."

I gestured to the stacked pizza boxes and said, "Please, help yourself. There is pizza and drinks, and if you are up for it, you can probably get in on that basketball game."

Butchie smiled, opened a lawn chair, and pulled a drink out of the ice chest. He opened his phone and handed it to me to look at something. It was a message for *Katharine* but sent to the email that Butchie monitors for me. He manages my bookings for major events, group readings, and other business stuff.

The message read, *I noticed we live very close, and I would like to meet you for coffee. You look like you need a friend like me. I want to share something with you, and only you.*

I looked inquisitively at Butchie while he answered the email message.

Thank you for reaching out, but Katharine cannot meet for coffee.

I looked at Butchie and said, "Thank you for looking out for me."

Butchie looked at me in disbelief and snapped, "Come on, Katharine, I'm leaving for a couple of months tomorrow. Now, I've got to worry about a creepy guy trying to get you to have coffee with him."

He wasn't jealous or anything like that; he was just being very protective of me. He's like Kevin Costner in the movie *Bodyguard*—he tries to balance loving me and protecting me at the same time. I walked behind him and began lightly massaging his shoulders while saying, "You don't need to worry about anything. The house has cameras that are monitored and cover every angle of the perimeter."

He calmed down and said, "Make me a promise, Katharine. You don't leave the house unless someone's with you."

I soothed his request by saying, "I promise."

Butchie turned around and looked me straight in the eyes and popped a kiss. "Okay, that's good enough for me," he stated. "It's going to be hard staying that far away and not worrying about you here."

A stack of mail sat on the corner of my desk from earlier in the day. There was a unique gold envelope lying on top. I quickly discarded most of it in the recycling bin and opened the gold envelope. It didn't have a return address, but I could sense Sierra's energy all over it. The card inside had a picture of a beautiful beach with a sunset. A piece of paper embossed with a fancy S fell out. I opened the folded paper.

Dearest Katharine,

I hope your day is a beautiful one. You are such a gift to me and so many other souls. One of the things I first felt when I learned about you was just knowing you would change my life. I hadn't brought this up before because I didn't know how. I did hear you say that when people meet, there's always something for them to learn from the relationship. It might be a spiritual evolvement or a balancing of a spiritual lesson. I believe our connection is both.

There were times when I felt anxious. So, I either thought about what you said or thought of you and felt comforted. I will chalk it up to us being part of each other's spiritual family. I remember when I inquired about your family. You said you were the family's black sheep, and your life experience is not always essential to the family you're born to. The importance lies in the family you make. It's the people you consider your family, even without biological relations. I feel that way about you. I hope this card conveys that you're making a difference in my life.

Love always,
Sierra

I kept a special box beside the bed with greeting cards and notes. I often opened the box and looked at some of the encouraging stuff when I became emotional about work and felt like quitting. I pride myself on being a secret keeper to everyone I read for, so this is a place where I conceal these cards.

I went to my bedroom, opened the nightstand drawer, and grabbed the box. I placed Sierra's card inside, and slid it back into its hiding spot.

Chapter 4
No-Child Policy

While Butchie and I finished breakfast the next day, I psychically got flashes of beautiful cars in my mind—just random classic vehicles and flashes of a man carefully shining each one with a cloth.

Butchie's voice interrupted, "Hello, Katharine, where are you? Are you even paying attention to what I'm saying?"

"Yes, I got everything you've been telling me," I answered.

He said, "I may regret asking this, but what has got your attention?"

"I keep getting random flashes of classic cars and flashes of a guy who seems sad in losing them. I'm sure it's about a client I'm reading for today." I insisted.

There was a card lying next to Butchie's plate. He put his hand over it and slid it across the table. While smiling, I quickly opened it. It was a gift card for Carter's luxury car service.

"Thank you, Butchie, this is very thoughtful," I said.

He modestly explained, "While I'm away, this should cover any possible misses on the school bus for Zach or a ride into Houston."

I nodded in agreement and replied, "Thank you, you know it will get used."

I glanced at my watch and realized I was cutting it close to getting home for my nine o'clock session. The session was with a client named Davy, whom I had a brief reading with at a charity event about two years ago. I had given him my contact information in case he wanted another session later. I remember when I sat down with Davy for the first time.

I like to use oversized note cards with my contact information for when I do *automatic channeled writing*. People appreciated the cards as a great souvenir from the night and gave them a reminder of what needed to be remembered from our session.

When I sit down with someone at an event or a party, each reading is usually about twenty to thirty minutes long. So, I make notes and do *automatic writing* on the cards. Many people end up reviewing the cards later and setting up a private session with me. That is why I remember Davy. When he asked me about his husband-to-be, Ian, I saw that the spiritual contract between them needed to be balanced.

When I got to my desk, I sat down and grounded to prepare for the session. I knew this call was for clarification and validation. I began the FaceTime with Davy.

He held up the card with the *automatic writing* and my contact information while smiling.

Davy began, "I don't expect you to remember the reading you gave me two years ago. There were a lot of people there, and it was a large event. And I know you've read for thousands since then. But you wrote something on this card from our session that struck me as odd, but I did exactly what you told me to do, and it paid off."

My spirit guides stepped into the space to help. I remembered instantly what I had written on the back of the card. His spiritual connection to Ian needed balance. Once it was in place, the spiritual contract would clear for every lifetime. The spiritual guidance was to have a written contract before going into this marriage.

Davy was giving up his hopes of being a father. He knew going into this marriage with Ian that he would never be a father.

I knew that was a big deal for him and it weighed heavily on the relationship.

Ian had a car collection, which he claimed were the only babies he would ever want. The memory of seeing Ian's spectacular car collection had put me into another daze and I must have gone into my *signature* unconscious pause again.

Davy immediately pleaded for my attention, "Katharine...Katharine...Hello? Oh...I'm sorry; I thought the screen froze up. Are you okay?"

Suddenly, I popped back into *this* world and said, "Yes, I'm fine. I remember our session, and I remember how you were planning to marry Ian despite the fact that he didn't want children and that his car collection was his babies."

Davy lowered his head toward his desk, as if disappointed. He glanced up and briefly smiled as he read out loud the notes on the card that I had written when I first met him.

He began, "The marriage will be short-lived. Ian's no-child policy will never change. Since you are being asked to give up the dream of being a father, you need to add this stipulation in case Ian ever wants to end the marriage."

He paused for a moment to collect himself and then continued reading the notes I had written. "The car collection at the time of marriage and any other car acquired during the marriage will become the sole ownership of Davy McLean. The building built for these cars and the property the building sits on will also go to Davy McLean. This will be difficult for you to ask, but one day, you will know why."

Davy held the card to his chest and admitted, "I did not want to believe what you said since Ian was very convincing of his love for me. But when we sat down to sign the prenup, I realized you were right. So, I told him I would waive all rights to the other property and money if this one claim was added to the agreement."

I wanted to hug Davy right then because I knew this was a monumental leap of faith for him.

Davy added, "I wanted to meet with you to give an update on this but also to ask what is next in my life?"

I explained, "Davy, your spirit guides are saying the energy around you is shifting. Ian will try to fight to keep the cars, but the young man he is interested in will encourage him to divorce you quickly. The connection Ian has to the new love interest is one-sided, and this guy will string Ian along."

Davy's eyes began to tear up as he nodded in agreement with me. "You're so right, Katharine. I found out Ian had been conversing with a twenty-year-old guy in London for some time now."

I responded, "Davy, I know you are upset right now because the pain and shock are still so fresh. The connection between Ian and this young guy won't last long. This guy is not at all interested in Ian. He enjoys the gifts and the thrill of the chase, but he doesn't intend to move to Connecticut. The only reason why he's urging him to get a divorce from you is because he's trying to postpone moving to Connecticut with Ian. He keeps telling Ian he won't live with him if he stays married to you. The desire to have this guy move in is pushing Ian to get the divorce, which, of course, benefits you."

I could hear Davy quietly sobbing, and I tried to console him with my words.

"I understand divorce is tough on everyone," I soothed. "But you need to see that you've set yourself up in a lovely way. Ian had no intention of ever giving you anything, and he was going to have you sign the prenup without the car clause. Thank goodness you added it. This car collection is worth millions. Let's talk about your future moving forward."

I paused and allowed his spirit guides to show me some future events.

I explained excitedly, "Your spirit guides are showing me that you will be a father of three. All the babies will be yours and your partner through surrogacy. When you marry again, it will be forever. In a few years, you will look back at this as an experience that made you appreciate your beautiful life."

I had a busy day, but I had forty-five minutes between my subsequent sessions. So, I ran downstairs and into the backyard to water all the plants and vegetables. I could hear the phone ringing inside the house, so I turned off the water and returned inside. I noticed it was Sierra calling.

I answered, "Hello."

She replied, "Hi, Katharine, it's Sierra. Do you have a minute? I want to talk to you about a few things."

"Sure, Sierra," I said. "I have forty-five minutes until my next appointment."

She explained, "I spoke to Dr. Vasquez about changing my name, but she told me it wasn't necessary. So, I'd like to talk to you about it, okay?"

I answered, "Please, Sierra, start however you want."

She began, "When my father and mother were dating, they were crazy in love, and it stayed that way until my father passed. While they were dating, my father bought a Ford Sierra. My mother told me I had been conceived in that car. I don't like the name Sierra and wanted to know if there was another name you feel would resonate better with who I am."

"Sierra, you can change your name to whatever you want," I stated. "Some celebrities have shortened, added to, or completely changed their names. My opinion should not matter, but I love your name; it fits you. You may have been named after a car, but Sierra is beautiful name. Besides, if you had been born earlier, your parents might have named you Pinto after the 1970's Ford Pinto. Could you imagine—Pinto Delmar?"

Sierra laughed hysterically, then said, "Don't joke with me, Katharine. I mean come on, even you use your middle name instead of your first. I'm leaning more toward a name like Michelle."

I knew Sierra was insecure about many things, so I had to make sure she didn't get overwhelmed by insignificant details of her life. I responded to her with more psychic reasoning.

I recalled, "When I have read for you psychically regarding the men in your work, I noticed the lure you have over them; it's this exotic temptation that you exude from head to toe. It's your name! It's your brand, Sierra Delmar."

Sierra seemed to understand what I was trying to convey, but I needed to go a little deeper.

I suggested, "Let's try something different. Go stand in front of the mirror and state 'My name is Michelle Delmar'."

I heard Sierra push the chair out from the desk and get up. There was a moment of silence as I knew she was looking at herself in the mirror.

She laughed nervously, saying, "Hi, I'm Michelle Delmar."

There was a short pause, and then, more confidently, "I am Sierra Delmar."

I declared, "You are viewed as exotic! The men who are drawn to you crave that exotic look. They see it as an experience to explore. When you stand in front of the mirror and say, 'Michelle Delmar', it doesn't have that same impact as Sierra Delmar. I want you to see yourself as the person you want to be. Many immigrants felt they needed to change their name when they got to this country. They needed to be something different. But the name doesn't make you who you are. Your intent makes you who you are or who you become."

Sierra seemed satisfied with the explanation and turned the conversation in a different direction: "I see your point, Katharine. So, do you agree with what I do?"

My spirit guides encouraged me to give the nonjudgmental view I'm usually true to.

I explained, "The experience you choose is not for me to judge. Only you can determine what is right for you. It is my honor to help with anything along your spiritual path. Your path and experience here is your choice, and no one else's. When we choose to incarnate in any lifetime, you and your *Higher Self* decide what we do with our experience. I know there will come a day when you decide this isn't what you want to continue doing, and you'll find something else that brings you joy. Until then, we will continue to work through whatever you want to talk about."

Sierra was tearing up when she asked, "What about you...I mean, do you like *your* work?"

I could feel my heart full of light as it was beaming out to her.

I answered, "Yes, I do. I find that, with everyone, I naturally have love and respect for them on a deeper level than I can explain. Even if I tell everyone I meet that I love them, they would be unable to comprehend what I truly feel because most people don't see everyone in that way."

Suddenly, the alarm on my phone let out a loud jingle, letting me know I had an appointment soon.

Sierra heard the alarm as well.

"I guess time is up!" she declared. Katharine, I want to thank you for being a part of my life. Sometimes I get a strange feeling that you're somehow my savior or something."

I affirmed, "Sierra, it's my honor as I learn so much from everyone I read for."

I logged onto my Zoom account and waited for my client to appear. A few minutes had passed while I was sending Zoom links out for the next day's sessions. My spirit guides suddenly caught my attention and told me to Facetime my client, since she had forgotten about our session time. I quickly exited Zoom and began to Facetime my client, Kennedy. The screen opened with a view of the inside of Kennedy's car. Behind her shoulder, I could see a small dog and a toddler in a car seat. Kennedy turned the phone toward herself to be in full view of the camera.

She spoke, "Hang on, Katharine. I'm ordering some food."

I could see that she was at a fast-food restaurant, and the girl taking her order seemed to be having a rough day. While waiting for her to finish her order, I set the timer to stay on track since I only had a fifteen-minute break between Kennedy and the next appointment.

Kennedy declared, "They are super busy today, and the line here is longer than average for this time!"

She was unaware of the time, so I reminded her, "We have forty minutes left for the session."

After the food bag came through the open window, Kennedy said, "One moment, Katharine."

She parked her car, pulled out a few fries, and devoured them while handing a bag of food to her toddler in the backseat.

She turned the car off, took a deep breath, and exclaimed, "I'm ready now for our session!"

Without missing a beat, she continued, "My husband and I have been going through a rough patch."

She looked down in the food bag as if she lost something and inquired, "Do you see us working through this, or do you see me deciding to leave him?"

Kennedy continued digging around in the bag, randomly pulling out ketchup packets and throwing them on the floor.

She huffed, "Oh, no, they left out the dipping sauce! Hang on." She leapt out of the car and ran to the restaurant.

As I sat waiting, I could hear her child talking to the dog. I could see cars periodically pulling out of the drive-through. I looked down for a moment and started some *automatic writing* since our session had little time left. I proceeded by channeling all she needed to know about her marriage and what she could do to improve it. There really wasn't anything I could say that would give her the motivation to change. She wasn't willing to put much effort into making changes, which would force him out of the marriage.

I heard the car door open, and Kennedy hopped back in the driver's seat. "Sorry, Katharine. I ran into someone I knew, and she chatted with me for a minute. Okay, so no more distractions. What do you want to tell me about my marriage?"

I announced, "Kennedy, I have two pages of automatic writing with lots of information. But there is nothing I can tell you that you'll take seriously. I can see you push your husband to the breaking point. You will not find anyone else as good as him. You will continue to draw in men that just use you. Your husband will be consoled by one of your friends, and they'll end up together."

Kennedy didn't seem to grasp what I had just said. She just looked at me, puzzled, and took another bite of her sandwich. She took a long slurping draw from the straw in her drink.

Finally, she spoke, "I'm still trying to figure out which one of my friends would want him. I mean, I've complained about him to every one of them. And they all seemed to agree with me. So, I know you might be wrong on that. Besides, I am the hottest chick in my group of friends, and I can tell that all their husbands want me too."

The alarm on my phone went off, letting me know the session was up, and not a moment too soon. I sat in awe for a few seconds, trying to digest the selfish words I just listened to.

Kennedy looked perturbed but still had enough breath to ask a question. She blurted out, "What does my future look like?"

"Kennedy, our time is up, and I have to prepare for the next session," I protested. Anyway, I wrote two pages of notes while you were in the restaurant. I can snap a picture of them and send them to you in a text. If you have trouble reading my writing, just let me know."

She became more upset, and huffed, "I had to order food and it's not my fault this place forgot my sauce!"

I just sat there in silence, hands together, and praying she would just stop.

Kennedy took a deep breath and said, "Do you think we can talk later today so I can ask more questions?" she pleaded.

My spirit guides stepped in to tell me, *Kennedy doesn't have any regard for anyone else, and that's why no relationship she ever has will ever work.*

Kennedy continued before I could answer her question, "When I booked this appointment, there seemed to be many times to choose from. Obviously, you can't be that busy."

I said, "I *am* busy because I take other appointments that are booked through other sources. Please review the notes and keep them in a place so you can look them over at the end of the year."

Kennedy's hand moved toward the phone, and she quickly ended the FaceTime.

I glanced through my text messages while hearing my guides tell me that my next session had an emergency. I realized that Zach and Breezy wouldn't be home for another hour, so I checked the hotline for callers waiting. I didn't have anyone in line, but I logged in to accept calls anyway while I finished some office stuff.

After a few minutes, the phone rang with a hotline caller.

"Hi, this is Katharine. How may I help you?" I answered.

The man on the other end of the phone replied, "Hi, my name is Dominic. I have a few questions about my work."

I invited Dominic to ask his questions.

He said, "I work at this church. I'm a priest, and I've been in love with another priest named Scott who has been there for some time. We had a good connection. On several occasions, I felt it would turn into something more."

He stopped talking for a moment to catch his breath and then continued, "But since the last time we talked, he hasn't wanted to connect with me again. So, I have a few questions."

Dominic paused to collect his thoughts and then said, "The first question is should I stay at this church? Scott has been at the church longer than I have. It seems more people request him for funerals. I seem to do more of the weddings and house blessings. I was wondering if you see me doing more funerals at this church?"

I responded, "Dominic, your spirit guides are saying that there's much more for you to learn at this church. You will have more opportunities coming up at this church. You *will* be doing more funerals. There'll be more requests for you over the next few months."

I could sense that he had another question. His spirit guides showed me his heart and how much his heart was connected to Scott.

I asked, "Dominic, is there anything else you want me to look at?"

"Yes," he replied. "Do you feel that Scott and I will ever have an actual relationship?"

Immediately, his spirit guides told me that Scott was not interested in continuing this long-term relationship.

I clarified, "I'm sorry, Dominic, your guides are showing me that there's no opportunity for something long-term with this relationship. You don't have a spiritual contract in place. It's not something you plan while you're here on earth. It's something that's contracted and planned way before you get here. But I do see you with a good person in the future and having a great connection with them. Although, this person is not a priest. This person has an occupation outside of the church."

I continued, "The exciting part is that they adore you because of what you do, and you have a great amount of respect for one another. You may have some feelings of resentment toward

Scott. But I want you to keep in mind that it was just an experience. And there's nothing you need to feel angry or upset about."

Dominic hesitated, "Interesting you say that, because I felt I should leave the church. I already feel uncomfortable being around him. There are four priests at our church. I suspected he's been engaging Edward, the newest priest who recently joined."

Dominic's spirit guides urged me to tell him that he's correct about Edward.

I said, "Your spirit guides are saying you're right that Scott had a connection with Edward long before he had been assigned to your church. It was Scott who had requested Edward to be sent there. Your spirit guides want you to continue your work there and not discuss your past connection with Scott. You need to do well there so you can improve. You are the next priest in line for Scott's position, so you will step into that lead role when he leaves."

Dominic challenged, "Are you sure Scott will leave?"

I explained, "Your spirit guides are telling me that he will leave to avoid any trouble from the past relationships he has had there. You need to see this as an example of what you shouldn't do while working there. The connection with your future significant other is unrelated to the church."

Dominic seemed to gain an interest in what I was telling him, so he said, "Please go on."

I continued, "He will work completely outside of your profession. You won't allow yourself to be entangled in the relationships within the church. This decision will help you to continue your work there. It looks like Scott will be leaving in the next few months. At that point, you can choose to change out Edward so there are no weird feelings with the other priest you will begin to work with."

Dominic praised, "This is the best news ever. Do you see how I will meet my partner?"

I replied excitedly, "I see a handsome man walk in and shake your hand in a formal greeting. He is part of the legal counsel that comes in to talk with the staff regarding Scott's departure. I am unsure of his name, but I see Hawaiian in his energy field."

When I got off the phone with Dominic, I realized I only had a few minutes to get to the bus stop to greet the kids. Some people were walking down the street quickly to try and beat the rush of kids about to get off the bus. I passed an older fellow walking two Pomeranian dogs. The guy looked like an historical version of Santa Claus, complete with a white beard and walking cane. I made light conversation with him as I passed.

He cackled, "You should find someone your own age. Don't waste your time with me."

I had to laugh because I didn't realize being pleasant to someone would be misconstrued as coming on to them. I chalked it up to flattery.

I continued to move past him towards the bus stop as Zach's bus pulled up. A mob of kids got off and started running down the street. Zach and I walked and talked with a few of his friends as we headed in the same direction. Then Zach and I turned off the main road toward our house.

Zach looked up at me and said, "Mom, are you going to make meeting me at the bus stop a habit? I'm excited and glad to see you're not panicking about being away from home."

Suddenly, I felt a rush of fear run through my entire body as I realized what he was saying. Then I started to calm down realizing I had been getting away from home more often and was ok. It seemed like the *universe* was guiding me toward a cure for my anxiety of being away from home. I didn't recognize it due to my busy days. I smiled at Zach, and he looked back at me as if he had been monitoring my behavior and noticed some changes.

Suddenly, I heard my spirit guides say, *the little girl spirit down the street is out front.*

My eyes darted in the direction of the house with the little girl's spirit, and sure enough, she was out front.

"Hey Zach!" I exclaimed. "The little girl's spirit is out front of the house. Let's get the car and drive down there and see if we can help get her into the light."

"Okay, Mom, let's go," he agreed.

I ran through the house and into the garage while smashing the button to open the garage door. I backed the car out into the driveway, and Zach jumped in. I continued to back down the driveway, forgetting to close the garage door. I turned onto the main street.

We noticed Breezy and her friend walking from the bus stop. I slowed the car down, and Zach yelled out the window, "We're going down to see the little girl's spirit. We'll be back in a little bit." We drove off while Breezy was in mid-sentence. Zach just waved as he laughed at her disgusted expression.

"Zach, do you see how the little ghost lingers out front? This is where she took her last breath on the stretcher of the ambulance," I explained.

I parked in front of a house with a *For Sale* sign two doors down from the little girl's spirit.

"Come on, Zach," I prodded. "Get out of the car and keep your eyes out for the other spirits who come in to help the little girl get to the light."

Zach was so excited; we had been hoping to get the little girl spirit across for some time. I moved in close, but not too close, so as not to draw the homeowners' attention.

I called in Archangel Azrael and *my* angels to help bring the little girl's spirit to the light. There was a group of angels with Archangel Azrael. I didn't recognize many of them. They weren't looking at us but were focused on the little girl's spirit. The spirit was waif-looking which matched what I had been told by my spirit guides about her human life of neglect at the hands of her family.

The angels spoke lovingly to the girl's spirit, and suddenly, a deceased woman entered from a portal that appeared. She opened her hands to the child. Zach and I stood in silence as we watched the little girl's spirit move further than I had ever seen her before.

As she moved through the large portal to the woman, the angels, and Archangel Azrael's accompaniment followed, and the massive portal of light closed. I glanced at Zach as I stood there in tears and felt the hurt and pain the little girl's spirit encountered during her existence here.

Zach asked, "Mom, we did a good thing, so why are you crying?"

I pulled him in for a hug and turned to walk toward the car. I explained, "I'm crying because I wish I could've saved the little girl when she was alive."

After we got back to the house, Breezy had already started making dinner. She had taken a tablecloth from the cabinet and placed it on the picnic table. She had planned for us to eat outside. A feeling of gratitude poured over me for what I had just experienced with the little girl's spirit. A river of tears just started pouring out.

"Excuse me," I said. "I need go to my room for a few minutes."

I got to my room and sat on the bed. I let the tears pour out and thanked the angels for coming forward to help that little girl's spirit. I asked permission from God and the angels to help me with any of these types of situations in the future.

I wanted to do whatever I could to help spirits, and their loved ones have peace.

After dinner, we all got into bed and watched *The Parent Trap*. We had seen this movie several times already, but it always brings me comfort and laughs, and I needed that now. Perhaps it was Dennis Quaid's smile or Lindsay's natural acting ability. Whatever it was, we all loved it.

After the movie, I reached over to turn off the phone. I noticed several text messages pop up. The one that stood out was the one from Butchie that read:

> We are filming a night scene. I won't be out until after 4:00 a.m. I'll call when I get up. Please answer, even if you're in a session. I want to know that everything's ok! I love you.

After turning off the phone and the lights, I glanced at the TV. Lindsay Lohan, who plays Annie's part, said, "She's drunk! She's never had more than one glass of wine her entire life, and she chooses today to show up totally zonked!"

I reached for the remote and set the sleep timer to turn off the T.V. in thirty minutes. My mind went back to the word *zonked* as I realized I had missed something that my spirit guides said after I listened to Lindsey deliver that line.

Dang it, I thought. *What was it that I missed? What was it? I am so tired. I can't even put coherent thoughts together.*

I glanced over at the wall and saw my spirit guides standing there. I looked at them, expecting to hear a repeat of whatever was said after I listened to the word zonked. My spirit guides began sending a sleep frequency to which my mind no longer cared what was being said. My eyes closed on their own.

I woke up entirely rejuvenated and refreshed. The stream of frequency my spirit guides gifted me was more than just sleep.

I stood in front of the bathroom mirror and squeezed out some toothpaste, missing the bristles completely as it dropped into the sink. I topped off the toothbrush again and commenced to brushing.

Breezy and Zach walked into the bedroom. They were already dressed and looked ready to go somewhere.

"You're not even dressed yet?" Breezy grumbled. "Here, I'll pull something from your closet for you to wear. We need to get going. Marilyn will be here shortly. Remember, you volunteered to drive her back from the dental appointment? She's going to be sedated. We're going to walk to the shopping center while you and her are in the dental office."

Zach looked concerned and asked, "Don't you remember?"

I spit out the toothpaste and laughed. "Of course, I remember," I replied. "Okay, let me pull myself together. I'll be down in a few minutes."

At that moment, we heard Marilyn's horn out front. The kids ran downstairs and hurried outside. When I got out there, Marilyn jumped into the passenger side, so I got in the driver's seat. Marilyn looked at me and imitated an English accent, "Ok, James, we're ready. Take us to the dentist and be snappy about it."

We all laughed as I backed the van out of the driveway and drove up the street. I turned and looked at Marilyn while she popped a pill and took a swig of water.

"What was that?" I asked.

She explained, "It's something the doctor told me to take before my dental visits or medical tests to help with my anxiousness."

"Okay. So, the dentist makes you anxious?" I queried.

Marilyn replied, "Yes, I am incredibly anxious."

I thought about it for a moment. I guess we all have something that makes us anxious. I never really felt that Marilyn ever judged me about my own anxiety. She always seemed to figure out how to get me to a calm place when I panicked. If the dentist was the only thing that made her anxious, then that's a blessing. Sometimes, I felt terrible for Marilyn having a friend like me, who gets nervous about being out in certain places. Although, she never seemed to let it bother her.

After Marilyn's appointment we all went to lunch at one of my favorite restaurants.

Marilyn's energy looked very filtered, which was an indication of intoxication, or drugs present in the body. Of course, there were drugs in her body because the dentist gave her a sedation. When we got to the restaurant, Marilyn got out of the car and walked to the entrance. Ramsey pointed down to her feet and said, "What happened to your shoe, mom?"

He was right. She was missing a shoe. *How was she missing a shoe?* I thought.

I opened the passenger door to see if her shoe slipped off her foot into the van. Nope, no shoe.

I called the dental office, and asked if, by chance, she left her shoe there.

The receptionist started laughing immediately and said, "Yes, we found her shoe in the waiting room. She must have walked out of it on her way to the door."

I told her to hold on to it and we'd return to pick it up later.

I looked at Marilyn and said, "You left your shoe at the dentist's office. We've got to go back and get it."

She slurred her words, "No, no, no, I'm fine. I don't need to go back and get it. Let's get the kids fed."

I said, "You can't enter this place without a shoe."

Marilyn giggled, "Don't worry about it. I have a plastic bag here. I'm just going to tie it around my foot."

Laughing, I said, "What? Tie it around your foot. Are you serious? No. People are going to notice that."

She insisted, "No, no, no, I'll be fine. I'll tie it around my foot, so I'm not barefoot and sit at the table."

"Okay, great," I hesitantly agreed.

So, we walked into the restaurant. The kids and I strayed to the counter to order our food.

I glanced over at Breezy and said, "Do you remember the part in Parent Trap where Annie said, *...and she chooses today to show up totally zonked?*"

Breezy laughed and said, "Yes, I was thinking about the same thing. When we tell Marilyn this tomorrow, she won't believe us. We're going to have to get a picture."

I turned to the table to snap a photo of Marilyn, but she was gone. I glanced around frantically, wondering if she had gone to the bathroom. I finally spotted her grazing off the salad bar with a grocery sack tied to her foot.

Breezy was laughing hysterically, and I realized this was the time we needed to get the photo. She'll never believe this any other way. Breezy snapped a picture of Marilyn while I urged the boys to stay in line.

"I will be right back," I said.

Marilyn picked up a carrot stick and dipped it into the ranch as I approached. It's always hard to manage people taller than you, but I guided her back to the table and told her she needed to sit down before the manager comes over and asks us to leave.

I got back to the boys and placed our order. When we got in the car, Marilyn insisted on going home, but I told her we needed to get back to the dental office so I could pick up her shoe. She looked down at her foot and realized that she didn't have a shoe on, even though we had been telling her that for the past hour. We picked up the shoe and then drove her home. I figured she could pick up the van the next day.

When we returned to our house, I got settled back in and took some work calls.

Later in the evening, while lying in bed, my phone chimed with a new text. It was from Marilyn, and it read:

> Katharine, thank you so much for being a great friend and helping me through my anxiety issue. And sorry for being so zonked today. Love Marilyn.

I put the phone down and thought for a moment. I began to laugh, as I realized what It was that I had missed from my spirit guides last night while watching *Parent Trap*. They had been trying to convey to me what was going to happen today with Marilyn. They kept showing me the word *zonked*. This was a valuable lesson for me: Pay closer attention to what my spirit guides tell me.

Chapter 5
Kissing Homeless

I put on a hat for shade in preparation for mowing the yard. While I was pulling out the mower from the garage, a car came barreling down the street, whipping around the cul-de-sac and not breaking at all. It had a strange device attached to the top, and I was curious as to what it was.

Of course, my guides chimed in and said, "It takes street photos for mapping directions."

I didn't know what that meant, but I thought it might somehow be connected to Google regarding how they do street views.

I noticed a few other neighbors were working in their yards. I waved to Mary across the way and then started up the lawnmower.

As I finished mowing the front yard, I psychically got a glimpse of a woman I previously did a reading for, Lyla, from California. She was twenty-two, very wealthy, partied every day, and had no real ambition in life other than when the next party was.

The vision I had was of her kissing a homeless person. That's not an exaggeration or anything. I witnessed him sitting against the wall with tattered clothes and looking weary. This person was filthy, and they were certainly homeless. *So, why was she kissing him?* I thought.

It had been a while since I heard from her. Whenever she did call, it was through the hotline, and she always seemed to be hosting some party.

I tried not to give it too much thought and continued to work in the yard. I had booked a light day with work to do some things in the yard. It was relaxing for me to use the leaf blower and lawn mower and do yard work. I had an appointment at 2:00 p.m. By the time I finished mowing, cleaning up the yard debris, and chatting it up with the neighbors, it was 11:00 a.m.

That gave me just enough time to shower and clean up for lunch and still have plenty of time to do a few other chores around the house.

During lunch, the vision of Lyla kissing the homeless guy continued in my mind. That evening, I got a few more psychic glimpses of it.

Once I returned home from lunch, my spirit guides urged me to get on the hotline. I had only been on call for about twenty minutes when I received an alert for an incoming hotline call. Lo and behold, it was Lyla!

"Hi, Lyla. I haven't heard from you in a while," I answered.

She didn't even return a salutation but just started talking. She blurted, "John's been in rehab a few times, but it didn't seem to work. One of the times, he was forced into it by his parents. The other, he was court-mandated because of disorderly conduct. I feel bothered by something we have been doing lately, and sometimes it feels wrong."

I could hear her take a long drag from a cigarette and then a loud gulp of a beverage. There was a long pause. I was remote viewing her, and I could see she was holding a canned energy drink. I knew how easily she could lose track of why she called, so I asked, "Lyla, what do you want me to look at?"

I didn't sense that she required psychic guidance, but she seemed more in need of a confession.

Lyla began purging, "Well, John and I had been going out more than usual, just like we did last year when he got in all that trouble. I do everything he wants me to do to get his love and affection. We still hang out with the same group of friends. Lately, when we would go out partying or clubbing, we would make bets with each other to do crazy things.

She continued talking at breakneck speed, "Everybody in the group is already wealthy, so we don't bet with money. Sometimes it's just cigarettes or something fun, you know? Maybe even a stack of pancakes. So, the other night, while we were at the club, we were all so wasted. When we left, you know how there were so many homeless people just hanging out on the streets? Well, one guy was sitting on the sidewalk all day and night, and people would buy him tacos. He's pretty dirty. When I say dirty, he hasn't showered in a long while. When we left the club, John dared me to kiss him. I'm like, okay, what harm could it do?"

She took another long drag from her cigarette and proceeded, "I could do a little kiss on the cheek, I thought, maybe even the top of the head. Then I took out a napkin and wiped my lips. But when I leaned in to do it, John yelled, 'French kiss him, and we want to *see* the tongue action.' So, I leaned in and kissed him just like that. I was so drunk. If I had been sober, I would never have done it. I was so disgusted thinking about it after waking up the next morning. It was the grossest thing I've ever done in my life."

She continued, "Some of the other things he asked weren't so bad. We went to listen to my favorite DJ. He dared me to dry hump her thigh. That wasn't a big deal. I did it. But kissing this homeless guy, I don't know what to do. I know John needs to get back into rehab. The last time he went into rehab, he just made it a party. He hung out with movie stars. A few people from a variety of bands, and oh yeah, there was that lady who was married to that popular rocker who committed suicide."

I watched the whole kissing event unfold in my psychic eye. At the same time, she paused, took another drag of her cigarette, and swallowed the rest of her energy drink. She continued talking as though she was trying to get into the book of Guinness World Records.

"I don't remember her name right now," she continued. "But John said she tried to sleep with him. It's evident to me he turned rehab into one big party, just like he does everything else. I could never break up with John. I love him, love him. I'd do anything for him."

She gagged, "I still get sick when I think about kissing that homeless guy. I want to throw up right now. One of the other girls with us was only concerned about partying. I've talked about her before with you. She's the one who made a comment about me being 'another trust fund baby.' Someone dared her to get under the blanket with some other guy, who I believe was relieving himself at the time. And she did it. None of this seems to bother her like it bothers me."

She slowed her pace a little, "I'm beginning to think if John loved me, he wouldn't ask me to do stuff like that. I wouldn't do it if I were just hanging out with my friends or on my own. Or if John had never come into my life. Sometimes, he does it to see if he can get people to do whatever he wants. It's like a magical time for him. I had always told him it doesn't matter how much money we have if we don't live long enough to enjoy it."

Lyla continued, "I don't think he hears me. I believe what he hears is that we need to keep enjoying life. Every day, it's about him looking good. Resting from his hangover and doing it again once he can stand upright. The other night, after the kiss with that homeless guy, he was kissing all over me. It didn't even phase him. I hadn't even brushed my teeth yet. I was too fucked up even to do anything. And he thought we were having sex. I swear, he thought we were having sex. He wasn't even hard, but he was going through the motions like we were having sex.

She went on, "I just let him do it. I just wanted to go to bed and forget it all. Besides, the room was spinning. And I just wanted to be done with the day."

I heard Lyla's refrigerator open, and she took a long draw from her cigarette. Again, I reminded her of my services and asked, "What would you like me to ask your spirit guides and angels?"

She took another drag of her cigarette and said, "I don't know, Katharine. If you could guide me, how do I get him into rehab and keep him as my boyfriend? I love him and don't want to give up on him."

I quickly intervened, "Ok. One, you've got to come from a place that's not you. It would help if you came from a place of your well-being. John is not able to see it for himself. It would help if you guided him to a mirror and stripped him down naked with none of his fancy clothes. Then, ask him to tell you why he wants to destroy his body. What does he feel like he's gaining, and why doesn't he want to use his time to make his life the best it could be? Then you will have to do the same for yourself when he is not there."

Lyla seemed amused but interested.

I heard her light another cigarette and take a long drag. Lyla softly replied, "Katharine, I want you to scan my body and see if I need to know anything."

When I glanced into her body and saw her energy field, I noticed a soul waiting beside her, waiting to come in. When I see this in the energy field, it usually means a pregnancy is coming. When the soul is entirely over the body, the pregnancy has happened.

It showed up as an overlay in the energy field. This is not to be mistaken for the soul being inside another's body; it's just an overlay to show me that the pregnancy has occurred. With Lyla, I recognized that the pregnancy would happen soon.

I informed her, "Lyla, I see a baby spirit waiting to come in, and it looks like a girl, so a pregnancy is coming within the next few weeks".

I heard her set a to-go cup on the kitchen counter. Suddenly, I saw a rush of red color in her energy field.

Lyla whimpered, "I'm scared, Katharine. I don't think John could be a good father, and with the way things have been, what if I get drunk and the pregnancy is not John's?"

She began crying.

I knew none of Lyla's friends would speak honestly to her, and while I felt strange doing so, I needed to do it anyway.

I calmly assured her, "You have two choices when you go out. You can get so drunk that you miss the enjoyment and the celebration of your life, or you can decide to be in control of your actions. As I see you in delivery, this child will be born, and the baby will be healthy. It will be John's."

Lyla exclaimed, "No way! I don't want to do that at this point in our life. This has given me so much to think about."

I concluded, "Please understand that when I say I see you keeping it, that is not an order or demand. It is a fact. There is no way you could ever turn away a baby of John's, knowing the child will have some learning difficulties due to John's drug use."

It was time for my 2:00 p.m. appointment, and I needed some sunshine, so I took the iPad to the patio table for my next Facetime. The sky was clear, and I could hear all the birds chirping back and forth to each other as if they were trying to entertain me.

Some clients joked that it sounded as if I was in a bird sanctuary. The sudden Facetime notification seemed out of sync with the beautiful bird sounds, fulfilling my attention. My guides stepped into the area, as did the client's spirit guides, who appeared on the small phone screen.

"Hi, my name is Joanna Ramirez," a voice began. "I'm a little nervous talking to you. I didn't feel nervous when I made the appointment, so I don't know what's happening now." She smiled, and I smiled back.

"It's okay," I reassured her. "You're fine; there's nothing to be nervous about. What I like to do in sessions is allow you to go through all your questions first. And then, as you're asking your questions, your guides may have me write a few things down, which is called automatic writing. I jot a few things down, and then at the end of our conversation, I fill in anything else you need to know."

Joanna smiled and calmly said, "That does make things easier. I didn't prepare any questions. But I do have one particular reason for the appointment. My daughter plays on a soccer team. She has soccer practice Tuesday through Saturday unless there is a game. Over the last month, I've occasionally caught a lady looking strangely at me while at soccer practice."

Joanna sighed, "She seems to be looking at me more when my husband, Javier, shows up to practice. He only shows up once or twice weekly but never stays for the full practice. Most of the time, he shows up toward the end. I was wondering if she somehow knows my husband. You know, like in an intimate way? Sometimes, I get the feeling he's cheated with her."

She continued, "There's nothing of any evidence that proves he has. We have sex regularly, at least once or twice a week. So, I guess in this session, I want to focus on what is happening with that woman. I need to know if I am crazy or paranoid. Should I be looking into this more?"

She said, "He only goes to work. He never hangs out with friends or family unless I am there. I know he works hard for our family. He is so exhausted that sometimes he comes home and goes straight to bed."

Joanna paused for a moment while looking down. Her eyes were filled with tears when she looked back up at me.

I asked, "Joanna, by any chance, do you know the woman's first name?"

She seemed to be contemplating the question and said, "I'm not quite sure. Maybe Tia, Thea, or something like that."

Several light beings came in and surrounded Joanna. That's when I knew there was much more to see than she thought.

I said, "Joanna, since you don't know or are unsure of her first name, please take a moment and picture her face."

At that moment, Joanna's spirit guides transmitted a frequency of the image of the woman who Joanna was worried about. I psychically got that she was not the one having an affair with Joanna's husband. While still viewing Joanne, I communicated with her spirit guides. I asked them to explain a little more.

Who is her husband having an affair with? I asked.

I could no longer hear the birds chirping, only the massive silence. Joanna's spirit guides relayed, *Many women. The woman staring at Joanna only knows about one of the affairs. Javier is cheating with her neighbor.*

Suddenly, her spirit guides showed me what Javier does during his workdays as a TV cable guy. He visits several different customers throughout the day, some for work and some for pleasure.

He visits some customers more frequently than others, obviously, the ones he services more than cable T.V. He has been doing this over the last five years. I had to pause and consider everything before I presented this information to her.

Silence broke, and I said, "Joanna, I need to explain what your spirit guides are showing me. This should answer all your questions, although you may not be happy. Your spirit guides showed me your husband wearing a work shirt and jeans, entering various people's homes. He is driving a truck that has spindles carrying different types of wire cables. It appears he is a cable TV provider."

Joanna seemed shocked and said, "Well, that's right. He works as a contractor for a local cable company, installing or troubleshooting. He shows me all the written work orders every day."

Joanna's spirit guides softly told me that Joanna was not prepared for what she was about to hear, but this was the best way for her to find out. I explained to her what the spirit guides had shown me as a typical day for Javier.

I explained, "He stops at a few different places and either installs or works on the cable TV. But when he finds a place where a woman lives alone, he becomes very friendly with them and eventually has sexual relations."

I continued, "He's built quite a group over the last five years. All these women are sixty years old or older. That's part of what he finds enticing with this routine. Your spirit guides said Javier seeks these women because he feels it's his best opportunity. They all seem to fall for Javier because they lack getting attention from anyone else. Many of them just lie on their sofa and talk to him as he installs their cable.

He becomes more and more personal with them in conversation as he works.

I watched Joanna's expression of discontent as I said, "The guides are telling me that you have seen him watching porn containing grannies or older women."

"Yes, that is true," she confided. "But Javier told me he was sending it to someone as a joke."

I inhaled deeply and stated, "Joanna, your husband does contract work for a cable company. That is true. But there are several customers he has become intimate with. Do you understand what I am telling you?"

I noticed the shock and disbelief on Joanna's face, but she needed to hear this. I explained, "The woman at soccer practice has been struggling to tell you. She has witnessed Javier visiting her neighbor over the last year and a half. The neighbor woman is sixty-eight years old."

Her spirit guides told me Joanna was about to abruptly end the session. Suddenly, Joanna's hand moved toward the screen, and the Facetime connection disappeared. I turned the iPad off and began to ground where I was sitting.

When I finally emerged from meditation, the birds were singing what seemed to be the same melody they had been playing before. I suddenly heard my guide say that Breezy was home. When I turned around, she was standing by the patio. I gestured for her to come over.

Breezy said, "I didn't want to walk up if you were looking into something important."

I looped my arm through hers and said, "No, I was coming out of grounding. Why don't we pick some veggies and make pizza tonight topped with homegrown goodies?"

Breezy smirked, saying, "I'm one step ahead of you. I mixed the dough and set it aside before I walked out here."

While laughing, I said, "I know. I psychically saw you make pizzas when I first looked at you, that's why I suggested it."

Later that evening, I talked to Butchie on the phone for a few hours and fell asleep. All I remember before falling asleep was the soothing tone of his voice.

The constant ringing of my phone shattered the silence in the bedroom. My upper body bolted straight up like a mechanical robot. My eyes weren't even open yet when I reached for the phone.

"Hey Katharine, this is Sierra," the voice burst out.

"I know it's two in the morning, but I'm glad I could reach you. I need your help!" she exclaimed.

Sierra informed me, "The wife of a guy named Frank that I had been servicing, texted me. Shockingly, she was able to get my number. Usually, my clients are very secretive."

"Anyway," she continued. "I received a text from Frank's phone asking me to meet him at his house. He said he'd leave the front door open, and I should make a drink, then go upstairs to the bedroom and get ready. He would only invite me to the house when his wife was on a long-lasting trip. This way, he had time to get everything cleaned up afterward."

Pausing momentarily, she continued, "I felt weird about it, but I did it anyway."

As Sierra talked, her spirit guides opened a viewing portal, showing me that Frank's *wife* had been waiting for her in the house. I focused back on Sierra talking.

She recalled, "Everything seemed fine as I entered the house. There were drinks poured and a tray of food out on the counter. I bypassed the food and grabbed a drink, heading up the stairs. I had my *weekend bag* in my hand as I moved up towards the room. I felt odd even though I could hear jazz music playing and everything else felt normal."

Sierra paused for a moment and took a deep breath, "Hold on a second, Katharine."

I asked, "Are you okay?"

"Yes, I just needed a moment," she clarified.

She continued her story, "I walked into his bathroom and couldn't shake the feeling that someone was watching me. I heard a noise, and when I turned around, I saw Frank's wife standing in the doorway of her closet. I didn't run or get scared. I still had my drink in one hand and the *weekend bag* in the other, and I asked her, 'Are you the one that requested my services?'"

Sierra paused and then said, "Without hesitation, she lunged at me. She held a large candle holder, swinging it at me like a *Louisville Slugger*. I managed to miss being hit, although she broke a glass window. As I came down the stairs, I threw my drink toward her. I don't know if it broke or if she got hurt, but I bolted out of there. I ran across the yard to the street. I frantically hopped in my car and took off like a *bat out of hell!*"

Breathing heavily, Sierra continued, "She didn't look good, Katharine. I'm terrified! Did I hurt her? Is she going to call the police on me? What's going on? Did he just randomly give her my number to clear his conscience?" Sierra was puzzled.

As I looked into the situation psychically, I parroted what Sierra's spirit guides told me. "The wife had gone through his phone while he was sleeping, Sierra. She managed to take out all the phone numbers and call each one. There were other women besides you from whom he had received *services*. Franks's wife contacted them, as well. She went down the list, scheduling a visit to see them face-to-face. You were last on the list."

Sierra cursed, "That sick bitch! She's a psychopath!"

I interjected, "Sierra, that's not the only thing she did. She went through his phone and randomly copied the photos that he had taken of his secret sexual escapades."

"Thankfully, there's none of you," I assured her. I do see a legal situation coming out of this for the wife, and the photos that she collected will be used as evidence."

Sierra seemed relieved, "OK, great! Do you see *me* having any legal trouble over this?"

I answered, "Not at all."

She quivered, "I'm scared, and my heart is racing. My pulse is thumping on my wrist, and my ankle hurts because I broke a heel trying to get down the stairs."

I thought I should interject something positive, so, I said, "Sierra, look at it this way: There was no harm to you, no harm to her, and you didn't drop any of your belongings there, which could have made things difficult for you later."

I continued, "I think the main thing we should be asking here is, *where's* Frank?"

Instantaneously, a male spirit beamed right in front of me, like they do in *Star Trek*. I instantly knew that it was Frank.

I hesitated, "S...Sierra... I ...I'm sorry to tell you this, but your client Frank is standing in front of me *in spirit*. He told me that he had come home from work four nights ago, and his wife started asking him a bunch of questions. She had gone through his phone the night before while he was sleeping. She found a bunch of suspicious names and decided to do a little research on them. She was able to learn about all the secret sexual encounters he had been having."

I parroted Frank, "My wife was so upset that she got in her car to back out and leave. I tried to calm her down as I walked in front of her car to the driver's side. She stepped on the gas pedal and ran me over. Her anger was so uncontrollable that she continued pushing on the gas pedal even after realizing she had hit me. That's what killed me."

I advised, "You need to contact the police about what happened tonight. You will not have any legal issues."

Suddenly, Frank's spirit chimed in and said, *My physical body is still lying on the garage floor. Once you call the police, they'll be able to find me, and they'll recognize the liquid in the glass that she tried to poison you with. She had put poison in the drinks that were waiting for you at the foot of the stairs.*

I relayed to Sierra what Frank shared, and I could tell she was emotionally distraught over this news. Then I said, "Please go to the police and tell them everything. I'll stay on the phone with you as long as you need, or you can call me afterward."

There was a moment of silence in the air.

Suddenly, Sierra exclaimed, "I can't believe that bitch tried to poison me! I mean, really? The nerve of her. Well, I'm definitely going to the police now!"

Chapter 6
A Slap of Confidence

Macy Graham was my 1:00 p.m. appointment. While I waited for her to call, I sent a text reminding her of our appointment. She was now fifteen minutes late. Macy was usually quick to respond with a video call.

Macy's face popped up on the computer, "Hi, Katharine, I'm sorry it took so long. I was trying to figure out how to share my screen, but I have it all figured out now. There's a video I need you to watch before our session. I want you to tell me what you think."

"Sure, Macy," I said. I waited for her to start the video, which was from the front porch security camera. There appeared to be a ghost in the footage.

Macy pleaded, "Katharine, did you notice that? Can you tell me who that ghost is?"

As soon as I psychically went in to feel the energy of the presence at her house, the angels around her told me there was not a lingering spirit on the porch.

I looked up at Macy and parroted word for word what the Angels said to me. "There are no lingering spirits on your porch."

"Well, Katharine, it's something," Macy rebutted.

She became very emotional, and her voice elevated as she tried to fight off an all-out cry.

Macy blurted out, "What is it? It's something. What's that image?"

She must have realized she was yelling and calmed down by taking several deep breaths. Then she looked up and said, "I wouldn't be so concerned, but my husband, Don, shared the video footage with me. He agreed that it's my grandmother coming to talk to me."

She replayed the video for me and used the pointer to show the zoomed-in apparition.

Macy continued, "Do you see where the ghost is standing? The plaque on the wall behind that image was from my grandmother, who used to make crafts and sell them at shows. She made the *Welcome* sign, the *Stay a while* sign, and the *Sit for a Spell* sign—all of them! I know it's my grandmother."

She paused abruptly and stared at the computer as if I didn't understand what she was showing me. It was hopeless. Macy's spirit guides stepped forward and said, *There's no spirit there. However, her grandmother does visit with her, although this is not her grandmother in the video. The image in the video is just an illusion that her husband created.*

I knew I was going to have a difficult time explaining this to Macy, but I needed to.

"Macy, your spirit guides told me that Don created this illusion. Your husband has doctored the video," I stated.

She refuted, "What? There is no way. He's the one who showed me the video. He told me he only showed it because I know more about ghosts than anyone. Why in the world would he want to fake a video? There's no way he would do something like this. Can you give me one valid reason?"

Macy paused and stared at me through the computer screen with an angry look. I realized she wasn't upset at her husband, only at me. I sat in silence for a moment while the spirit guides and angels transmitted a soothing frequency to keep me calm. I remote-viewed the day of the video, and I began to explain to Macy what I was seeing.

"I'm seeing your husband at the computer," I began. "Don is reading an e-mail from someone with whom he shared some footage of your front porch. He doesn't know this guy. It looks like this is the guy that Don hired to create the illusion on the porch."

I was still watching the remote viewing when Macy interrupted, "My husband is cheap and would never pay someone to do something like this. I mean, he nearly has a heart attack at restaurants when he sees the prices on a menu! And I'm talking fast food restaurants."

Immediately, more images of the past several weeks flashed before me. I saw things that Don was secretly doing behind Macy's back.

I went on to explain what I had remote-viewed, "Macy, I saw a woman who lives right behind you that your husband is interested in. It looked as though while you were investigating the ghost on the porch or sitting out there waiting for a ghost, he was quickly having some intimate time with her."

She replied, "Katharine, you don't understand! The woman behind us was recently abandoned by her husband and had no one to help her. Don has been helping her fix things around the house. She didn't even have a working AC; my husband fixed it. The spirit guides told me that Don did not fix the AC himself. He paid someone to do it. I knew this would be the proof Macy needed to believe any of this.

I revealed, "Macy, you can check the credit card bills from your husband's card. Your guide told me that your husband paid for the neighbor's AC repair. Don didn't fix it himself."

Macy looked at me through the monitor like I had no idea what I was saying.

Shockingly she said, "Okay, I will check the credit card bill. As far as my husband, where other women are concerned, he is just being helpful. That's the kind of person he is."

I knew I had to be careful in my approach. So, I looked at Macy with a soft smile and said, "Macy, have you ever seen Don fix an AC unit? Has he ever worked on *your* AC unit?"

Macy thought for a moment. She seemed to look very disgruntled, but I couldn't determine if she was upset with me or her husband.

She abruptly replied, "I think I've gotten all I needed out of this session."

The video connection ended abruptly, and I glanced out the window. My spirit guides told me that Macy would find out that Don did pay for the neighbor's AC repair. She would also learn about his affair and soon catch him in the act.

My spirit guides said, *Macy doesn't like you right now, but she will contact you again.*

That certainly didn't make me feel good—not that Macy didn't like me, but that she would contact me again. Her energy was much too high and intense for me.

After taking a short grounding break, I looked at my phone and saw a few texts from Sierra Delmar. The first one accompanied a photo of an adorably tiny filthy border collie lying on the floorboard of a Maserati.

I quickly looked through several other photos of this sweet boy whom Sierra referred to as Owen. Then, I focused on the text messages.

The first text read:

> I met a friend for fun and found this boy wandering the street. What should I do with him? I know you will know, so call me.

The second text read:

> You're probably in a session, so I decided to take this sweet boy to a vet. I had him examined and left him for neutering and teeth cleaning.

A third text:

> This lovely boy needed a name. So, please refer to him as Owen. I named him after Owen Wilson. They both have a crooked little smile that makes you realize you have found a friend.

I laughed thinking about Owen Wilson in the 2005 movie *Wedding Crashers.*

There were several other texts from Sierra. I decided rather than text her back, I would call her.

Sierra answered, "Hang on, Katharine, I'm formalizing Owen Wilson's stay at the Gold Coast Vet Treat and Retreat."

I could hear a woman in the background tell Sierra that Owen would be groomed and ready for pickup on Thursday. As I heard her say that, I remotely saw a woman handing Sierra a shopping bag that seemed loaded with things for Owen.

I heard Sierra's shoes clicking on the floor and a bell jingling as the door opened for Sierra's departure.

"It's been quite the day," Sierra announced. "I didn't want to take Owen to the shelter and couldn't leave him to suffer on the street. So, I thought what would Katharine do? That's when I sent you a text. My friend I was having lunch with took us to a veterinarian's office around the corner when I didn't hear back from you."

I giggled and said, "That is great! I would have done the same thing. I'm proud of you."

I could sense that Sierra wanted a session with me.

"Katharine, do you have time to chat?" she asked. "I have some things I would like to go over with you."

I heard a car door open, and her heels clicked against the concrete as she walked to her door. She keyed in the code to her door and walked in. I could hear heels clicking on the marble now.

Sierra set some bags down and said, "Give me a second to get in and take my shoes off."

I replied, "No worries, take your time."

She began, "Katharine, I have this job coming up that requires travel. It's tentatively set for a six-week stay but give or take a few days. The client is a writer and married. The length of my stay will depend on whether his wife decides to join him at some point. Do you see me staying the whole six weeks?"

Sierra's spirit guides showed me the number 9. As I tuned in deeper to their frequency, they told me that the guy Sierra was referring to was very devious.

I paused to tell Sierra what her spirit guides said, "Sierra, they told me you would be there for nine weeks. Your guides also told me that this guy is devious."

I hesitated while the guides showed me some more events.

I told Sierra, "I got a vision showing me that you are afraid, and you're left tied up in the dark."

Sierra became a little agitated and replied, "Stop it, Katharine! I don't care about that. It's all part of the act I'm hired for. Please don't look at what we do. I only want you to answer my questions."

I looked at Sierra's spirit guides while they conveyed, *there is a spiritual lesson and advancement for her and you, too.*

I felt a little anxious during this reading, which tends to be a forewarning of the person I'm reading for. But she already blew me off, so I just continued the session as usual.

"Sierra, what else do you want to know about the trip?" I asked.

It sounded like she was opening a box. I could see her pulling items out. She kept talking while being occupied with the contents of the box.

Sierra began rambling, "I have a list of things I can and cannot bring on this trip. He has given me a list of things I am not permitted to have access to. Unfortunately, one is my phone. If you say that I am there for nine weeks, I can't imagine not having a phone for that long. I mean, I couldn't imagine going without my phone for a day, for that matter."

She paused and giggled, "So, I purchased a burner phone."

Sierra continued, "In the contract he had me sign, I agree that my phone will be turned off and locked in his safe. Today, while I was out, I picked up a burner phone with extra batteries. I plan to hide the burner phone on a trail somewhere before I get to the final destination. He knows I like to jog, so he agreed I could continue my daily running while he worked. Although, he clarified that I can't go anywhere else. I'm hiding the phone to stay in contact with my sister Marisol and let her know I'm okay. She worries about me."

She took a long pause, so I remote-viewed her to see what she was doing. She was lying on the bed with her legs drawn up toward her body while she was lightly touching the scar on her big toe.

Suddenly, Sierra declared, "I told Marisol about you and how talking to you has helped me so much! Marisol didn't care much for Dr. Francine Vasquez, but she likes you."

I could hear classical music begin to play in the background softly.

Sierra seemed inattentive to the music and continued with the questions, "Do my spirit guides say if I do anything else with my life other than the work I am doing now?"

I explained, "Your spirit guides say that your spiritual experience now is soul growth from the trauma of your early life and other lifetimes. By the end of this year, you will feel more mature and able to see yourself evolving spiritually."

Time escaped me as we talked for the next forty-five minutes about places that she might like to live and about her first love, the guy she had lost her virginity to. There was such a deeper level to Sierra that you couldn't help falling in love with her.

I always cheer for the underdogs of love, worthiness, and happiness. Those are the souls who may never know just how much I love them. After the call, I received a text with a photo of a bed that Sierra ordered for Owen. Then another picture of Owen on the vet's exam table popped on my phone, looking right at the camera.

Oh my gosh, I see it! This border Collie does look like Owen Wilson, I thought.

My most interesting session today was with Mike McLean, who had reached out a week ago and asked if I could do a group session. Of course, I agreed because I read for families all the time. But he stated that this one was very particular. I didn't ask him for details. I just wrote the appointment down and didn't look into it before the session. Sometimes, it's exciting and a nice change, not knowing what I'm reading for.

When we started the video call, two men sat beside Mike. Dan Susman and Tom McMann identified themselves as detectives. They explained that they were looking into this case regarding a woman who scammed Mike McLean out of a large amount of money. Dan appeared to be in charge, although it didn't seem that they knew what to expect. Dan opened a file folder while Tom took notes on what seemed to be some type of form.

"How does this work?" inquired Dan. "I mean, how do you work? What do you need?"

I smiled and answered, "You can say the name of the person, and please, no last names. If there is a building or street, then all I need for you to tell me is the numbers on the building or street."

"Okay," Dan seemed puzzled.

"Anita!" he yelled.

As soon as he said the name Anita, Mike's spirit guides showed me a male energy.

I must have given a weird expression because Dan immediately said, "What's wrong?"

"Hold on a second", I said.

I looked again at what the spirit guides were showing me. Sure enough, it *was* a man! The image of Anita that Mike had fallen in love with was not the person he had spoken to on the phone. It was not the person he had been messaging with or the person he sent money to.

Mike spoke up, "What is it? "

"Why did you say the name Anita?" I inquired.

Mike looked at me without knowing what to say.

"Your guides showed me a man's energy," I said.

Then I asked, "What image do you get when communicating with Anita?"

They showed me photographs of a woman they had taken off the Internet. The image was different from the one my guides had shown me.

I explained, "The person you had been messaging was a man portraying himself as Anita. The image your spirit guides showed me does not belong to Anita. It belongs to this guy you've been messaging."

Tom looked at Dan and asked, "Can you describe the facility to which we tracked the IP address?"

I looked at what the spirit guides were showing me and visually followed them to the space.

Mike seemed physically sick and yelled desperately, "Please, what do you see? Tell us!"

I looked at each of them one at a time and declared, "I don't know how to describe this place other than it looks like a crappy house. It appears to be constructed of cinder blocks. There are screens on the door opening, but not a real door. There are curtains over the window but not hanging on rods. There are four computers set up on a makeshift table that look like it might have been a door. The computers are lined up along chipped and cracked walls."

Dan took a deep breath and asked, "Do you get a sense of where this is?"

I listened for the spirit guides to tell me or show me something. I noticed Mike's face beginning to sweat profusely. I tried to ignore his nervous energy as I focused on what the spirit guides showed me.

I looked at Dan and stated, "It's in Miami."

Tom chimed in, "Does this guy live there?"

I remote-viewed the room and didn't see a bed. As I made my way through the next area, I could see old broken-looking chairs, but there were no beds or blankets.

I looked at Tom and said, "There are no beds or blankets here. There are no rooms other than this one, just another small area. Paper cups and plastic wrappers from food items are strung all over the place. There's a toilet in the corner. It doesn't look like anyone lives here, but this is where they work."

Mike looked like he was going to pass out. His anxiety was through the roof.

Dan stayed focused and continued asking, "Can you go back to the man you saw posing as Anita and look to see where he lives?"

I asked the guides to show me where this man lives. I began to explain what I was viewing.

"The house is a mansion with gates around it. There is a driveway paved with an intricate design and palm trees in the yard."

Dan asked, "Do you get a name?"

I heard the spirit guides saying something and tried to mimic it.

"Ma...Mateo," I announced. "I am unsure if I am pronouncing it right, and I don't know if it's his first or last name."

Dan looked over at Tom, who nodded and said, "Katharine, you have been very helpful. Is there anything else that we have not asked which might be important?"

I remote-viewed again and reported, "This looks like a family-run business, and this is not the only con they are making money from. The small house with the four computers is in a gated junkyard of old trucks and cars. It seems they are running a chop house for stolen vehicles as well. I can see a street sign with a name. It looks like King. Yes, it's King Street."

Breezy patiently waited for us to take a few bites and then asked, "So what do you think?"

Zach answered with an Englishmen accent, "This is hotel resort quality. Do you have anything like this at your hotel, Butchie?"

Butchie seemed to miss us more than he thought and said, "There are deserts here that may look good but they're missing the love that goes into making them like you're having."

Looking at Butchie, I said, "Tell us the most awesome thing that has happened since you've been in California."

He laughed while beginning to blush, "Well, I was standing around waiting for the art department to make some changes to the set when an actress walked up behind me and slapped me on the butt. I was talking to another actor on set, and when she slapped me, I quickly turned around, and she winked."

We all laughed since Butchie was always proper about his work. I knew he never would've expected anything like that, and I could not resist the urge to tease him.

"So, tell me, was that the slap of confidence you needed?" I asked.

Butchie's face turned red as he proudly replied, "You know everyone loves a person in uniform."

When we ended our video call, Breezy and I watched a little TV while she worked on her school project. It was the last week of school, and it seemed there was much more work being assigned than at any other time during the year.

She was taking a forensics class as an elective. The project she was working on required a diorama of a murder scene. She got up to go to the restroom, and I inspected her work. There was a female figurine with a slash of red paint across her neck, and it appeared to be trailing from the kitchen. Although it was a model, it looked realistic.

Breezy sat back down and asked," Do you think I will get a good grade on this?"

I thought about it, then asked, "Are you asking me psychically or just in general?"

Breezy quickly answered, "No, not psychically! You know I wouldn't ask it like that. Just tell me if it looks good."

I didn't quite understand the purpose of the project, but I told her that it looked great. She didn't seem appreciative of my comment. Her way of venting is by responding to me in German because she knows I don't understand it. Apparently, she didn't think I looked at her project, so she said, *"Du sagst nur, was ich hören möchte,"* which translates to "You only say what I want to hear."

After she did this, I laughed and uttered some German words of my own that were out of context.

Sometimes, to make Breezy laugh, I'll say something like, "*Das auto,*" which translates to *the automobile* in English.

She usually gets a kick out of my attempts at speaking German. If *Das Auto* doesn't do the trick, then I'll say something like kindergarten in my best German accent. It's actually a German word, although we use it differently in English. It's funny,

I promise, and I get laughs from Breezy, Butchie, Carter, and Marilyn when I do it.

They all speak perfect German since three of them had lived in Germany. Butchie lived in Germany for seven years and took German classes in college. Breezy learned in four years of high school and conversed with her stepmom, who is a native German.

I had been practicing a few words to shock Breezy one day: *wunderschöne Tochter*, which means beautiful daughter. I decided to save it for the right time to surprise her.

Breezy and Zach wanted to go to bed early because they were extremely tired and excited for school the next day. They both had class field trips that they were looking forward to.

I got cozy in bed with a cup of sleepy-time tea. As I sipped the tea, I thought about the day's highlight—seeing how Sierra saved Owen. That sweet boy showed up right where he needed to find Sierra.

As I allowed my eyes to relax and my body to sink into the bed, the phone rang. It was Sierra calling. I answered but told her that I was already in bed. She pleaded, "I don't need you to look into anything; I just want to talk. Would that be, okay?"

"Sure," I said. What do you want to talk about?"

She began telling me about places that she liked visiting as a child, dreams she had had, and places that she liked to eat.

There was just something so endearing about Sierra, even though most people who hear what she does for a living tend to go right into judgment. But I could see the true essence of her and who she was. She's one of the few people I've worked with who actually wanted to improve their spiritual life. She changed the outlook of the way she was raised and is now open to the truth.

We ended up talking for several hours. At one point, I woke up at 1:34 a.m., realizing I had fallen asleep during our conversation. Maybe Sierra fell asleep, too. I wasn't sure.

The next day, I sent her a text with an apology. I didn't hear back from her for a few hours but wasn't concerned about it. When I did hear back from her by text, she said:

> Lol. I fell asleep, too, but I didn't know you did.

On the last day of school, Marilyn came by to pick up the boys and me. Then, we headed over to Breezy's school to pick her up. The night before, Breezy warned me that she had a lot of stuff from her locker and several completed projects to bring home.

When we arrived, it looked like she was sitting on every project she made this year. I told her there was no way we could take all of it with us. I told her to pick out a few projects and throw everything else in the trash. Marilyn popped the back of the van; Breezy loaded up the few projects she wanted to keep and closed the hatch with her backpack. We saw Ruby, Breezy's friend, wandering around, looking for her ride. She wore a homecoming mum from October with all the bells and trinkets. I was surprised the artificial mum held up so well.

Marilyn offered Ruby a ride and she accepted after calling her mom for permission. I was pretty sure Ruby's mom had forgotten to pick her up considering I had just seen her at Target.

I glanced back at Ruby sitting in the row behind Marilyn. "What about all the projects you did this year? Did you bring any home?" I asked.

Ruby answered, "No, I didn't want to bring them home. After each project was graded, I just trashed it. I cleaned my backpack today at school so that everything was organized."

Marilyn pulled up to a few more girls so Breezy could say goodbye, and then we headed to lunch. The boys were oblivious to everything going on. They were having fun in the back talking and playing Pokémon cards or something.

On the way to lunch, I noticed a few texts on my phone. I answered all of them back. I didn't book any appointments for the day, but that didn't mean I wouldn't end up having a session. I usually end up with at least one emergency session on days like this.

I snapped a picture of the van to show Butchie how packed we were and how we were having fun. I didn't expect to hear back from him, but I immediately got a text:

> I'm glad you're having fun. The girl doing my make-up loved the picture, too.

It always seems to feel different when school is out for the Summer. There are endless possibilities for your day: being able to sleep in, staying up late, and going places in the middle of the day. There is something magical about summer days.

We seemed to be on a repeat pattern during the summer. Marilyn picked us up every few days, and we all went somewhere. We had a lot of fun. I often wished to drive to all these places, but some of them were too far for me to get in my comfort level. It worked out for Marilyn to drive anyway since everybody fit comfortably in her van. And I only had a four-seater car.

Sometimes, Marilyn had me drive her van on short rides that I was comfortable with. Driving Marilyn's van became so much fun. It was always exciting when we loaded everybody up and headed out on a big adventure. Well, maybe not a big adventure, but when we started the day open to possibilities, there was always some type of excitement.

We got home at 9:00 p.m., and after settling down, I got a text from Matt Winterbottom, one of my best friends in Utah. He started as a client, and we became friends over our fifteen-year relationship. It's interesting how some people are just meant to be in your life, and everything clicks between you. You find that moment of realization when you feel you've known that person forever.

Mike called about his dog, Powder. She is a blond and white Maltese Yorkie mix. He asked me to look at Powder because she had not been eating lately. When I scanned her body, I saw the kidneys highlighted which usually means there is an issue. I urged him to take her to the vet and request they check her kidneys.

Mike texted me later to let me know that the vet said Powder's kidneys had shut down. I felt bad for Mike and told him I would send prayers for him and Powder.

The day was coming to an end, so I texted Butchie to call me when he had time. I didn't have anything pressing and I just needed to hear his voice. Perhaps he would have some crazy story about today. I knew this trip was good for him. It allowed him to live like a local for a couple of months and experience a different environment.

We talked for an hour, and I felt slightly down after we hung up. I thought about how nice it would be to set aside my fear and go places, but the worry of having a panic attack prevented me from even trying. I didn't want everyone else's trip to be jeopardized because of me.

In a way, Butchie inspired me by showing how he could easily jump on a flight and feel comfortable anywhere, even in another country. Perhaps that was just a learned behavior from the Army. I laughed as I envisioned the Army enlistment ads: *Be like Butchie, hop on a plane or out of a plane; Airborne is the only way.*

He has been on every flying machine and apparatus except for a rocket. And knowing Butchie, he wouldn't mind signing up for that, too.

I went to my bedroom and saw my precious dog, Padme wedged between Breezy and Zach. I also realized Padme's son, Anakin, was lying on my pillow.

As I slid into the bed, Anakin repositioned his body to spoon my back. He turned and licked Zach on the chin. I wasn't sure if I could sleep with everyone in my bed, but I was so tired that I just closed my eyes and faded away.

I woke up to the smell of waffles and the sound of the blender whipping up a smoothie. When I got out of the shower and started to dry my hair, I noticed the phone had a message from Sierra:

> Please call me within the next 10 minutes.

I glanced at my watch and the time the message had been sent. There was still time, so I called her.

When Sierra answered the phone, it felt like she was somewhere else. It was much different from the energy of Chicago, different from her building, or from any other place I could recognize.

Sierra told me that she had arrived in Oregon a few days earlier and had been busy with her client.

She said that on the way to his house, she had the taxi driver stop on the side of the road beside some old buildings in a blueberry farm. She walked into one of them and hid the burner phone in a plastic Ziploc bag with the two extra batteries she had bought. She stored two numbers on the phone: my number under "K" and her sister Marisol's number under the initial "M."

Sierra clarified, "My client agreed that I could go jogging every morning, so I hid this phone to check in with you and my sister."

"I appreciate that, Sierra," I stated. "But I don't like that you took this job."

"I know you don't," she giggled. "Although a quarter of a million in six weeks will feel good in my checking account. Besides, how am I going to care for Owen in the pampered way he has gotten used to?"

I felt very nervous about all this. I wanted to talk some sense into her and convince her to leave immediately.

Suddenly, I heard the dried grass under Sierra's steps crackle as she said, "I will send you a super cute picture of Owen I took before I left. He is staying at the doggy retreat until I get back. There's a video camera in Owen's room so I can check on him during his outdoor playtime. My client agreed to let me check Owen's live feed video with my phone he put in the safe, but I can't send the photos until I get home."

I heard Sierra's breathing shift, and her energy quickly changed as she quietly exclaimed, "Katharine! Someone is coming! I must go."

The phone call ended abruptly, and I stood there looking through a remote-view, watching Sierra running toward an empty road. To say I felt better hearing Sierra's voice would not be the truth. I felt so much more anxiety now. It seemed like it was coming from me, even though my spirit guides told me it was from Sierra. I had to shake it off, so I quickly showered and got dressed.

When I made it downstairs, Ramsey was kneeling on a barstool, waiting for the waffle maker's light to switch off, indicating the waffles were ready.

"So, did anybody offer to make the waffles for you?" I asked.

Ramsey answered, "Zach made me two waffles, but they had blueberries, and I was in a chocolate chip mood."

I could see beyond the kitchen window to the backyard where Zach was sitting with a plate of four piled high waffles, a glop of blueberries, and a bottle of syrup in his hand. Marilyn was standing near the garden talking to Breezy.

I continued talking to Ramsey while glancing outside, "Well, Ramsey, you seem to have everything handled. Is the smoothie on the counter anyone's in particular?"

Ramsey answered, "Yeah, my mom made two, one for her and one for you."

Ramsey and I walked outside. He sat at the picnic table, and I walked over to Breezy and Marilyn.

"Thanks for the smoothie, Marilyn," I said.

She turned and smiled, "How about we go to Herman Park in Houston, ride the train, and have dinner before returning home?"

I had a sudden surge of panic when I thought about leaving my house and going out to Houston, but then I looked at Zach's face, and his aura color changed to a light shade of green. This let me know he was hopeful for a yes, probably since Marilyn would drive, and she helped calm me down.

I thought about the anxiousness I had been having with Sierra. A drive into Houston to see some uncommon sights was just what I needed.

I told them, "Well, c'mon, let's fill our water bottles and get moving."

I noticed everyone's aura color had changed to a beautiful yellow. Zach wolfed down his waffles, and Ramsey was trying to keep up. Everyone was in high-speed mode to fill their water bottles and get into the car. I'm sure they were in a hurry because they didn't want me to change my mind.

I became very anxious on our way to Houston. Traffic wasn't bad but just being away from the house caused anxiety. I was nervous about being around all the other energies I might encounter at the park, museum, or wherever we were going to end up at and not being able to retreat to my safety zone.

It way ok, though, and I fought through the anxiety; the smile on everyone's faces and the shock that I agreed to go was enough to help me power through. Before we left, I grabbed a tote and put a few magazines and a small orange photo book in it. I always took photos with me on trips so when I felt panicked, I could look through them for comfort. I always chose pictures of events and happy times the kids and I had experienced. When I would take a deep breath and look at those photos, my anxiety would usually calm down, and I would avoid a panic attack. I also brought some essential oils, snacks, and a notebook.

The park was beautiful, with a variety of people and an array of activities going on. It was a perfect time. I noticed a bit of anxiousness, but I realized it wasn't coming from me. For some reason, my mind kept getting flashes of Sierra in a compromising position. I just couldn't determine if it was real or play. She reprimanded me the last time I mentioned it, so I just tried to shake it out of my mind and continue with the fun day at the park.

Chapter 7
Out of Balance

I was lying in bed, trying to figure out what just woke me up. My heart was racing as I continued laying there, and all I could hear was the constant pounding of my heart. My eyes suddenly focused on an oversized portal full of light above my body. I felt my body heating up like a volcano getting ready to erupt as beads of sweat dripped from my forehead. It was strange because the air conditioner was on 69 degrees. *It should be nice and cool in here. Why am I so hot?* I thought.

I felt my spine straighten as if there was a stream of direct energy flowing through it. I kicked off all the blankets and just lay there, allowing my legs to cool off. I had difficulty remembering what I was dreaming about before I woke up.

Quickly, I remembered my spirit guides talking to me. And then I remembered seeing Sierra arguing with a man.

Who is this guy? Was I asleep? I thought. I was desperately trying to calm myself down. *What is it about this energy that is making me so anxious?*

The portal was still hovering above me, and thousands of colorful, tantalizing lights were flowing around the room.

The spirit guides near me noticed the portal was closing and desperately continued to add light around my energy body. I closed my eyes and lay there for a bit, trying to go back to sleep to recreate the dream I had earlier.

I began to feel the coolness of the air on my chest and shoulders, realizing it was a little too cold. The spirit guides backed away and were now fading into the ethers. I turned to my side and pulled the sheet back over me. I tried to keep my eyes closed, reflecting on the light show I had just experienced.

What was the purpose of the vision I just saw? I asked myself.

I was eager to find out, but my spirit guides were hesitant to explain. It became evident to me that this was a spiritual lesson I needed to experience. They didn't want to show me the connection to the vision again. I just couldn't figure out what was causing the panic attack. I fell asleep without realizing it.

Suddenly, I felt a door close on me. My fear of being locked in a small space got the best of me, and I quickly opened my eyes. I glanced around the room, calling in my spirit guides and angels in a frantic tone. They appeared and began to put light into my body. I kicked the sheet back off, propped myself up, and tried to calm down.

I looked down at my feet and focused on grounding to the Earth.

I'm okay. I'm okay. I repeated over and over again in my mind. *I'm not closed in. I'm in this open area. I'm safe.* I assured myself.

I looked to my spirit guides and asked them if this was all just another dream or if there was something I needed to know.

They smiled back at me and disappeared. Right then, I knew that something extremely challenging was getting ready to happen, and I was being prepared for it in an unusual way.

I reached for my watch and realized it was only 4:30 a.m. I didn't know if I could go back to sleep, so rather than just lie in the dark, I turned on the TV. I looked for something funny to watch to. My thumb erratically tapped the remote until I stopped on an Adam Sandler movie.

I lay there thinking about the spirits I had recently talked to and the people I had been reading for. Then I thought about Sierra. I had been waiting to hear from Sierra for a couple of weeks. She'd gotten to the point of texting me every day, but it suddenly stopped. I'd been a little concerned about her welfare.

I thought about remote viewing her, but then I remembered her request that I not look deeper into her interactions with clients. I still felt something was off.

I flashed back to the stack of books in Sierra's room, all of which were from the same author. I suspected she hadn't read any of them because they appeared brand new and barely touched. And I intuitively knew that this was the guy Sierra was with now.

I had the onset of a weird emptiness overcoming me, and I was sensing a sudden ominous energy. I was starting to get worried about Sierra's welfare, but I didn't know what to do.

I called Butchie to see if he was available to talk. I told him that I was concerned for Sierra. He didn't know much about my private conversations with Sierra or what she did for a living.

I told him I was worried about the trip she was on. Butchie is always trying to keep me from worrying too much about my clients, so he just brushed it off and said I shouldn't get so personally involved. He reminded me that Sierra was a grown woman making her own choices and could handle herself.

Then he said something insightful: "I didn't expect this connection with Sierra to be a spiritual lesson for you, too."

Dang it! I thought.

I knew he was accurate because that was the guidance I got when I first received Sierra's request for a session. My human perception quickly dismissed it as a lesson in acceptance since what she did for a living made others feel shameful of her, although it didn't bother me. I knew she would eventually evolve into something different when she was ready. Something was happening within the dynamics of Sierra stepping into my world.

This day was super packed with sessions. I checked my emails, and there was one from the hotline where I offered psychic readings. The email urged me to be available more often this week since I had some complaints from callers who were unable to arrange a call with me.

I realized I needed to spend more time on the hotline over the next few days since most of my days had been spent reading for scheduled appointments. I never tell callers from the hotline how they can reach me outside of it. If the caller finds me through the hotline, I believe in not biting the hand that feeds me.

The fact is, I don't even give my last name. It's better since most calls usually last between three and twenty minutes anyway. I have continued doing readings there to maintain spiritual guidance for a few of my favorite callers. And there are a few that always call on Christmas or Mother's Day. They don't have any family left alive and wish to communicate with their loved ones on those days. There is a particular woman that I have been taking calls from every Christmas for the last several years. No sooner than I log in the hotline to take calls, she rings. Just like clockwork.

There was no indication that this day would be anything out of the ordinary with hotline calls, so I switched the indicator to *available to take calls and* settled into my Herman Miller chair. I took a few calls that only lasted a few minutes each and then checked my calendar to see when my first regular session was scheduled for. I realized the first session was going to begin in fifteen minutes, so I went to the kitchen to get a glass of water and eat a banana.

The phone rang right on time for my session with Dr. Brooke Rossi. I had not met her yet, but I was intrigued by the call.

"Hello," I answered.

Excitedly she said, "Hi, Katharine, this is Brooke."

"Hi, Brooke; it's nice to meet you. What can I take a look at?" I queried.

Brooke began, "I'd like you to look at some things at work. One of my associates has worked with you before, regarding a personal relationship. She was amazed at how insightful and helpful you were, so I wanted to see if you could help me."

She continued, "I am so in love with a man named Hudson. He is everything perfect I imagine in a partner, and he's a fantastic lover. However, he struggles with dissociative identity disorder."

She paused for a moment to catch her breath. Brooke seemed intensely infatuated with this man, but I could sense that something was off about this whole thing.

Suddenly, her spirit guides interjected, *this man is a patient of hers.*

Wow! I didn't expect that. I thought.

Brooke whispered, "I didn't meet him under normal circumstances. He came to me for help as a patient, and it became intimate."

I felt she wanted to use me as a confessor rather than a psychic.

"Brooke, what exactly is it that you want me to take a look at?" I inquired.

Brooke paused again, and I could tell she was debating whether to hang up. She was wondering if her confession was a mistake.

She hesitated, "Katharine, please take a look at our relationship. Do you see it last?"

"Yes, I do. Until the day of his last breath," I assured her.

"Oh, good. So, you see us together for a long time?" Brooke queried.

I insisted, "No, that's not what I said. I see you being together until his last breath, which doesn't appear to be too long from right now. His passing occurs during the year he is twenty-eight."

Brooke shrieked, "What do you mean, Katharine? He's twenty-eight! So, what are you telling me? He's going to die this year?"

"Yes, it looks like it's a short time from right now," I consoled.

She asked, "So, how long do you think he has?"

"Hang on a second," I instructed. "It looks like it's only a couple of weeks from now, maybe three weeks."

She huffed, "What happens? Does he walk in front of a subway or something?"

Brooke's spirit guides had already opened a portal. They were showing me what had previously transpired in their connection and what would go on until he passed. He would continue as her patient, and they would have sexual relations during his appointments. She would press on with charging the insurance company for sessions and keep writing him prescriptions for his personality disorder. I was baffled that she claimed her love for him despite her selfish actions.

"Katharine, are you still there?" Brooke inquired.

"Yes, I'm here, I acknowledged. "I'm sorry. I was looking at what your spirit guides were showing me."

I relayed, "Here is what they're saying and showing me: You're continuing to bill his insurance, you're engaging in sexual activity during his patient visits, and you're continuing to write him prescriptions."

I insisted, "You're not so much in love with him as you are with his disorder!"

I paused for a moment as I heard her begin to cry.

She sniveled, "While I was in school, I learned about dissociative identity disorder. I was so intrigued about how the subject could identify as a person one moment, and in the next, a different person with a completely different set of values. The whole subject was fascinating to me."

Brooke continued, "When I began practicing as a psychiatrist, I fantasized about someone coming into my office with this disorder. I had a female come in at one point with a borderline personality disorder. Then, one day, when I was feeling sad about the same old patient problems, a beautiful man walked in. He looked like a model who had popped out of the cover of a GQ magazine."

She proceeded, "And you know what? He struggled with the disorder to the point that he wanted to commit suicide. We worked through it together. Do you know what it's like to have a breakthrough like that? It was amazing! That's when I fell in love with Hudson. He needed the medication to keep himself balanced, so I had to write the prescription. But the relationship continued to develop into so much more. I was instantly attracted to him. He was so good-looking and sweet. Each personality carried a different life or existed separately from the other personalities. In one of our sessions, I witnessed one of his other personalities—Vernon."

Brooke laughed, "Vernon is Amish, and it was during this session that we had sex. I didn't expect it. He was the one that started engaging with me, but I couldn't stop. Everything about him changed. It was like a fantasy coming true for me. I was with this gorgeous man who was at that moment, identifying as Amish Vernon, a carpenter, who only wanted sex with me. He had never had sex before in his life."

Brooke seemed to catch herself, realizing that the professional ethics committee would be screaming at her if they found out.

I interrupted, "Brooke, I understand how you became so consumed with this unusual experience. In my profession, I certainly don't hold anyone in judgment, so I'm not going to tell you that this is wrong. But I'm sure your profession has strict codes and ethics to comply with, or you could lose your license. I am only here to answer your questions with intuitive insight and relay what your spirit guides are showing or telling me."

I continued, "I am being told that while Amish Vernon had not had sex before, the owner of the body he occupies did. The personality, identified as Hudson, has had sex with hundreds of women *and* men.

"The sexual activity that Hudson's body took on is based on all his different personalities," I explained.

I declared, "He doesn't want to take the medication. When he's alone with you in your apartment, you make him take the medication. It's making him sick! He's not long for this world. Which means his Higher Self is going to choose to cross over."

Brooke was crying intensely.

She protested, "You must be wrong! He's only twenty-eight years old. He is so happy when we're engaging together. I have been with every one of his personalities now. We are together outside of appointments, and he spends most of the time at my house..."

I interrupted, "Brooke, I wish I had better news. But I can't change what I'm seeing. There's no change possible. This is a warning for you to prepare yourself as he completes his transition. He will be pronounced dead in his home."

Brooke asked, "Why does he die at his place when we have been spending time at mine?"

My guides highlighted Brooke's lack of concern for Hudson's crossing over. Her only concern is why he's not in her bed when he dies. This saddened me.

As I glanced into Hudson's energy, Archangel Michael appeared and attested, "Hudson's Higher Self wants a restart and longs for the confusion of this life to be over. His Higher Self has chosen for his death to be at his place because of Brooke's selfishness."

I finally answered Brooke, "He will be at his home by choice. It doesn't look like a fallout between you two. He just wants to be at home."

Brooke vowed, "I will make sure he doesn't spend any time at home. Over the next couple of weeks, I'll keep him with me. I'll keep him in good spirits. There's no way I want to lose him now that we found each other."

I could tell she didn't want to accept anything I had said. And she certainly was not going to consider her deviant behavior as unethical. Intuitively, I knew this was not the last time I would hear from Brooke. It appeared that Hudson had learned a valuable soul lesson. Still, Brooke was just at the beginning of experiencing the consequences of her selfish decisions.

When I got off the call with Brooke, I saw a text message from Marisol, Sierra's sister:

> When you get this text, please call me. I haven't heard from Sierra, and I'm distraught.

I called her immediately.

She answered, "Hi, Katharine, I'm Marisol, Sierra's sister. She left for a job in Oregon, and I haven't heard from her since. Have you heard from her?"

"Yes, I received one call from her," I clarified. "She called me from the burner phone after arriving there."

Marisol asked, "How long had she been there when she called you?"

"Sierra said she had been with him for a few days," I remarked.

She asked, "Katharine, this seems weird, but can you look at her now?"

"Marisol, I know Sierra's alive," I consoled. "I feel her energy. If she had passed, she would've already come to visit me in spirit. But I did make a promise not to psychically look in while she's working. It was the one thing she was earnest about in our conversations. When Sierra first asked me about taking this job, I felt uneasy about it. I didn't want her to take it."

I continued, "I told her not to take it, but her only concern was if she would be fine afterward, and I heard yes. I must trust that answer from her guides. I also have to honor my word about not looking in at her psychically while she is *working*."

I knew Marisol didn't like that answer and she would be upset with me.

She protested, "Katharine, you don't understand. It's not like her to go this long without calling me. She knows I worry about these strange jobs she takes. My friend, Toni, is a detective here in Chicago, and I plan to ask her to investigate this. She can check on what's happening and if Sierra is okay. Perhaps she can look into Sierra's client and find out where he lives."

I cautioned, "Marisol, I don't think it's that easy. I remember the guy's name from glancing over the book she had of his, but he probably leases his place under a different name. This man is very wealthy and some sort of celebrity. Those types of people don't usually lease in their own name. There were some rules he requested that she follow for this job, and secrecy was paramount."

I stressed again, "I promise you; she is alive, at least right now!"

Marisol confessed, "Katharine, you must forgive me for not trusting you. This is my sister. She's the only family member I have left. I can't just leave it alone."

I assured her, "Marisol, I understand what you're telling me. But even if I only knew a person briefly, they always showed themselves in spirit when they passed. I know you don't know this, but I care about Sierra. I feel like she's right on the brink of wanting to change occupations and do something different. I'm hoping for something that's not so dangerous."

When we ended the call, I sat there momentarily, struggling to keep the promise I made to Sierra not to look in on her.

I realized that I had a session starting in twelve minutes with Baker Mayes, a new client. I ran down the hallway to the bathroom. Sitting on the toilet, I thought about the call with Marisol. The concern in her voice was troubling. Marisol had known Sierra to take these types of jobs before, and yet she was so worried about this one. *What was it about this particular client that worried me so much?* I thought.

I realized I had finished peeing and was still sitting on the toilet. I flushed the toilet, washed my hands, and grabbed a towel from the counter. My phone was lying on the vanity, and I could see the video open to Baker smiling. He was propped up in bed. His aura was very dim and covered in dark grayish matter from head to toe. His energy leaked from his field in a small stream over his crown. Instantly I knew he was not long for this world. I also didn't feel like I needed to be the one to deliver that news to him now.

In the background, I heard a female voice with a hefty Puerto Rican accent. She seemed to be complaining about something. Baker's smile appeared forced. He was a very handsome blond-haired man in his mid-fifties. I noticed from his face and aura that he had cheek implants. The implants never merged with his body's energy. This was not the cause of his illness, but it did seem to have thwarted his immune system from overexertion.

I began, "Hi Baker, it's a pleasure to read for you today. What would you like me to take a look at?"

Baker started to speak, and the unidentified female voice seemed to fade in and out, as though she were walking from room to room.

He explained, "The female voice you hear in the background is one of my tenants, Anne. I was given your contact by a friend that you've read for several times. He told me that you are an ordained minister and can perform wedding ceremonies. Is that something you still do?"

I giggled slightly and said, "Yes, it is. I don't do it very often."

At that moment, his spirit guides appeared in the room. Several angels gathered around him, and a beautiful male spirit stood beside him. He identified himself as Baker's husband.

I said, "Baker, a guy standing next to you is telling me he is your husband; his name is Joe."

"Yes, that's my Joe," he confirmed. "Ask Joe if it is okay if I marry Anne."

As I focused on the male energy identified as Joe, he laughed and said, *Yes, it's okay for you to marry her. I know you don't want to lose the building.*

I knew exactly what Joe was referring to. Baker explained that he had only been given a few weeks to live. The building he owned was a small apartment building with eight tenants. When his husband, Joe, passed away, it took him a long time before he could just leave the house and go to the grocery store.

He was so sick with grief that one of the tenants would bring him food. She complained a lot but always cared for him and looked after his needs.

At that moment, I heard someone saying something in the background. I couldn't quite make it out, though. Baker continued explaining that when he passes, his family, who has had nothing to do with him for most of his adult life, would sell or tear it down.

Rather than have it torn down, he wanted to marry Anne so she could get the building. He did have a Last Will & Testament drawn up but felt the marriage would ensure the family wouldn't fight for it.

"So, Baker, do you want me to perform a ceremony today?" I asked.

He quickly replied, "Yes, absolutely, as soon as we can get Anne in here."

He elevated his voice as he called to her. She was busy cleaning a room down the hall.

Baker explained, "We must get her to sit down as soon as possible and get on with the ceremony."

He walked over to the bed in the living room and lay down. Anne pulled up a chair as close to the bed as possible and sat down. She began to tear up and reached for a tissue. I introduced myself to her, and she smiled.

"Is there anything you'd like to say, Anne?" I prompted.

She quivered, "I never asked for this. I never expected this. Baker is so kind to me. There were times I was struggling. He knew I was working. He always gave me extra time to pay the rent. When he became sick, I never thought anything of it; I thought it would just go away. I looked at him as if he were a family member."

She explained, "I don't spend much time with him, he's usually in his room. I never looked at this complex as being individual apartments. I saw it as one big house."

Baker looked over at her and said, "That's precisely why I want you to have this apartment building. My family has always been greedy; I don't want them to fight for it. Besides, it's what Joe would've wanted to do."

At that moment, I heard Joe's spirit say, *This building is too beautiful for it to be demolished; all the work Baker and I have put into it should be appreciated by someone.*

I understood entirely what he was saying. He wanted to protect part of the legacy he and his husband, Joe, had with this beautiful building.

So, I looked up at Anne and Baker and asked, "Will anyone else join us for the ceremony?"

Baker asked Anne to go and get Trevor, one of the other tenants, from across the hallway.

Anne returned with Trevor, who was carrying a guitar. Trevor nodded and started playing *Annie's Song* by John Denver. Someone else quietly entered the room.

It was a woman carrying a bouquet of beautiful flowers. She handed the flowers to Anne and gave her a kiss on the cheek.

The woman said, "Hi, I'm Anne's daughter, Beatrice."

I noticed that Baker's smile had grown, and he was being comforted by Anne holding his hand. I looked at Baker and asked if this was everyone. They both nodded and smiled.

I conducted a straightforward ceremony followed by a couple *I do's*.

Anne reached around Baker to hug him as his eyes filled with tears. Trevor began to add words to John Denver's song, which he had only been playing instrumentally to this point. It was the perfect song for this moment.

Although there was no passion or intimacy between the two, there appeared to be a long-founding love. With Joe's blessing, it made it so much better for Baker.

A woman arrived, carefully carrying a cake with beautiful icing flowers. Even though Baker was ill, it looked like a typical wedding celebration. I looked at Baker and asked if there was anything else he would like me to do.

He said, "Yes. I'd like to know what *the other side* is like."

Joe stepped forward in spirit, and I began to parrot exactly what Joe wanted Baker to hear. By the end of the conversation, Baker looked lighter, happier, and fulfilled.

He was enjoying the day, and although this was not a passionate relationship, it was one of honor and integrity.

Trevor came over to the screen as I was ending my call with Baker. He told me how much he loved Baker and how much he loved Joe. Trevor had been living there since 1992. He explained how much he appreciated that they didn't raise the rent like other's had done on this block. And he told me how all the tenants would chip in to maintain the common areas as if they were the owners themselves. They all worked together as a team.

When Trevor walked away, I told Baker, "The most important thing you can remember is that it's not always the family you're born to, but the family you make. It's Joe's beautiful heart you found in this life. And it's the family you formed in this building. That is your true family."

I asked him to ground with me as I guided him through the release of trauma connected to his biological family.

When we ended the video session, I thought about that John Denver tune, *Annie's Song*. I realized it had taken on a new meaning for me today. I remember hearing the song another time before; it seemed so romantic. But at this moment, it felt more honorable because of the selfless act that I had just witnessed.

We were invited to Marilyn's house for dinner that evening. After we ate, Marilyn and I sat by her pool, dangling our feet in the water.

"I worry about you and the things you experience with your work," Marilyn shared.

I rubbed her shoulder and said, "Please don't worry, Marilyn. There are some days I think I should walk away from it all. Then, the next day, I experience something that validates my work."

Later that night, when I got off the phone with Butchie, I lay there thinking about my day. I felt fortunate to have the people in my life that I do.

I turned to my right side and looked along the wall where the souls usually lined up for the next day's readings. It's funny because my kids won't lean against that wall because they know spirits await to communicate with me.

When I tell some people about the waiting spirits, they think it's scary. I don't see it that way because I'm so used to it. For me, this occurrence is the same as anyone else watching people standing at the bus stop awaiting their ride.

Suddenly, my phone was blowing up with text messages from Ms. Gibson. I picked up the phone to read the texts:

> Katharine, are you up?

> Katharine, please help. I need your help!

> Katharine, please, please call me!

> Katharine, I need help.

I finally called Ms. Gibson back. "What's going on, Ms. Gibson?" I inquired.

She answered, "Katharine, the attic has fallen where the raccoons live. The whole ceiling in the back half of the house is caving in. Some *kits* have fallen and landed on the broken sheetrock. Chili, the large mama raccoon, had babies."

I didn't know the raccoon terminology, but I realized that *kits* are baby raccoons.

"Katharine, there are some *kits* on the floor in that back room," she frantically continued. "What do I do? How will their mother find them?"

I didn't want to step anywhere near a worried mama raccoon. Besides, I recalled a picture of Chili that Ms. Gibson had shown me. She was a large raccoon, somewhere around twenty-five pounds.

"Calm down, Ms. Gibson," I encouraged. "It's okay. What I want you to do is have your brother go around back and open the window to that room. The mother raccoon will find her babies. Everything will be okay."

"Are you sure about that?" she asked.

I reassured her, "Yes, I'm optimistic. A mother raccoon will come to the spot where she left her babies. She'll see the floor has dropped out and look at where they are. They'll cry out to her, and she will put them somewhere else."

She sighed, "Katharine, this is a big mess. I just had my housework done. And I am trying to figure out what to do here. Why did it fall? Do you have any ideas?"

I suggested, "Ms. Gibson, knowing the mess raccoons make, living in the attic, I'm sure it finally fell in from the saturation of their urine and defecation."

She seemed shocked, "That can happen?"

I explained, "When they urinate and defecate, it dries up and stays there. Raccoons tend to make a designated area in which they reside. Wild animals don't intuitively go outside to use the restroom. They make a spot in your attic. It would help if you Google diseases you can get when living in a house of urine and fecal matter. There's a lot. I'll send you a link to the Google page on this."

Ms. Gibson paused as if I had just given her highly classified information, "Katharine, how do you know this stuff?"

"Outside the spirit world, I Google the things I don't know, I explained. "I just sent you a link to the problems humans develop when exposed to pathogens from poorly managed animal feces."

"Ms. Gibson, check your text. Did you receive the link?" I asked

"Yes, I just got it," she confirmed. "This isn't very pleasant, Katharine. I'm looking at all the health problems that could develop, and I seem to have all of them."

At that moment, I received a text from Ms. Gibson. It was a photo of the damaged ceiling and a few faces of raccoons peering downward, listening to the little kits scream.

I called Ms. Gibson and let her know everything would be okay but that she should not keep raccoons in her house.

She disputed, "I know you say that, Katharine, but I can't send them away. They're just looking for a handout."

"Ms. Gibson, you keep the babies from learning to fend for themselves. What are they going to do when you're gone?" I counseled.

She deflected, "I don't know, Katharine. Hopefully, whoever lives in my house later will feed the raccoons."

I knew something was wrong with her thinking, but I was too tired to dissect it tonight. We ended the call and I breathed a sigh of relief.

Suddenly, I had a flash of Macy Graham and the fake ghost on the porch. *That's weird*, I thought.

Later that night, as I turned off my phone, I saw a text from Macy Graham that read:

> I am sorry for how I talked to you. I caught him screwing the neighbor. I hope you have thirty minutes tomorrow so I can tell you what happened.

When I finally began to relax and drift off to sleep, I heard my spirit guides whisper, "You will be working with Toni, soon."

I was too tired to even think of who Toni was.

But the moment before I faded into a dreamscape, I realized Toni was the detective from Chicago that Marisol had mentioned.

Chapter 8
Tripping Relief

I love lying in the yard and don't even care if neighbors drive by. They're used to seeing me do it. Not that I'm laying out in a bikini or naked, trying to get attention. I just love having the cool grass on my back while feeling the energy of Mother Earth saturate my body. I enjoy feeling the vibration of the world. I tend to do this as a soothing mechanism when something's bothering me emotionally.

It had been several weeks since I heard from Sierra, and I was getting increasingly concerned. We had been making real progress on the spiritual level before she left for this trip. I was finding it extremely difficult to maintain my promise of not psychically looking in on her. She asked me to refrain from looking into the work she does with clients, and that was the part of our contract I was not willing to break! At least not for now.

Sometimes, I would get glimpses of things she was feeling. I wasn't purposely looking, it just happened unwarranted at random times. It was an eerie feeling that was hard to shake.

Butchie decided to extend his trip in LA. He had known about a film class and managed to sign up for it. He mentioned that we should consider creating films about my work to help educate others on the spirit world. He believed I was an angel hiding my identity as a human. He was so convincing to others that they would often ask me if it were true. I would laugh and tell them he was just in love with me.

As I continued enjoying the relaxing feel of the Earth under my back, I noticed the kids walking out of the house dressed as if they were going out somewhere. Breezy was carrying my purse, which I understood that to mean we were leaving.

I didn't remember making any plans for today other than going out for an iced tea later; then, I heard Marilyn's van squelching around the cul-de-sac. She stopped in front of the house as I lifted my head. Breezy and Zach were standing over me.

"Come on, Mom, get up," Breezy pleaded. "We're going to lunch."

Zach squatted down to help me get up.

I declared, "Come on, Zach, I don't need help; I'm not old yet."

I stood on my feet while Breezy put the purse over my shoulder. She looped her arm through mine and guided me to the car. Zach was already four feet in front of us. He aggressively slid the van door open and did his best incredible Hulk impression while Ramsey laughed.

He threw his backpack on the seat and jumped in the back with Ramsey. I climbed in the front while Marilyn looked at me suspiciously.

"What were you doing?" she asked.

Everything happened so fast, and I was still absorbing the energy from the ground.

I felt loopy as I answered, "The ley lines! Yes, the ley lines. I was recharging my body with the energy from the Earth's ley lines."

Marilyn responded, "I don't know what all that means, but a new restaurant just opened nearby, and I'm starving."

"All right," I laughed. "Let's go. What type of food do they serve anyway?"

"*Italian!*" boasted Marilyn.

"Oola-la! Italian. I like Italian," I exclaimed.

I faked a smile and pulled myself away from worrying about Sierra. I realized I couldn't worry about everyone that I conducted sessions for. *God, I'd be up all night.* I thought.

I used to do that constantly: I would worry about clients I had read for. I would send light to them and pray that they would listen to my warnings. I would continually check in on them after their reading.

It became exhausting!

Worrisome!

I wasn't fun to be around because I constantly checked on everyone and tried to save them. That was years back, though.

I glanced at the faces in the van, and I saw everybody so happy. I wanted to relish this moment with them.

"I'm choosing to be happy today," I whispered.

"What was that?" Marilyn asked.

I said a little louder, "I'm choosing to be happy today."

Marilyn looked at me and commented, "That's what I thought you said. But you seem happy to me, *every* day."

She clarified, "Butchie has told me that you have seen some dangerous situations, but you seem to manage it all well."

Breezy interrupted, "Mom, don't let me forget about my backpack and project in the back of the van. It's been there since the last day of school."

Marilyn laughed, "Trust me, I'll make sure you take that creepy murder diorama out of the back. Carter saw it the other day when they loaded up Ramsey's baseball gear. He noticed you got an A on the project. But that doesn't merit taking up all that space"

After lunch, Marilyn whipped out five tickets, and the boys went crazy.

She fanned herself with the tickets and bragged, "Carter got us tickets to Comic-Con."

The boys already knew.

Ramsey burst out with excitement, "We need to go in costumes!"

Marilyn looked at me and asked, "So what do you think?"

I smiled, "I don't feel like I need to wear a costume, but I'll support *you guys* wearing costumes."

Zach bragged, "Ramsey and I already have our costumes."

Breezy interjected, "I know something that I can wear."

"You do?" I asked.

"Yep. I'll show you when we get home," she said.

Marilyn chimed in excitedly, "I have one, too."

"You do? Where did you get it from? Halloween?" I asked.

She explained, "It's one of the costumes Carter bought."

I agreed, "Okay, then, I'll try to come up with some kind of costume. Let's run home, get our costumes, and head to Comic-Con."

I was so excited to go to Comic-Con. It was my first time. I was thrilled to see everybody dressed in their costumes. When Marilyn returned to pick us up, she wore a Wonder Woman costume and looked gorgeous—Ramsey dressed as Batman. Zach was in a Luke Skywalker costume, and Breezy was dressed as Poison Ivy. I put together some clothes, quickly styled my hair, and became Princess Leia from Star Wars.

On the way there, I remembered I had an appointment with Macy Graham in the next hour. I couldn't believe that I had forgotten. I realized I got lost in the excitement of going to Comic-Con for the first time.

I texted Macy to tell her I was not at the office, but I would be available if she still wanted to FaceTime by phone. I told Marilyn to go inside with the boys and I would meet her after my call.

Breezy waited with me in the van.

When I connected with Macy, she giggled about the costumes she saw Breezy, and I wearing and repositioned herself on the sofa.

"Macy, what would you like me to look into?" I asked.

She confessed, "I didn't want to believe you when you told me that my husband was sleeping with the neighbor. I felt if he was cheating, I needed to get proof. I let him think my daughter and I were camping on the porch waiting for the ghost. I even set up cameras and filming equipment that I had rented."

She continued, "Renting the camera equipment was just in case you were wrong, and my grandmother's spirit *was* on the video. My daughter and I even put our sleeping bags out and sat in the chairs. Hubby came out and checked on us a couple of times. But I had this urgency to go and check on *him*. I walked around the house rather than through the house so that I wouldn't make any noise. And so I wouldn't set off any notification alerts from the cameras. While walking around that side of the house, I noticed the back door of *her* home open."

As she spoke, I psychically knew the back door was *not* open. Somebody might have unlocked it, but I let her continue the story of going through the neighbor's house.

"I could hear them in the other room," she confirmed. "When I walked in, he was screwing her. The crazy thing is, they didn't even notice me standing there. I snapped a photo and screamed some names at both of them. I went home, but he didn't return to our house until morning. He claimed he loved me, but he also knew I was mad and wanted to give me a chance to calm down. So, he didn't say much else."

Macy stated, "I had a couple of questions for him. He answered them, but I wanted to hear your answers for comparison."

She began, "He told me she came onto him first. Is that true?"

When I looked in psychically, her spirit guides said, *yes, the neighbor was the first to come on to him.*

I told her, "Macy, your spirit guides are telling me that your neighbor was the first to come on to your husband. But people make passes at each other every day, and he could have turned her down."

She agreed, "Okay, Katharine. Here's my next question: How long has this been going on?"

I explained, "Your spirit guides said it's been on and off for the previous year and a half. She wrote it down on the paper where she'd been taking notes."

I commented, "I suppose his answers are on that paper, too."

She declared, "That's all I needed. Can we save the other half of this thirty-minute appointment for a few days from now? I've got some thinking to do."

I acknowledged, "I understand, Macy. No worries. I want you to know that you should see this as a blessing. It's not your job to fix him or to feel like you need to stay with him. It would be best if you just moved on from him."

She didn't seem enthused with this answer. I could tell by her energy that she wanted to hold onto him. But there wasn't anything else I could give her.

She sighed, "Thank you. I appreciate you, Katharine. I hope you have fun today."

I ended the call and Breezy and I made our way into the NRG center. NRG Houston hosts just about every significant event in the city. I was uncomfortable going into crowded places. My anxiety would increase as I noticed people's energy fields, deceased people around them, and illnesses within the body.

I tend to see all the bad things they've done even when I'm not trying to. A lot of people think that it's such a cool thing to have these abilities. But in this case, I see it as a double-edged sword. It's not pleasant to see the dark secrets of others when you're just trying to have some fun with your family and friends.

Marilyn immediately spotted us as we made our way through the door. She came over and pointed to where the boys were. She'd been watching for the door and watching the boys at the same time making sure we didn't get lost trying to find them. The boys were in line for the meet and greets. The first ones we met were William Shatner and Jason David Frank.

We continued to experience one fantastic activity after another. The boys loved the games and watching everyone in costumes. We took some group pictures with some of the exciting backgrounds.

A few hours later, I began fighting off a severe panic attack as I tried to hide it from the kids.

While digging around in my purse looking for some gum, the small personal defense alarm that Butchie gave me turned on. It sounded like a fire alarm was going off in my purse, and I struggled to turn it off. The sound induced a full-on panic attack, and I needed to get outside. I had managed to survive around all these people's energy but at that point, I was finished!

I could tell Marilyn's feet were hurting from her bulky, heeled shoes. She motioned to me that she was ready to go. We gathered the kids and headed to the van. I could tell everyone had a great time showing off their costumes and mingling with the other fans.

The kids' happiness soon replaced the anxiety I had been experiencing from the unintentional shifting energies of people.

We stopped at a Smoothie King on the way home for a small delight. At 5:00 p.m., we pulled up to the house. Ramsey and Zach had a sad face, and I could tell they didn't want the day to end. So, I agreed to let them set up the tent in the yard.

We all stayed in costume for a while, except Marilyn's boots, which were tossed to the back of the van when we left the event. We just lounged back in the zero-gravity lawn chairs and watched Ramsey and Zach put their tent up in the front yard.

Their energy field was a beautiful yellow. Zach and Ramsey continued pulling out more garage items for their tent. As I watched everyone relaxing and the boy's playing, I felt grateful for the day.

I was thankful that my panic attack didn't cause me to leave the event before everyone had fun. The anxiety was not as bad as it usually was, however, it had been very present. Even with all the distractions, I had a good time.

I noticed my phone ringing in my purse. I reached down and pulled it out to see who was calling. I didn't recognize the phone number but knew it was a Chicago area code. My guides told me it was Toni calling—Marisol's detective friend.

As I answered, there was a momentary pause, and then she said, "Hello, Katharine, this is Toni Chavez. I am a detective here in Chicago and a personal friend of Marisol. She told me that you know Sierra Delmar. Her sister hasn't heard from her in a while, and I was wondering if you could help us locate her."

My anxiety started to build, and my heart began racing. I paused for a lengthy time while thinking about what to say next.

Toni inquired, "Hey, Katharine, are you still there?"

"Yes, I'm still here" I answered. "I don't know how much help I would be to you."

"Are you familiar with Doctor Francine Vasquez?" Toni asked.

I replied, "Yes, I am. She was the one who referred Sierra to me several months back."

Toni stated, "We've spoken to Francine, and she seems to be cooperating with us."

I thought for a moment about Dr. Vasquez and the statement Toni just made about her cooperating. It didn't feel right to me. Something just felt off about it all.

She went on, "So, as I was saying, I need help locating her. Law enforcement in Oregon has no desire to help find Sierra. They told me there are no signs of foul play. She entered Oregon alone, and they don't want to waste the personnel and resources looking for someone they don't believe is in trouble. As you know, it's not like Sierra to go this long without calling her sister or at least sending her a text message. That's why Marisol is so worried."

I replied, "I can completely understand that. But what can I do?"

Toni asked, "Do you know the name of the man Sierra went to visit?"

I explained, "Sierra never gave me his name. I saw a stack of books by her bed that I believe he had written. It appeared that he sent her those books along with a few gifts."

"Do you recall the name on the books?" Toni asked.

I consented to her question, "Yes, the name was Stover Prescott."

Toni was shocked.

"Are you sure about this name?" She asked.

I revealed, "Yes, Toni, I'm certain. One of the first times we had a session, I remember seeing the books stacked up and some gifts nicely wrapped as if she had just opened the box from the delivery. She asked me about the job that was coming up. My guides told me the name on the package was the client for the job."

Toni continued to inquire, "So, what did you tell her when she asked about the job?"

I stated, "I told her I didn't want her to take the job. I told her I would not suggest that she go on the trip. She didn't care. She told me it was a massive amount of money, and this is what she does for a living. Also, I think she was a little enamored by who this person was. She never gave me his name and I didn't ask. She didn't know I saw the books stacked in her room with his name on the package label.

Toni asked, "So, explain again how you saw the stack of books?"

I replied, "By remote viewing. When I see things, I can either look from the standpoint of the room itself, as if I'm there, or I can look through the eyes of the person I'm reading for."

"That's very interesting," marveled Toni.

I could see doubt all over her face, but I shook it off just like I have with hundreds of others.

What she thinks doesn't matter, I thought. *Besides, I've worked with many people who have become believers.*

Toni continued, "As I said before, Oregon law enforcement does not want to look for Sierra. They said there's no sign of foul play. Is there any way you could meet me in Oregon? I could arrange a ticket for you."

Suddenly, I had this feeling of major panic running up and down my body. *There's no way I'm willing to be enclosed in a plane*, I thought.

I mean, there were times I have flown before. But at this point, no, not now. No way. Especially not after 9/11. For some reason, if the employees at the airport saw me as a Middle Eastern-looking person, I'd get a pat down. I knew that wouldn't bode well with my anxiety.

I exclaimed, "Toni, there's no way I could fly!"

Toni was confused, "What are you talking about? Are you disabled or something?"

"No, not physically," I explained. "But I have major anxiety. It would take so much effort to get me on a plane. You'd basically have to drug me, but please don't do that."

Marilyn and Breezy had been listening to my conversation and realized what was happening. They imitated holding a steering wheel while mouthing to me, "We could drive."

I don't know what happened to me; maybe the Universe took over the control of my body, but I quickly said, "Toni, the only way I could go is if we drive."

Toni was perplexed, "Aren't you in Texas? That's a two-day trip by vehicle."

I responded without realizing the consequences of my agreement, "Yes, I am in Texas."

Apparently, Zach had been listening in on the conversation as well because I noticed he was on the iPad, seemingly calculating the trip. Suddenly, he whispered out loud, "It looks like it takes thirty-two hours to get to Oregon."

Toni must've heard Zach's calculation in the background and stated, "Actually, Thirty-four hours to the exact destination by my calculation."

She paused then exclaimed, "That will be a long drive for someone like you that has such anxiety! How could you possibly drive that distance?"

I declared, "Toni, I definitely won't be the one driving that distance, but I do have two other people who will."

My heart was pounding out of my chest. I was so anxious. Beads of sweat formed on my chest and neck just from me thinking about the trip.

I laid back on the ground to try and relax.

What the hell was I thinking! I thought. *Am I in a nightmare? Did I just actually agree to all of this?*

I saw my spirit guides and angels form a circle around me and beam light into my direction. I welcomed the shower of light by raising my arms toward the sky and opening my palms.

Toni was still on the phone, asking, "Hey, are you still there?"

"Yeah, I'm here. At least I think I'm here," I answered.

I was so confused about what was transpiring that I could have been in another world or dimension playing out someone else's experience. It was so surreal for me.

"OK," Toni said. "I'll send you my itinerary and where I'm staying once I figure it out. Do you know exactly where this guy lives in Oregon?"

I answered, "No, I don't. But I do remember seeing a note card. The note card beside the books read: *Let's play in Sherwood*. I instantly knew it was Sherwood, Oregon."

Toni acknowledged, "Thanks, Katharine. I'm going to fact-check that by researching places he has rented. If they're in Sherwood, I'll see what I can find."

Toni was still confused about how I could remotely view things and how I am able to see specific things, people, and events without being there.

Suspiciously, she asked, "If you have not been to Sierra's place, how did you see a note card?"

I explained again, "I get a view of things from the eyes of the person I am reading. So, if they are looking at something like the note card, I can see it too."

When I got off the phone with Toni, I suddenly felt petrified. I was still in disbelief at what I had just done. Marilyn put her hand on my arm to try to calm me down. She knew this was going to send me into a panic mode.

Breezy and Zach were looking at me in disbelief, and I knew they were thinking: *who the heck is this woman? How did she agree to drive across several states with such a crippling anxiety? Where's our mom?*

I was thinking the same thing!

I looked at Marilyn and whimpered, "Are you okay with making this trip?"

Ramsey jumped up and exclaimed, "We're ready! We *neeeeed* a road trip. Come on, Zach, let's get our bags."

Marilyn looked at me and said, "I'm with you, girl; Breezy and I can take turns driving. Let's get moving. What appointments do you have set today, Katharine?"

I replied, "Well, I have a session that starts in about an hour. It's a follow-up from another reading. It's only thirty minutes, and then I have a follow-up session from a few months ago for another thirty minutes."

"Okay, are these both FaceTime calls?" She asked.

I stated, "They are, but I can ask them if they'll do a phone call."

"Okay, great. Breezy, get the snacks together," Marilyn ordered. "I'll bring some drinks. We'll get everybody loaded up. And we need to get on the road soon to make good time."

She continued barking orders, "Breezy, you need to work on figuring out where our first stop will be. We'll need to stop every six to eight hours to rest, even if we pull over for just a few hours. And, of course, we'll stop for meals when we can."

I joined in, "Okay, great. I'll start this first session here, and then I'll do the other thirty-minute session in the van."

"Perfect," Marilyn concurred.

Breezy leaned over to me, "Mom, are you really doing this?"

I could tell by the look on her face that she didn't feel I was going to be able to go through with the trip. I wasn't even confident myself. Although I was seriously nervous about this trip, I cared about Sierra and knew I had to do something.

Perhaps this was what the universe wanted all along—to pull me outside of my comfort zone and show me that I could *move beyond the closet.*

After grounding, I moved inside to start my first session with Father Dominic. I got a FaceTime call from him.

"Hi, Dominic, how are you today?" I began.

"Fantastic!" he beamed. "I've got some great news, and I wanted to follow up with you after our last session. You told me I would be meeting someone. You also mentioned it would be through work. It all came to pass, just like you said, and the guy's name is Gabriel Akana. He's an attorney, and he's dreamy. Do you remember the session we last had?"

I answered, "Yes, I remember little bits of it, but not everything."

Then I explained, "When giving information, I tend to be in a trance state. I focus on relaying the message concisely and often don't remember it afterward."

I could tell that he was pleased.

Dominic acknowledged, "Very well, then let me catch you up. Remember the priest at my church named Scott, who everyone requested to do the funerals?"

"Yes, I remember," I responded.

Dominic continued, "He had been there longer than me, and many people liked him. He and I enjoyed a few nights together.

Then, there was nothing. It seemed like he did it with everybody who worked there."

"Ok, I remember that as well," I interjected.

Dominic gushed, "Well, anyway, he's gone! And I'm the lead priest now. I've brought in good people to work here. The new employees and priests care about the church. The archdiocese hired a law firm to come in and prepare the staff to answer questions that may come up from the parishioners."

He took a deep breath and continued, "Well, one of the lawyers who came in was Gabriel. The moment he shook my hand, I felt this electricity. It was amazing. And then I thought about Archangel Gabriel."

Dominic was overjoyed and full of life. He had an oversized smile, and he was beaming with a light that showed pure love.

He rejoiced, "When he said his name was Gabriel, I almost lost myself. I felt I was in heaven. Everything in my life became easier. Our conversations just flowed so smoothly. We visited several museums and had a great day together the following week. We picnicked together. We hiked together. We golfed together. We have so many things in common. He is every bit of the person I've dreamed about being with. The surprise was that he was a lawyer. I never thought I would ever date a lawyer!"

He finally paused to breathe, and I inserted, "I'm really happy for you, Dominic. So, what would you like me to look at in this session?"

He stated, "I was so shocked at how accurate you were in our last session that I figured I would ask what else is in store for me. Well, I'd like to know how long you see me staying at this church and if it's worth it for me."

As I went in to look, his spirit guides and angels came forward and said, *He is safe staying there for now, and it will be much easier than it has been over the last couple of years. As the church grows and expands, he will find other things to do along the way and in about six months, he'll leave the church.*

When I told him this, he didn't seem too bothered.

So, I said, "I am glad you don't seem bothered by what I am saying."

Dominic replied, "No, not at all. It feels like a relief to leave the church eventually. The only troubling spot is telling my family I won't be a priest anymore. That's going to be the most challenging part. I think because, at that point, they will have to come to terms with the fact that I'm gay. Right now, they're not quite sure. They've never brought it up to me. But I won't hide my relationship with Gabriel if they confront me."

I continued relaying to him what the guides were telling me and what I was seeing psychically.

I added, "You will be getting married in Italy. Gabriel is in love with you, too."

He giggled, "I can't wait! I'm so excited! Katharine, you are a godsend. I appreciate all that you have done for me."

We spoke for a few minutes longer and then ended the call.

After the call, I went upstairs to pack for the trip. I could hear Breezy downstairs going in and out of doors. It sounded like she was packing quickly, loading up everything from the house. I thought about how nice it would be if she put that much energy into cleaning her room. The front door opened and closed loudly.

She yelled upstairs, "Marilyn's here. Let's all load up."

Zach came running down the stairs. He was carrying two bags: a backpack and a duffel bag. He threw everything in the van and jumped inside with Ramsey.

I walked downstairs with two pillows, a blanket from my bed, a large bag, and my phone chargers. I watched Breezy load a bunch of stuff into the back. I got into the bench seat in the back of the van. I was already beginning to get nervous—feeling closed in.

What was it that Zach said? I thought. *I guess it was thirty-four hours. I hope I can go all the way there with no problems.*

As I tried to rationalize with myself, I looked around at everyone's faces. They all seemed so excited to be going on this trip. I realized they weren't so focused on *why* we were going on this trip but on the fact that we were going on *one*. Breezy got into the passenger side up front.

She turned to me and said, "Ruby is going to be taking care of our pets while we're gone. She can stay the night at the house. Is that Okay?"

I remarked, "Sure, sure, that's great. Hey, I was thinking that since that map takes us through Utah, and we don't want to stop for long overnight stays, we could pull off at Mike Winterbottom's place to rest for a while. He always said we could stay with him if we came to Utah. I can text and let him know we'll pass through Utah on our way to Oregon."

Breezy looked over the map and said, "That's all we can do is pass through. So, text him and let him know we'll come by. It'll be good to stop there, take showers, and take a break before we head through Idaho."

I heard Zach telling Ramsey a little information about Mike. Then he pulled out his iPad and selected a movie to watch. Breezy and Marilyn were talking in the front while they plugged in the address on Google Maps for our destination. I tried not to focus on anything else because the thought of leaving the house and being so far away was starting to make me feel nauseous. I was seriously debating whether I could do this. Everything was happening so fast, and I didn't have time to process what was really going on, which was probably a good thing.

I had never seen the kids so excited about anything. I realized that I was going to have to really try to make this trip work.

The alarm on my phone alerted me that I had five minutes before my next session with Johnny Lenhart.

I announced out loud, "I have a session that starts in five minutes. It will only last thirty minutes, but I need everyone to be quiet until it ends."

I tapped in the number to my iPhone, and it began to ring. Johnny answered after a few seconds and said, "Hello, this is Johnny."

I responded, "Hi Johnny, this is Katharine. What did you want to ask about today?"

He explained that his sister and wife were there as well, and he would put me on speaker for everyone to hear.

Suddenly, I heard, "Hi, you can call me Bonnie. I'm his sister."

Johnny followed with, "My wife's name is Dara."

I replied, "Hello, Bonnie, Dara, and Johnny. I didn't realize this was a group session. But I'm excited to read for you. What would you like me to take a look at?"

Johnny took a deep breath, and I could sense he was trying not to hurt anyone's feelings.

He emphasized, "Bonnie and Dara seem to have trouble getting along. It appears that Bonnie doesn't like my wife."

Bonnie interrupted, "It's not that I don't like her, but why did you have to marry someone from Indonesia?"

There was a quick pause, and I heard a soft delicate voice that must've been from Dara.

She whimpered, "I'm sorry, I'm sorry, I'm sorry."

Johnny protested, "Sis, it's wrong for you to be so prejudiced. Maybe you can talk to Katharine and ask her about the situation. Ask her about our relationship."

"Okay, very well then," Bonnie grunted. "Katharine, do you see Johnny and Dara lasting?"

When I looked into Dara and Johnny's energy fields, I heard their spirit guides say, *Dara will always love Johnny, and they will have four children together. After Johnny passes, Bonnie and Dara will live together.*

I sat there for a moment processing the information I had just received. I knew Bonnie was so upset about the marriage that there was no way she would accept this information.

My guides urged me to share their information but to leave out the part about Johnny's passing and them becoming best friends and living together.

How will I word this? I thought.

I stated, "Okay, Bonnie, when I look at Dara's energy, I can tell she is immensely in love with your brother. She sees him as the man of her dreams. He's tall, he's handsome. She loves everything about him."

Bonnie piped up, "I bet! He's a doctor. What's not to love about that?"

Johnny ordered, "Please stop, Bonnie."

"Bonnie, what is the issue you really have with Dara?" I asked.

She paused for a moment and scowled, "I don't like that she's a mail-order bride. So many women here in *this* country wanted my brother, yet he chose a foreigner!"

Johnny sounded hurt as he whimpered, "I found an attraction to Dara. And besides, the women I have met here seem *only* to notice that I'm a doctor. They're only out to marry a wealthy man. I wanted someone who would truly love me."

Dara interjected in her beautiful accent, "I love your brother. I love my Johnny."

Johnny exclaimed, "Most everybody in Miami acts the same. They're so shallow. I wanted someone who would care about me. When she fell in love with me, Dara didn't know I was a doctor. Yes, I arranged for her to come here to get married. But I don't regret it for a moment."

I disclosed, "Bonnie, your spirit guides shared that you came to the United States as a baby, and you weren't born here."

Bonnie murmured, "Yes, that's correct. My brother and I were adopted. Our parents were doctors, and they didn't want to give birth to children of their own. They felt it was important to adopt. Although Johnny and I were born two weeks apart, we became brother and sister."

"But that has nothing to do with this marriage!" Bonnie raged. "It has nothing to do with the fact that he has a mail-order bride!"

I tried to reason, "Bonnie, you only choose to call her a mail-order bride. She is a human being. She loves your brother. He loves her. Right now, the only person who is angry about this is you. And you know what? That's destroying *you*, not him, not her, and not their relationship. It only empowers their relationship. Their relationship is long-lasting—longer than any relationship *you* will ever be in."

I paused for a moment and then assured her, "I see there will be a day when you and Dara will be best friends. I want you to be open to it. Open to seeing her as the person your brother sees."

Suddenly, her spirit guides chimed in: *Ask her what her birth name was.*

I quickly inquired, "Your spirit guides are urging me to ask you for your birth name. Can you tell me?"

Bonnie answered calmly, "My birth name is Bong-Cha. It means superior daughter."

I went on to tell Bonnie that her spirit guides had told me that her birth name was very rare here and that she should be proud to have been born with it.

Your spirit guides said, *parents are less likely to name their child Bong-cha because they don't want them to grow up with a superiority complex.*

"That's very interesting. Bonnie, you do seem to have a superiority complex," Johnny declared.

Bonnie began laughing. Johnny started laughing too, and disclosed, "You always told me you were superior. I guess there's some truth to it."

She divulged, "I guess sometimes I do behave like I'm entitled."

Johnny said, "Of course you do. It's the way we had been raised. It's the benefits and the opportunities we had been given. But my love for Dara is so strong, and I know her love for me is the same. She never even knew I was a doctor when we began talking. She thought I worked at the family business. She had no idea it was a family practice."

"Johnny, I know you say that, but are you sure?" Bonnie asked. "I just want the best for my brother."

He confirmed, "I know. And I appreciate that, sis."

I interjected, "Is there anything else you want me to look at in this session?"

Bonnie asked me a few things about work and their practice, and Johnny asked about their home. Everyone seemed to have found peace with each other and been satisfied with the session, so we said our goodbyes and ended the call.

I let everyone in the van know I was off the phone and talking could resume.

I sat back in the seat for a little bit and tried to relax. My anxiety was starting to build up again as I was looking out the windows and seeing different things that I normally don't see. I realized we were way out of my typical driving range.

The silence was broken when Breezy turned around and looked at me and said, "Hey, are you doing okay?"

I replied, "Yes, I'm just feeling a little nauseous."

I pulled out a small photo book from my tote and began looking at pictures to try and get my mind off the drive.

Marilyn shouted, "Why don't you get on the hotline and take some calls. Those are never long. That'll get your mind on work.

If you're reading for other people, you won't be focused on this trip."

I remarked, "That's a great idea, Marilyn. I'll get on now."

That was a perfect idea, and it seemed to work for a while.

I immediately received a couple two-minute-long calls. Then Robbie called.

I answered, "Hi, this is Katharine. How may I help you?"

"Hi Katharine, my...my name is...is Robbie," the voice seemed unsure. "Umm, I'm anxious right now."

I listened for a moment, and I could hear his spirit guides say that he had taken something, and he feels like he's going to die. So, he wanted to talk to someone because he's scared.

I asked, "Well, Robbie. Is there anything you want me to look at on a psychic level?"

"Yes, there is!" He exclaimed. "Umm...am I going to die?"

I clarified, "This hotline doesn't let us answer medical questions, but maybe you can phrase your question differently."

He paused, thinking, "Umm...umm...what do you see me doing tomorrow?"

I focused momentarily on Robbie's energy to see what he would be doing tomorrow.

His spirit guides told me that he was not going to die. But he's going to learn a very, very valuable lesson in keeping his body clean.

I relayed, "So, Robbie, your spirit guides said that you are not going to die. I can see you doing laundry tomorrow, washing your sheets, and buying a vacuum."

He laughed, "Wow. You are making me feel better. I do need a vacuum, and I absolutely need to wash my sheets. I probably haven't washed them in about five weeks. I'm also afraid because of what I took."

He continued to ramble, "I feel like I'm getting better than I did. I've been tripping all day long. And I saw an ad for this hotline. I looked through the faces, saw yours, and just felt drawn to call you. Your photo seemed so reassuring."

I encouraged him, "Well, now that you know you will be doing laundry tomorrow and buying a vacuum, I hope you feel more confident about your life."

"Yes, I do feel better," he admitted. "I have been putting off buying a vacuum. And I glad that I will be around to go buy one."

He was still a bit anxious and asked, "I don't want you to get off the phone with me yet. Is that okay?"

I replied, "Sure. But you're being charged by the minute on this hotline, so it could get pretty expensive."

He reassured me, "Yes, I'm okay with that. Even if I talk to you for quite some time, it doesn't matter. I have lots of money. Just stay on the phone with me. I don't want to be alone. I don't have anybody else I can call."

I declared, "Here's something you should think about, Robbie: Your spirit guides said the only reason this happened was for you to learn a lesson."

He concurred, "I understand that completely, Katharine. I'm usually the kind of person who won't even take an over-the-counter pain reliever. I don't know what got into me lately."

I explained, "Well, Robbie, it's weird that people would take anything another person gives them unless it's from a doctor. And yet they read the labels on prescription bottles with such caution because they're afraid to put it in their bodies. Just look at it this way: this is the amazing body you'll need to carry you through your entire life. You want it to continue functioning at its best."

I paused momentarily and then emphasized, "Most people don't realize the importance of caring for their body until an illness happens. I know you are going to be fine. After all, you're buying a vacuum tomorrow, and that seems like fun."

He laughed, "Yeah, Katharine, you're funny if you think buying a vacuum is fun."

I added, "It is. It just depends on where you go. Target is always my choice. So, you said you've felt like you've been in a slump lately. And that's why you took what your friend gave you."

I asked, "What was it that made you feel depressed?"

He sighed, "Mainly my job. The supervisor was changed out and promoted somehow. I ended up with this female supervisor, and all she did was complain, complain, complain! She would change the protocols constantly. It was so stressful. Exerting myself was all I could do to make my numbers, and then she would change the protocol again. A couple of guys at my company were planning to leave and I have been considering it as well. But I've been there for a while, so I would hate to leave."

I encouraged, "Robbie, sometimes when an antagonist comes into your life, an opportunity for growth opens. I believe you need to apply for other jobs. It doesn't cost you anything to apply, and it would be worth finding other options. I think you should follow the guidance of the universe. Just be open, and many doors will unlock for you."

Robbie acknowledged, "I know what you're saying is true. But Katharine, I am still feeling anxious. What can I do for this?"

I glanced in front of me and noticed Ramsey and Zach were watching the movie *Elf* with Will Farrell.

I realized what could help Robbie, "Maybe you should watch something funny. Get your mind off this serious stuff. I do that whenever I feel anxious or I'm having a panic attack. I watch something that's just stupid funny and forget about everything else for the moment. It helps to clear the energy of what was bothering me."

"Okay, maybe I will try that. Is there a movie you could suggest?" he asked.

I was getting guidance from my spirit guides that Robbie didn't want to hang up.

I suggested, "Well, Robbie, two movies are my go-to films to make me laugh. One is *Dodgeball*, which is super funny. And the other is *Happy Gilmore*."

Robbie laughed and agreed, "I like both of those, too. I'll put them on and listen to them in the background as I try to calm down from the day."

I glanced at the time and realized we had been talking for forty minutes now.

"Robbie, we've been talking for forty minutes now," I commented. "That's quite a lot of money. Maybe we should end the call. You can try watching a movie and doing some light housekeeping. If you have any issues, you can always call me back."

Robbie shrieked, "No! I don't want to hang up with you. I don't care how much it costs. Look, I make great money. I could stay on the phone with you for the next few days and will be financially fine. Please don't hang up on me."

I declared, "Okay, so listen, Robbie. I need to tell you, I'm actually on a road trip right now."

Robbie asked, "So, are you driving and talking to me? That doesn't seem safe."

I replied, "No, I'm not driving and talking to you. I'm actually in the back of the van. My best friend and my daughter are in the front seat, and my son and his friend are in the center seat."

Robbie's voice perked up, "Oh, that's awesome. So, you guys are on a road trip? Where are you going?"

I divulged, "Well, we're going to Oregon. We live in Texas, and we're heading towards Dallas at the moment. We're making that our stopping point before heading onward to Oregon."

He was surprisingly excited, "Wow, what part of Oregon? I sure could tell you some stuff about Oregon."

"Really? You know a lot about Oregon?" I inquired.

"Yeah. I've been camping there. I've been camping in Washington too. I mean, there's just so many beautiful stopping points there. A lot of cool parks and trails," Robbie insisted.

I added, "That's what my son Zach was telling me. Zach looks up places to visit and has unmasked several off-the-beaten-path trails in Oregon."

Zach heard me say his name and asked, "Hey, Mom, who are you talking to? Is it Butchie? Tell him I said hi."

I quickly put the phone on mute and answered back, "No, not Butchie. I'm still on the work call."

He looked up and inquired, "Are you talking about me?"

I said, "No, I just mentioned we're going to Oregon."

Marilyn pulled off the road and into a gas station. She yelled to the back, "Anyone who needs to go to the restroom, get out now. Our next stop won't be until Dallas."

I let Robbie know I needed to go to the restroom and if he wanted, he could call me back in about ten minutes.

He pleaded, "No, I won't hang up. Please don't hang up on me."

Not wanting to upset him, I urged, "If you hold on, I will be right back. Is that Okay?"

He calmed down a bit, "Yes, that's fine, just set the phone down."

I got out of the van as Marilyn finished pumping the gas. We walked to the restroom together, and I told her a little about the call with Robbie.

She implied, "Oh, well, it's keeping you occupied from focusing on the road trip as long as you're reading for other people."

I watched Zach and Ramsey get back in the van with Breezy as we quickly left the restroom.

Marilyn saw them, too, and said, "How much do you want to bet one of those backpacks has fireworks in it now?"

I laughed, thinking about the boys and their sneakiness.

"Fireworks are the least of our worries on this trip," I said.

She laughed, "This is going to be a smooth trip. I suggest you stay on the hotline for the rest of the trip."

I gasped, "The rest of the trip! I don't know about that."

"Well, I think it's a good idea during *most* of the driving time," she restated.

We returned to the van. I realized Zach and Ramsey picked up the phone and had Robbie on speaker. Robbie was telling the boys about the haunted trails in Oregon.

"I'm back," I called out.

I questioned Zach, "Why did you pick up the phone?"

He replied, "I heard someone talking from it, so I picked it up and started talking to him. He told me about all these haunted places to visit on the way. Can we go see them?"

I countered, "We'll have to talk to Marilyn and see what kind of time we have. We can't forget exactly why we're on this trip."

He handed me the phone, but Robbie yelled, "Wait, I want to tell him one more thing!"

I agreed, "Okay, I'll put you on speaker."

Robbie beamed, "Hey Zach when you stop again, look for a bookstore somewhere along the way. You might even find a book or brochure at a gas station as you get closer to Oregon. There's a lot of books about haunted places in Oregon."

Zach and Ramsey seemed even more excited about this trip after listening to Robbie. They turned to their iPads and began looking up haunted places in Oregon. The call with Robbie ended at three hours and eleven minutes. When I finally looked outside, I noticed we were in Hutchins, Texas. I didn't want to focus on the location, so I closed my eyes and tried to take a nap.

Chapter 9
Last Night

I woke up to an automated German voice speaking. Breezy had her phone map app set to the German language. I adjusted the seat while trying to stretch my legs. Ramsey and Zach were watching a movie.

I yawned, "Hey, are you guys doing ok?"

They answered simultaneously, "We're ok."

I called out, "Where are we?"

Breezy proudly stated, "We're in Dallas near the museum. I'll exit somewhere around here and find a hotel for the night."

Marilyn turned from the passenger seat, looking back at me, and asked, "You good?"

I replied, "Yeah, I'm fine. Better now. I'm a little nervous about where we are but excited to get out of the van."

Marilyn gestured, "We're just about to exit right up there."

I realized from the German announcement on the maps app that we were arriving at our destination soon. I looked around to figure out how long until I could get out, and then I noticed the hotel. I figured there must be a convention in town because the parking lot was so full.

Marilyn turned to everyone and instructed, "Boys, grab your backpacks, and we'll get the other bags."

Breezy pulled up to the front of the hotel, and the valet came out to take the car. I noticed Marilyn's energy was showing irritation. She was unhappy with all the dirt that got on her van, so she asked the valet to wash it. She had a bit of an OCD streak about her. She liked everything to look brand new and clean.

The van did seem a bit filthy. We must've driven through a rainstorm while I was sleeping. Breezy and Marilyn walked to the counter to check us in. I stood to the side with the boys. They were whispering about something and seemed very excited. Their bright yellow energy made me feel good, and I knew they were enjoying the trip. While we waited, a German Shepherd entered the lobby, accompanying a girl in a wheelchair. Her energy was a bright green, which indicated that she was a great healer.

The mother walked behind her with a mild red energy field, which implied that she was aggravated about something. We heard the mother call out to the girl and the dog to stop while she grabbed the bags.

They stopped close to us, and Ramsey spoke, "Nice dog. Did I hear you call him Marvin?"

The girl laughed, "Yes. We call him that after my grandfather."

They proceeded to the check-in counter.

Ramsey looked at me and said, "It's nice when dog owners give them real names. It makes them seem like a person in a dog suit."

Zach laughed as if he had pictured someone climbing into a dog suit. At that moment, Breezy and Marilyn walked up to us.

Marilyn asked, "What's so funny?"

Zach joked, "A person in a dog suit."

Everyone laughed as we walked down the hotel hall towards our room.

Zach turned to me and stated, "I thought Ms. Gibson had food names for all her animals until we went over there the other day. She had a pet with a person's name."

That didn't feel right, so I asked, "Really? How do you know?"

He happily answered, "There's a new tombstone sitting among the small ones, and it reads Benjamin Sean. The other tombstones read Relish, Chip, or other names you find in a kitchen."

I must have displayed a weird look because Marilyn turned to me and inquired, "What's up?"

I explained, "Benjamin Sean is the baby Ms. Gibson had who only lived a few days."

Marilyn exclaimed, "She's too old to have a baby."

I clarified, "She didn't have the baby recently. She had it years ago. I think it was forty-five years ago. It's odd that she would put a tombstone up in her yard with his name on it."

Marilyn suggested, "Yes, that's very odd,"

She opened the door to our room, and we all trickled inside. Suddenly, Marilyn pulled me into the bathroom.

She looked at me with parental seriousness and said, "You've done great so far on this trip. I know you'll do great the rest of the trip, so I don't want you worrying about Ms. Gibson. We'll investigate that situation when we get back home."

When we exited the bathroom, the boys pulled the bedspreads to the floor and were lying on top of them. Breezy was sitting on the sofa and glanced up. I pulled the bedspreads off the bed.

I felt drained—more so than usual. I tend to feel exhausted when I've been in panic mode.

The room had two king-size beds, and I was ready to make best friends with one of them. We all took showers and then got into bed. It took every bit of strength I had left to pick up the phone. I sent Butchie a quick text but hadn't explained anything about the trip yet. I noticed an email from the hotline and clicked on it, half asleep.

I woke up to Marilyn asking me if I remembered what I did last night.

Surprised by her question, I hesitated, "What do you mean what I did last night?"

I looked out the window, and the sunlight momentarily blinded me.

Marilyn rattled, "You and Breezy fell asleep first, followed by Ramsey and Zach. I was up for about an hour after that, talking to Carter. Your phone rang right around 1:00 a.m. You reached for it on the second ring. When you answered it, you began answering questions. You told them what you were seeing, and then you hung up. You were back to sleep within just a few minutes after."

She began laughing, "I've never seen anything like it."

"Are you messing with me?" I asked.

"Nope," she answered. "Check your phone."

I looked at my phone, and then my spirit guides came forward and told me, *you took a call, which lasted six minutes. When you went to read the email from the hotline, your status on the hotline went to available. So, you were on all night.*

Sure enough, I quickly checked the call log to see when the call came in and saw that it was from the hotline.

I looked up at Marilyn, "Oh Crap! How did I do that? I was asleep."

My spirit guides said, *it didn't matter. You were channeling all the answers.*

I logged into my listing on the hotline and checked the feedback.

I glanced up at Marilyn in shock, "They left feedback."

"Are you sure?" Marilyn asked.

I exclaimed, "Yes, it's from the customer that just called me!"

All the kids seemed to wake up simultaneously, and they were looking at me, waiting for an explanation.

Marilyn said, "Don't leave us waiting. Read the input out loud."

I replied, "It shows a five-star rating, which was highly recommended."

I read out loud the comments that the customer wrote: *Fantastic reading! Katharine seamlessly tapped into my energy. She was able to tell me about my issues without me giving her any backstory. She was so tuned in that she knew why I called. It was remarkable and on point. Katharine answered all my questions with ease.*"

I was super happy after reading the feedback, but I wish I could remember something about this call.

I looked at Marilyn and asked, "Do you remember anything about what I told this person?"

She thought about it and said, "I remember you telling her the guy she's calling about has been taking twenty-dollar bills from her wallet each week. I'm not quite sure what you were referring to as you were saying things like yes, I am so sorry, and no, and answering with dates and times in the future."

I shook my head in amazement, and we both laughed it off. I laid back on the pillow.

Marilyn leaned in and whispered, "Let's make it fun for the boys. There's a cafe inside the Dallas Art Museum. We can get tickets, look around for about thirty minutes, have lunch, and then hit the road."

"That sounds good," I agreed.

Suddenly, I saw a message from the hotline informing me someone had arranged a fifteen-minute call. It was Roxy.

I told Marilyn, "You guys start getting ready. I've got to take this call."

She asked, "Katharine, how quickly can you be ready?"

I replied, "Just a few minutes. I took a shower last night, so all I have to do is brush my teeth, pull my hair back, and change clothes."

Marilyn declared, "Okay, great. Let's go, everyone! Start getting ready."

I logged into the hotline, and Roxy was waiting. When she got on the phone, she gave me an update about her relationship with Craig. Roxy's excitement was a nice change for her.

She began, "Katharine, I have made many changes since our first conversation. I'm no longer letting Craig use me. I am now asking for money. He bought me a new car."

I knew she didn't want to hear me explain what was wrong with this, but I had to let her know.

"Roxy, you misunderstood me from the beginning," I protested. "That's not what I was trying to convey to you. I wanted you to have pride in yourself. I was trying to urge you to be open to someone who was a good person for you, someone who would be with you for the right reasons, not someone who would just buy you gifts."

Her energy indicated she did not hear a word I had just said.

Roxy perked up, and without missing a beat, she refuted, "I know you say that, but this is a better fit for me than anything else. Besides, I love him."

My spirit guides told me that Roxy would one day see the situation from a different perspective, but not today.

I explained, "Roxy, when I look at your energy, it's not showing a love connection to Craig. The connection from his heart belongs to the person he's married to. You and Craig have connections at the sacral chakra to the root chakra which are mainly sexual."

Roxy's energy shifted to anger, and she screamed into the phone, "Katharine, I don't believe that! I believe he does love me! He is fucking me! We *will* be together!"

She paused, and I could remotely see she was looking at a giant sparkling ring on her finger. Her energy seemed to calm down as she became mesmerized somehow by the ring.

She beamed, "You should see this ring on my finger. I'll send you a picture of the ring and one of me and Craig together."

Roxy continued to talk about everything Craig bought for her place and about her new car. I looked up and noticed everyone in the hotel room was ready to go. The boys were sitting on the edge of the bed, staring at me.

When I got off the phone, I ran to the bathroom, changed clothes, brushed my teeth, and was ready within five minutes.

Zach protested, "Mom, I don't think you brushed your teeth long enough."

I responded, "It's okay, Zach. I'll brush them again after breakfast."

We were ten minutes into the art museum when the boys complained about hunger. So, I agreed to take them to the café and told Breezy and Marilyn to meet us whenever they were ready. We grabbed a table and ordered our food. I went ahead and ordered something for Marilyn and Breezy so we could save time. Towards the end of breakfast, we discussed the route to continue the trip.

Marilyn suggested, "Let's not stop at another hotel and just pull off at a rest stop or truck stop to nap. Our next full stop should be at Mike's for the night."

I pointed out, "That's a challenging drive. Are you sure you're okay with that?"

"Yes, I'll be fine," Marilyn confirmed. "Breezy and I will continue tag team driving. You continue to ride in the back and take those calls. I feel like it's proving to be an excellent distraction for you."

I agreed, "Okay. That sounds good."

We loaded back into the van, which was now clean, beautiful, waxed, and everything else Marilyn could hope for. She tipped the valet, and we were on our way again.

Once we got on the road, I called Butchie and left him a voicemail. I still hadn't told him what we were doing.

Marilyn inquired, "What did Butchie say about the road trip?"

I hesitated, "We left in such a hurry that I didn't have time to talk to him about it. I didn't want to tell him we were going to Oregon in a text. He might think something's wrong."

Marilyn exclaimed, "There is something wrong! Sierra's been missing."

I sat back in the seat and thought about Sierra and our conversations. Then I got a flashback.

It was the same flashback I had seen of Sierra in a dark space. She looked distraught. It felt like this was happening at that moment. I started to feel overwhelmed and began to panic.

Suddenly, my phone went off and startled me. It was Butchie calling. My spirit guides entered my space. It looked like they came in to comfort me.

"Hi, Butchie, I answered. "How was your day?"

It appeared that he was in a good mood. His energy helped to calm me down.

He replied, "It's great. I'm learning so much in this class and having a good time. You wouldn't believe this superb restaurant we went to. They had little elaborate tents everywhere. While it was outdoors, it looked like it was inside."

"That sounds sweet," I said. "You'll have to send me some pictures."

He sighed, "I wish you could go on trips too. It would be much more fun if you were here with me."

Zach and Ramsey urged me to put Butchie on speaker.

I was hesitant to share, "Well, there is something I need to tell you. Sierra took the job I had advised her not to take. And her sister hasn't heard from her in several weeks. She asked a detective friend of hers to investigate this disappearance. They were concerned for Sierra's welfare and asked if I could help."

Butchie consoled, "I'm sorry to hear about that. I'm sure you'll be able to help her. How are you going to do it? Remote-view where she is? I'm sure you can remote-view everything going on with her."

Zach and Ramsey became quiet as mice. Marilyn glanced back in the rearview mirror to look at the expression on my face. Breezy turned around and winced.

"Well," I hesitated. "The detective, who happens to be a friend of Sierra's sister, asked me to meet her in Oregon to help out."

Butchie chuckled, "Well, we know you wouldn't do that. Did you tell her there's absolutely no way you could go to Oregon?"

I began to panic. It suddenly sunk in what Butchie had just said, and I thought, *Crap, I really am on my way to Oregon!*

The whole van got super quiet. I didn't say anything. I needed to figure out where to begin. My heart was pounding out of my chest. I was way too far to turn back now.

Oh, God, I thought.

I didn't realize that I had just said that out loud.

Butchie sputtered, "What? What was that?"

Suddenly, I realized there was no turning back—not in the van *nor* telling Butchie.

I confessed, "I'm in Marilyn's van right now, and she and Breezy are taking turns driving. We've got the boys with us, too, and we're headed to Oregon."

He fell silent, and I knew he was probably a little upset with me for not telling him until now. I realized that he was more worried for me than upset. Butchie's a protector by nature, and if he's in a position where he can't shield me, he becomes concerned.

His voice elevated, and he was in disbelief, "What? What are you doing? You're actually in a van on the way to Oregon?"

I restated, "I'm not in just any van. It's not like a random white van pulled up in front of the house, and I got in because they promised me candy. I'm in Marilyn's van. She's about the safest person I could ride with outside of you and Carter."

Butchie seemed a little short with me, "Okay, fine. Can you put Marilyn on the phone?"

I took a deep breath and said, "Actually, you're on speaker."

Butchie paused to think and then asked, "How long is the trip from your house to the destination?"

Zach piped up, "Well, Google Maps says it's thirty-four hours."

I could feel Butchie's worry surpass his irritation as he contemplated what I had just hit him with.

He was puzzled, "You've managed to get in a van and somehow commit yourself to getting there. I'm sure there wasn't much planning or coordination, considering your hasty decision. Hell, Katharine, they should have just given you a tranquilizer and carried you on a plane!"

I didn't know what to say, so I just tried to calm him down a bit. I said, "Look at it this way; perhaps this will force me to work through my travel difficulties."

Butchie's pragmatism kicked in, "Yeah, I get that, but I wish I were on this road trip with you. Nothing draws more attention than three women and two boys on a road trip in a van without the protection of a man."

I was secretly fighting off a panic attack, but I couldn't let Butchie know, so I tried to be funny.

"Stop worrying," I said. "Besides, you're mistaken when you say nothing draws more attention. Many things draw more attention, like women traveling alone, a streaker, and a truck stop whose mascot is a beaver."

I added, "Besides when I get too anxious, I'll just have Zach pull up the ending of the 2008 movie *The Lucky Ones*, where you're marching behind Tim Robbins. It gives me that feeling you're going off to save someone. It will calm me down."

Butchie laughed, "Yeah, right, you probably haven't looked at that scene since I first showed it to you."

"That's not true," I countered. "I just showed it to Carter and Marilyn a few nights ago after dinner.

Marilyn concurred, "That's right, and you looked really sharp, Butchie."

He laughed, "I know what you guys are trying to do. It's working a little bit, but it's not going to make everything just go away. This is a serious situation, and I don't want anyone in that van taking unnecessary risks. It would help if you kept me updated on everything going on and everywhere you go. Please, always be aware of your surroundings."

I giggled and exclaimed, "Yes, sir, Major! All of this coming from a true military Anti-terrorist instructor."

When we got off the phone with Butchie, Marilyn insisted, "Don't worry, he's not upset. He's just concerned for our safety, and we know we'll be fine on this trip, right?"

I ensured, "Of course, we're going to be fine."

Breezy turned around and asked, "Mom, did you check psychically?"

I remarked, "Of course I did. I psychically saw some of the sessions I'll be doing next week, so I know we live through this week."

Marilyn looked at me in the rearview mirror, "I'm not sure if that's the best way to determine whether we will live through this."

I stated, "Whatever happens on this trip, we know we'll be fine. We're going to have a great trip."

Breezy challenged, "Are you just telling yourself that, so you don't panic, or do you really believe we will have a great trip?"

I smiled, "Look, I've managed to be in the car this long, and I haven't begged you guys to turn around. So, I'm guessing this will be a great trip. I need to text Mike and tell him when we'll be in Ogden. Do you have an ETA for that, Breezy?"

Zach interjected, "Ramsey and I have been working on that. It looks like we're eighteen hours and fifty-six minutes from

Mike's. If we stay at Mike's place, we can stay a full night, get up the next day, and drive. That would be a good stopping point, don't you think?"

"I don't know if it will," cautioned Marilyn. "Is everyone good with riding for eighteen hours? More importantly, Breezy, can you help drive that much?"

Breezy insisted, "Yes, we can take turns driving and sleeping. We can always pull-off to the side to take a short nap at that big Mormon truck stop at the base of Utah and Colorado."

"That sounds great," Marilyn agreed.

I glanced down at my phone and realized I had a text from a client. It was from Priscilla Price, a client who had hired me for several private parties and special events.

The text read:

> I don't remember what happened last night. Do you have a minute to call me?

I told everyone I needed to call a client and to be quiet. I didn't want anyone to know I was riding around in the back of a van, taking calls.

I laughed to myself as I briefly thought about Priscilla. The backstory is that she's worth sixty million dollars, and that's probably a conservative estimate. Wherever she goes, people cater to her every need. She's among the nicest people you'll ever meet at a country club. She's down to earth, and she's everybody's friend. She's a lot of fun to work for at these private events.

I always meet the most interesting people when I read at these private events. There are always a lot of athletes, musicians, and entertainers. I think just about everybody, who is anybody, knows where she lives.

When I called her back, she answered on the first ring.

"Oh my God, Katharine, thank you for calling me back!" Priscilla declared. "You're on speaker with JT and me."

She took a deep breath, "OK, girl, you're the only one I could think of to call. I need to know what we did last night. I mean...I uh...We...We remember having a drink at The French Room. We woke up with our clothes lying on my bed and a gift box next to us."

As I looked at Priscilla's energy, her spirit guides came forward. I asked them what she did last night. They quickly opened a portal for me to see Priscilla and JT leaving the French room. They had already had a couple of drinks. They got a taxi and went to another club.

They had another drink as soon as they got into the next club. They stayed for a while and entered the shop next to the club. I realized that I had seen enough to begin explaining what had happened.

I told Priscilla, "The guides showed me that you and JT had left the French room, got into a taxi, and went to another club. You went inside, had one drink, and when you came out, you saw something in the window of the shop next door that you wanted. You went into the shop, and JT bought it for you. They wrapped it up, and you got another cab and went to your place.

The gift that you found in your room is yours. JT bought it for you last night."

She declared, "OK, Katharine, but there's still a problem."

Priscilla and JT started giggling, "When we woke up, the bed was wet, but we had our clothes on, so what happened?"

I relayed, "Your spirit guides said to look underneath the bed where you and JT had laid back. JT had left the club with a drink. He got into the taxi with the glass and carried it to the room. When he passed out, the glass fell out of his hand and rolled underneath the bed, but not before spilling on the sheets."

Priscilla said, "Hang on, we're gonna look now."

She started laughing, and JT said, "Sure enough, look at the glass here. I can't believe I left the club with it."

Priscilla yelled, "I can't believe the taxi driver let you in the car with it!"

They sat there for a minute, laughing at each other and their experience. They had thought something much more severe happened that night. Priscilla was very grateful for my detective work and for solving the mystery for them.

JT praised, "Thank you so much; this explains everything."

I replied, "I'm glad I could help. I guess you could go ahead and open the present now that you know it's yours."

Priscilla giggled as she gave JT a smooch. They were acting like two teenagers in love.

She bubbled, "Thank you, JT, for the present."

He laughed and said, "I hope you like it. You picked it out, and I don't even remember what it is."

Priscilla began to open the gift while I was still on the phone. I heard her gasp, "JT, it's gorgeous."

She spoke into the phone and divulged, "It's a beautiful diamond bracelet."

I congratulated, "Oh, that's nice. Well, I hope you guys have a great night. If you have any other questions, feel free to text me back."

When I got off the phone with them, I laid back, closed my eyes, and relaxed for a bit. When I finally opened my eyes, I realized it was dark on this road and I began feeling very nervous. I looked over the seat to see what Zack and Ramsey were doing. They both had tiny lights fixed on the pages of the books they were reading. They were reading about haunted places in Oregon.

I certainly wasn't excited to visit haunted places and see *more* spirits. I thought for a moment that most folks get away from their work surroundings for a mental break and call it a vacation, but there are always spirits no matter where I go. I can never have a vacation in that regard. It's not the spirits that really bother me. It's more of the way they die that is hard for me to see.

Zach believes that going to haunted places gives me a chance to help the soul finally cross into the light. I think that's so sweet of him to think like that. But now that I was out of my everyday surroundings, I didn't want to look for work. I sat back in the seat, propped the pillows up, and looked out the window into the darkness. I was thinking about what Marilyn said about me just focusing on work and taking some calls. So, I logged into the hotline and put myself on as available.

Marilyn announced that we would be stopping at the next truck stop soon. We parked and got out of the van to stretch our legs and use the bathroom, but we realized the place only sold drinks, cigarettes, and lottery tickets.

We were all feeling hungry, so Marilyn suggested, "We can get back in the car and go find a place to eat. But you're going to have to hold your pee for a little longer."

We all agreed to wait and loaded back into the car. Marilyn got us back on the road in no time, and it felt like we hadn't even stopped.

A few minutes later, I got a call from Toni.

"Where are you now?" she inquired.

I started to explain, "We're about to...hang on a second. Zach, where are we right now? How far are we from our destination?"

Zach replied, "It looks like we're about twenty-eight hours away."

Toni asked, "Don't you think flying would have been better?"

I reminded her, "No, I can't fly. I'm barely able to do this ride. Please stop reminding me that I'm in a vehicle away from my house. You have no idea the anxiety I'm trying to fight off right now."

"OK, check in with me when you get to Ogden," Toni replied.

I hung up, and the phone immediately rang again. It was a call coming in from the hotline. I tried to shake off my anxiety and settled into the seat to take the call.

"Hi, this is Katharine. How may I help you?" I answered.

"Hi Katharine, it's Roxy," she acknowledged. I'm so glad to see you're on this late.

"It's always a pleasure to read for you, Roxy," I answered. What would you like me to take a look at?"

She exclaimed, "Well, Craig and I fought! I got him to go out with me. We went to dinner with his best friend. After dinner, we went back to his house, but he wouldn't let me go inside. We got into this huge fight, and his best friend tried to calm me down. He threatened to call the police on me. I had to leave. I got in my car to go, and I hit his boat in the driveway. You know, Katharine, I could tell his best friend wanted to have sex with me."

Her spirit guides indicated that she was lying about accidentally hitting the boat.

I confirmed, "Roxy, your spirit guides told me you're not telling me the truth. You meant to hit his boat because you were angry at him."

Roxy paused for a minute and then started laughing.

"Yes, you're right," she admitted. "I did hit his boat because I got upset with him. Screw him. Let him spend his money to fix it. He should've let me in the house. I was just trying to spend time with him and wanted to go inside and have fun."

Roxy screamed, "He didn't want to upset Emily, and I got mad!"

I explained, "Roxy, do you remember whenever I told you he would never leave his wife, and even if he weren't married, he would never choose you? You need to get to the point where you'll be open to someone else who will be there for you. And see you as the most critical person in their universe."

She admitted, "Katharine, I thought you were wrong. Why would he want her over me? I'm able to be physical with him. I'm able to do things with him that she can't do. I bought all the sexy lingerie. He can't do anything sexual with her. What is it about her that he loves so much that he can't find in me?"

I waited for her spirit guides to give me some guidance. They finally explained, *he loved her from the beginning, and the fact that she changed his life for the good, means everything to him.*

I relayed everything they showed me and repeated everything they said. It didn't seem to matter to Roxy. She wasn't responding.

Suddenly, I noticed that she wasn't on the phone anymore. The call didn't get disconnected. She just didn't want to hear the truth and hung up.

Within a few minutes after hanging up with Roxy, another hotline call came in.

I answered, "Hi, this is Katharine. How may I help you?"

I heard someone crying on the other end of the phone. The person wasn't saying anything, just sobbing.

I consoled, "It's okay. What would you like me to take a look at?"

"It's not okay, Katharine. My name is Laticia Flores," she wept. "I called you two years ago about the guy I was chasing. His name was Jose. I was attracted to him, and I thought we were soulmates. When I called you, you told me I would regret going after him. And I needed just to find someone else. Anyone else, just not him. I had been so drawn to him, and I thought you were wrong. You even said you couldn't read for medical or legal on this hotline."

Laticia surmised, "Looking back, I realize you were trying to hint that it would be medical. I did stop seeing him after he beat me up. I had already begun to see that he was not a good person. He ended up in prison for gang-related activity. It's been two years now. I just received a postcard in the mail letting me know he was HIV positive."

She continued, "I am now in a relationship with someone else, and we're expecting a baby. If I weren't expecting a baby, I would've taken the information about the HIV as my punishment for being with him in the first place. My mother warned me about him. Everybody warned me about him. Even the church was telling me to stay away from him. I guess this is my karma for dating him. This whole thing is my punishment from God!"

Leticia stopped talking and started to cry profusely. I knew God was not punishing her, and she would be okay.

I testified, "Leticia, God is not punishing you."

She rebutted, "Katharine, you don't understand. I remember being in an apartment with his friends, and they were all passing the needle around—it was the dumbest thing. And yet I'd wait for him, even though I didn't do drugs. I just thought he was the most extraordinary person. And now I feel so stupid."

I declared, "Listen to me carefully, Laticia. I want you to go to the doctor and get yourself checked out. But I want you to understand that when I look at your life further out, I see you holding your baby. I see you are pleased."

She slowly calmed down and said, "Okay, Katharine, I understand what you're telling me. You are making me feel better. I'll let you know what the doctor says. Thank you for talking to me."

The automated voice on the hotline announced that the caller did not add funds to continue the call.

When I got off the phone, Marilyn notified us, "There's a huge truck stop coming up with a store and a restaurant. We'll pull in there, and afterward, Breezy can take over driving while I sleep."

The place looked like a three-ring circus. There were families, truck drivers, locals, and many interesting people. It boasted a giant car wash and a beautifully lit store with a restaurant inside.

Ramsey asked, "Zach and I ate the carrots Breezy gave us earlier, so can we get something to go from that restaurant?"

Marilyn agreed, "Sure. Get whatever you want. Here's a card. Katharine, are you going in with them?"

"Yes," I stated.

I walked in with the boys. I ignored the unhealthy food they were ordering. While we waited, I rummaged through the brochure stand next to the waiting area. It had a lot of pamphlets with different things to see in Utah. Zach and Ramsey started collecting a bunch of them. When the food was ready, Zach carried the bag to the van while I bought some bananas.

It seemed weird buying bananas at a truck stop. The boys were the first ones loaded in the van and had already started their movie and eating their pancakes.

Marilyn returned to the van and looked at the boys, "You're going to have to get back on your oatmeal after this trip."

Breezy was just staring at them. Each had a tall stack of six pancakes covered with syrup.

She joked, "Those two are going to turn into pancakes or waffles by the end of this trip."

She climbed into the driver's seat, adjusted the maps app for Mike's address, and said, "When we get to Mike's, we can take showers and sleep in a nice bed."

Marilyn put on an eye mask and laid back before we pulled out of the truck stop parking lot. I decided to leave myself on the hotline. I laid back on the seat to look out the window at the sky. Marilyn was asleep in a few moments. I knew she was super tired. I could already tell earlier that day.

Breezy seemed to be driving well, and she appeared wide awake. I texted Mike to inform him we were less than six hours from his house in Ogden. I looked over the seat in front of me, and the boys were passed out. It must've been all the pancakes they ate.

I was fighting off the panic of feeling trapped in the back. It's difficult to explain to anyone who has never had a panic attack. It was so difficult to focus on anything else. I started to realize that everything outside the van was entirely dark. There were no lights on the road from roadside gas stations or restaurants—the only light was from our headlights shining outward in front of us.

The boys had finished their movie earlier, so there was no light in their area and no exit door for me to access quickly. The anxiety was really building up.

Come on, somebody call me so I can clear my mind of feeling confined, I thought.

Miraculously, the phone rang.

It was the hotline. *Thank God!* I whispered to myself.

I greeted the caller, "Hi, this is Katharine. How may I help you?"

"Hey Katharine, it's Roxy," she answered.

"Hi, Roxy. What would you like me to look at?" I restated.

She huffed, "Please look at Craig psychically. He put a restraining order against me. Do you see him dropping the restraining order?"

"Sure, Roxy, hang on, let me take a look," I replied.

As I began to look psychically, her spirit guides told me that this was his way of protecting himself. He felt like he had gone overboard with this connection and was worried that she would do something crazy to Emily.

I clarified, "Your spirit guides are telling me this is his way of keeping a shield between you and him. He believes you're crazy."

Roxy screamed, "I'm not the one who's crazy! *He* is! *He* started this whole thing with me. *He* wanted me initially, but now he's acting like there's nothing! I know he has feelings for me. Maybe he's acting this way because his friend is telling him I'm the one who's crazy, but deep down, he has feelings for me."

Roxy paused momentarily, and I remote-viewed her. I could see her checking the phone.

She abruptly asked, "Hey Katharine, will you be on for a while?"

Unfortunately, for the next seven hours, I thought.

But I answered, "Yes, I'll be on for a while."

"Okay, great. I'll call you back later," she acknowledged.

After we hung up, I thought, *wow, it's wild; just the prospect of Roxy calling me back makes me feel better.*

She was a familiar voice. Not exactly a friendly voice, but at least someone to keep my mind off this trip.

I've read for Roxy several times, and she can be shockingly crazy. She yelled at me during this last session and then called me back later and told me she was sorry and how much she loved me—*borderline sociopath!*

I texted Mike a photo from where I was sitting that showed Breezy driving, Marilyn passed out, and the boys asleep in the center section.

Mike replied:

> Looking forward to your visit.

I also sent the photo to Butchie.

Butchie's response was a little bit different. He replied:

> This photo makes me worry. Everyone is asleep, there's no lights on the road, and you've got a teenager driving. Who's got an eye out while she's driving?

I quickly responded:

> Breezy is a great driver. She had proper training at the local driving school, and I'm keeping an eye on things.

In my mind I thought, *at least in between calls and my panicking.*

He responded:

> Okay, text me when you get to Mike's. Be safe and I love you.

Chapter 10
True Confession

I woke up to the irritating chime on my phone going off. I glanced at my watch and saw that it was 4:00 a.m. I noticed the van wasn't moving. I brought my awareness to the call coming in from the hotline. I looked up while answering and realized we had parked outside a place called *Moe's Munch and Crunch*. It had a giant bowl with cereal pouring out of it, and only half of the sign was lit and blinking.

Everyone in the van was asleep except for me. I had kept myself on to taking calls after my late-night call with Roxy. So, I must have fallen asleep at some point throughout the night.

I answered, "Hi, this is Katharine. How may I help you?"

"Hi, Katharine, this is Lisa," she replied. "I'm a friend of Roxy's. She is in jail. She went to Craig's, and he called the police when she broke his windows."

I commented, "Oh, no!".

Lisa laughed, "I'm sure you know Roxy can sometimes be overly reactive."

I thought back to the times Roxy had blurted out profanities, broken objects, and stolen phones so the spouses couldn't connect with their husbands.

I said, "I am sorry to hear that happened. What would you like me to look at?"

"I'm not quite sure," she whispered.

She spoke into the phone as if she didn't want other people around her to hear. She asked, "Do you feel they will let her go with no charges pressed? Do you think Craig will feel bad for calling the police?"

I explained, "Lisa, I've had several conversations with Roxy and let her know Craig does not want to be with her. You're right; Roxy shows moments of irrational emotional reaction. It's something she's going to have to learn to control. This is part of the experience she has to work through—working with people in healthcare. The connection between Roxy and Craig was not meant to be long-term."

Lisa asked, "Do you see Craig pressing charges? Do you see the DA's office pressing charges? Do you see them holding her?"

While she was asking these questions, I heard my spirit guides say that Craig would not press charges this time. He only wants to scare her enough to keep her away. I relayed this information to Lisa, who seemed happy to hear it. She told me that she didn't believe Roxy would stay away.

I imparted, "Please tell Roxy I'm sorry she's going through this. Tell her to stay away from his residence because he will press charges the next time she's there."

Lisa thanked me for taking her call. By the time I finished, everyone in the van was awake. It was close to 5:00 a.m., so they wanted to go inside *Moe's* for breakfast.

Moe's was an exciting place. When you first hear the name, you automatically think it's probably some big guy in the back working at the grill. Actually, it's a tiny woman behind the counter running the place. The name tag says Moe's, and she manages eight different cereal dispensers. Also, a sign on the side reads: *Hot cereal and sandwiches served daily.*

The boys sat at the counter while Moe told them about her favorite cereal. Marilyn sat in a booth, and Breezy and I hopped in with her. While Moe made her way over to us, she set down three coffee mugs. I put my hand across the top and asked her if she had any teabags.

She poured coffee for Breezy and Marilyn and took my mug back with her. She brought it back, filled with hot water and a tea bag. We all placed our order, and Moe walked off to get everything ready.

A heavy-set man entered through the door. He must have weighed three hundred and fifty pounds. We watched him walk to a four-top table with one oversized chair and sit down. The chair did not match anything else in the restaurant. I figured it was for the heavier folks who visited.

I noticed a unique energy surrounding him. It wasn't from a deceased person but maybe someone he's physically connected to. I could see this person psychically, and they looked oddly familiar. So, I asked him if he knew Patricia. Patricia was one of my hotline callers who usually asked about her animals or about her boyfriend's safety on the road.

He looked surprised, "Patricia is my girlfriend. Do you know her?"

I replied, "Yes, I've talked to her a few times. I'm a psychic medium. When Patricia last called me, you had just talked to her about a kitten you found on the road."

He sat there momentarily and recalled, "Oh yes, Katie, no, Kathy?"

I smiled, "My name is Katharine."

"Oh yes," he cheered. "Yes, Kathy, it's nice to meet you in person. How did you end up *here* so early in the morning?"

I explained, "We are on our way to visit a client."

He proudly smiled as Moe set his breakfast in front of him.

He looked up at me and said, "Patricia will be disappointed she didn't get a chance to meet you in person. She credits you with teaching her about spiritual stuff. My name is Big John, and I was wondering if I could get a picture with you to show Patricia."

Big John pulled out his phone and handed it to Moe. "Would you mind taking a photo of us?" he asked.

"Sure," Moe replied.

He prompted, "I want everybody in the photo. Come on and join us."

Marilyn, Ramsey, Zach, Breezy, and I gathered next to Big John. Moe snapped a picture and returned to the counter. She turned the television on to a news broadcast. I missed the first part of what the newscaster said but caught the rest.

"...otherwise, he's completely recovered from the bicycle accident several weeks ago when he dislocated his shoulder."

When I looked at the TV, an elected official was being filmed. He was smiling and waving while standing next to his family.

I immediately felt Sierra's energy. *Is this the guy whose shoulder she dislocated?* I thought.

I got a clear *yes* from my spirit guides. It was the same guy.

As we got closer to where we needed to be, the universe validated that I was doing the right thing by taking this trip. I also got the distinct feeling that this was about more than just finding Sierra. It was about having the confidence to leave my comfort zone and try something different.

While finishing our breakfast, I got a call from a woman named Carrie Tindall. I've read for her previously regarding her daughter, her daughter's boyfriend, and her dislike for him. This call felt different. Her energy was a dark orange as if deep fear had set into her field. I stepped outside to talk more freely.

She fretted, "Hi, Katharine. I know it's been a while since we last talked. My name is Carrie Tindell. I'm living in fear of my daughter. I am afraid for my life. She and her boyfriend have been stealing from me. Her boyfriend takes things and throws them across the room as a scare tactic."

I consoled, "I'm so sorry you're dealing with this. What is it you want me to take a look at?"

"Katharine, every night I've been sleeping with my bedroom door locked and bolted. I had a couple of extra locks installed on my bedroom door, and I slept with a gun underneath the pillow," she shuddered.

I declared, "I'm so sorry, Carrie. The hotline requires me as an advisor to urge you to go to the police."

"I have gone to the police," she protested. "There's nothing they can do until she moves out."

"By you going to the police, it was documented," I maintained. "I'm so sorry you are dealing with this."

Carrie whimpered, "I wanted to ask you when you see them leaving, Katharine. You were the only one I could think of to call since my extended family wants nothing to do with me for fear my daughter and her boyfriend will harm them, too. Maybe I am too emotional over this. I feel helpless, and I want to end my life."

She insisted, "I've gone to community health centers for counseling regarding all the issues connected to my daughter. I have nothing left that she has not tried to get her hands on. She has stolen credit cards and run them up. She has stolen jewelry and sold it all. I seriously have nothing left of any value. What do I do?"

I instructed, "Carrie, there are two things you need to do. First, you are going to list your house for sale. Have friends help you pack up what you want to keep. Throw away the rest. Your home will sell within two weeks. Do not engage anyone who would tell your daughter your whereabouts.

I continued, "The next thing you need to do is conduct energy work on yourself. I can see a thick, spiritually bound anchor running from your thigh to your daughter's energy. This indicates the connection between you two will be repeated in every lifetime until you remove it. I will explain how to go in and work on pulling it out."

Carrie sobbed, "Katharine, can't you remove it? I'm scared."

I explained, "Carrie, this is something you need to do. It won't be gone until you release the fear. You will reestablish the connection each time a thought or worry is focused on the anchor still being there. It would be best to do this independently; spend some time today and work on it. Once you remove it, your daughter will have the desire to move somewhere completely different. She won't even want to stay in the same city where you live."

She asked, "Are you sure about this?"

I declared, "If you don't get working on these changes, your Higher Self will choose for you to exit this life soon!"

Carrie was upset, but she understood my sincerity and seriousness.

"Wait a minute, you're saying I could get sick?" she inquired.

I answered, "No, I feel like they do something to kill you. The same thing happens for every lifetime you have with her—your life gets cut short."

She sighed, "Gosh, Katharine, I don't know what to do. I trust you, so I will try this."

I insisted, "There's nothing left for you to do other than this. Once you clear the energy anchor, you will have more vitality. You will thank her for the spiritual lesson, the opportunity, and all you learned. But this will happen on a soul level, not in person. You will release it all with a deep breath. There's nothing you need to say. You will feel the emotions of it. After this, your daughter will decide to move."

Carrie sniffled, "They don't even like this city."

I stated, "Once she moves, you won't have anything else to worry about. It's not a big deal; this will be the final lifetime of feeling powerless. When you start the process, you will have to feel where you believe the anchor is connected energetically. I can see it in the upper thigh. When it's cleared, you will feel better physically. You're not going to feel as stifled as you have been."

She praised, "Thank you, Katharine. I won't be adding in funds to continue this call, but I will contact you in a couple of weeks and let you know how everything is going."

I concluded the call by saying, "Okay, Carrie, I know you can do this. Please be motivated to make significant changes. Nothing changes unless you take steps forward."

I got off the call and walked back inside the diner. Breezy and Marilyn discussed how much longer it would take to get to Mike's.

"We're only a couple of hours away now," Marilyn beamed. "Maybe not even that, depending on if we take the shortcut I saw on my phone."

"OK, awesome," I remarked.

I was ready to get back on the road and finish this. I walked up to the counter to pay the tab and overheard Moe explaining to the boys how this was her father's place. She said that he loved cereal, and she decided to keep the business going when he passed away.

We got back on the road, and I felt better about getting to Mike's house. I knew I would feel better once I got somewhere that felt like a home. I could take some time to ground myself without being in a moving vehicle.

We noticed how huge the houses were as we turned into Mike's neighborhood. They were almost a block long themselves.

Marilyn said, "Wow, check out these houses."

Breezy replied, "I know. They're incredible. These Mormons surely know how to live."

I suddenly thought about the many clients I've had sessions with who deal with trauma because of their ingrained Mormon beliefs. I try not to judge any particular belief system. Still, I've had to clear many religious clients' energy fields from spiritual stagnation.

I rebutted, "I don't know about that, Breezy. Many of these houses have two or three generations of family living in them. That can be a good thing, but there are a lot of interesting stories here in Utah about certain families. Not all are good, just like anywhere else."

We pulled up to Mike's driveway and pressed the button at his gate to announce our arrival. The boys were excited.

Zach blurted out, "This place looks like the White House."

Ramsey agreed, "Yes, I wonder if he has a butler and a housekeeper. I wonder if he's got any guard dogs as well."

I was smiling from the excitement radiating from the boys. I was happy that they were having a great time on this trip, even though my anxiety was through the roof.

I told them, "He does not have guard dogs, but he does have a tiny dog named Powder. He named her after Powder Mountain, where he found her when he was skiing. He had no idea how she got there, but he's cared for her ever since."

Ramsey asked, "Well, that's cool. So, is he rich?"

I answered, "Mike has a great job and can do whatever he wants. But he prefers to snow ski and water ski."

I'd never been to his house, but he and his daughter had visited our home. This was the first time I visited him.

Mike answered the intercom, "Hi, guys. Just drive on up."

The gate opened, and we drove through. We continued up a winding driveway that had a unique design of colored pavers. As we pulled around the back, the garage door opened. We could immediately see an array of bicycles mounted to the wall.

They were in perfect shape and looked ready for the Tour de France.

The bikes were housed in a pristine workshop designed for the highest-quality service and maintenance. Four vehicles were also parked inside and were presented as showroom quality.

Mike came out to greet us and hugged Breezy, Zach, and me. He then reached out with a handshake for Marilyn and Ramsey.

I confessed, "We're so glad to see you, Mike. But we're exhausted from this trip."

Mike walked to the back door and opened it. He insisted, "Oh, no worries. Go inside and make yourself at home. I must go to work shortly, but you can sleep, shower, and eat. I made a tray of sandwiches, fruit, and some muffins. When I get off work, I can stop and pick up dinner, or we can all go out for dinner. Do you have a preference?"

Marilyn spoke up, "I would prefer to eat here. I'm so exhausted."

I agreed, "I don't want to go anywhere else until we have to. I need some time to restore my energy from the travel."

Mike affirmed, "Okay, I'll pick up dinner after work."

Mike grabbed his office bag and said, "If, for any reason, you need to go anywhere, there's a key under the rock by the sage on the walkway."

Mike headed off to work, and we all settled down. We took showers, one by one, emerging from the bathroom feeling clean and wearing fresh clothes.

Each one of us found our own place to relax. I noticed Powder lying on the sofa. It looked like a giant square that could hold a dozen people. I crawled on the couch and laid next to Powder. Zach and Ramsey climbed onto the other side of the sofa with a few books about local ghost stories from Mike's Shelf.

"Hey, Mom. You should check out Mike's books," Zach suggested. "We could go to all these local places and clear out the ghosts."

"That sounds cool," Ramsey cheered.

"It doesn't sound great to me," I admitted. "We've got to get to Oregon, and there's not much leeway for stopping."

Breezy walked up and plopped down on the edge of the sofa. Marilyn was carrying an iPad and climbed onto the sofa beside me.

She pointed to the map on the iPad and noted, "We don't have time to stop at very many places. Once we leave here, it's about a ten-hour drive to where we're supposed to meet Toni."

I agreed, "Boys, we are still a long distance from our destination, so try to stay focused on why we're on this trip."

Breezy turned on the TV and said, "Let's just watch a show, relax, and fall asleep. Enjoy this place for a short while."

Both boys quickly fell asleep holding their books. Breezy was knocked out within minutes, and Powder was cozied up to Marilyn. Mike's sofa was so large. It felt like we were on a giant bed.

After looking at our location on the map, I realized how far we were from home. I thought about Butchie's concerns about the potential danger involved, and I thought about how much further we had to go. The anxiety began to build in my mind.

But then I thought about Sierra and what could be happening with her.

I began to question whether law enforcement would have ever investigated the fact that Sierra was missing, if Marisol hadn't known Toni. I didn't think so.

Toni pointed out that law enforcement would not make much effort to find someone in Sierra's line of work.

I also thought about all the validations that have popped up during this trip and the people we've met.

The hotline readings I've been doing along the way have provided a distraction and kept me busy. Still, I couldn't shake the eerie feeling I continued getting about Sierra.

I was still waiting to hear from Sierra. I promised her I wouldn't look in. I knew that she had gotten herself into some interesting situations before. It was tough to fight off the urge to peer into her energy and the space around her to see what was happening.

Suddenly, I had a flashback…

I remembered one of the situations I had psychically read for her: She was on a weekend trip up North. She had been invited to a private mansion by a world-renowned Grammy award-winning music artist. He had been seeing her for some time and would call her whenever he was in her town to meet up.

When she first had me look into this guy's energy, I instantly knew who he was. She described him as having a bit of a wild side. However, his erratic behavior didn't surprise me. I never really cared for him or his music. I suppose it was because I psychically knew he was a creep to women.

But I found his tendency to get into suspenseful situations most interesting. It was almost like he enjoyed the attention so much that he was willing to put women in danger just for his ego.

They had several great days of fun in a row together. He took her out shopping and dinner, and by night, he was eager to get tied up and beaten. They had planned a three-week excursion, but it was interrupted by a visit of one of the groupies he had been stringing along while on tour.

The visit could have turned into a heated battle very quickly. So, he told Sierra to pretend she was his assistant until he figured out a way to get the groupie to leave. Eventually, he convinced her he was working on an upcoming show that she hoped would breathe new life into his career. He offered to have his driver take her to the airport. The crazy thing was that as he hugged and kissed her goodbye, he told her his driver would stop by Lululemon to buy her something. That was all she needed to get her loaded into the car and back to the airport.

The music artist pulled Sierra aside and said that the woman was a wacko. The evening seemed to get back on track after the groupie was gone. He asked Sierra to get ready because he was excited to begin their play time. After a few glasses of wine, he admitted to enjoying the attention the groupie gives him but the visit to his private home was unexpected.

Later, while he was begging Sierra to discipline him, the doorbell rang—it was the groupie returning. The groupie entered the unlocked house and found her way to the bedroom, where Sierra had the music artist restrained to a soft platform on all fours with sex toys lying around him.

The groupie was furious because he had misled her earlier. She began running towards Sierra while cussing at him. Sierra screamed out for help. The groupie pulled out a knife and lunged toward Sierra, but she fell on the oversized platform. After hearing the noise, the house manager came running in and detained the groupie. He got on the phone and called the police. Sierra discovered from the house manager that this wasn't an isolated incident. The music artist tends to draw in crazy women like this all the time. He dupes them into believing they are special and the only one he spends time with. But when they find out the truth, incidents like this happen.

Sierra survived that incident, but as I sat there momentarily, I wondered how often she had encountered similar situations. Suddenly, I heard my spirit guides say it had been about a dozen times.

I just realized that Sierra had never really focused on the danger of her profession, only the money she could make. It was beginning to make sense now. The Universe had created an experience and lessons to be learned. But was it going to be at the expense of Sierra's life?

Mike returned home carrying several bags. He had picked-up dinner from an Italian take-out and was excited for us to experience his favorite food.

We ate dinner beside the pool while the boys urged Mike to tell them about local ghost stories. Mike loved the paranormal and enjoyed talking about the local hauntings. Later that night, we discussed the route we would choose for the rest of the trip. Mike gave us some insight into places we could stop to eat and rest.

At the same time, he warned us to be very careful. He explained that there are some great places to see but to keep in mind that there are a lot of shady areas as well.

He declared, "If you guys get in any trouble whatsoever, call me! I'll make sure you get the help you need."

Any other time I would've been concerned after that statement but not now. I knew I was doing exactly what the Universe had intended me to do. And I was comfortable knowing that. Now, that didn't mean I wasn't going to have any more panic attacks or anxiety on this trip. But I knew there was a higher purpose for all this and without a doubt, we were being protected along the way.

We were all up by 5:00 a.m. the next day. Marilyn was bright-eyed and bushy tailed, ready to go. I left a note on Mike's kitchen counter, thanking him for letting us enjoy his beautiful home.

Once we got on the road, everything seemed simpler and straightforward. I think enjoying the comfort of Mike's home balanced us all back to normalcy.

Right around 10:00 a.m., I got a call from Brooke Rossi, the psychiatrist in upstate New York, who was in love with the guy having dissociative identity disorder. Most people recognize it as a multiple personality disorder.

When I answered the phone, she was sobbing and couldn't seem to put a coherent sentence together.

I asked, "Brooke. What's going on? What would you like me to take a look at?"

As soon as I said that I could see the spirit of Hudson, the man she was treating and having sexual relations with. He came into the space around Brooke. He had a distinguishing light around him, so I knew he had passed.

She tried to speak, I…I…Kath…Hud…he…

Her words just couldn't break through the crying and tears.

"It's Ok, Brooke," I consoled her. "I know Hudson has passed. He's next to you in spirit."

She began to cry even more. The sobbing continued for another few minutes before she was able to get any words out.

Finally, she exclaimed, "Katharine, you were right! I couldn't save him. I thought my treatment would keep him from wanting to leave. I guess suicide was inevitable."

I tried to comfort her, "I'm sorry, Brooke. There's nothing you could have done to prevent this."

Brooke remarked sluggishly, "I agree with you. There seemed to be something that, no matter the treatment, Hudson always wanted to leave. He couldn't stand himself. Or, in his case, any of the personas he identified with. After he passed, I had a busy work schedule with new clients, and I couldn't take time off."

She gasped for air, "It was three days later, and I had a meeting with a new male client. My eyes were red, so I camouflaged them with makeup. I had not read the new patient's records before meeting him, so I needed to at least find out what I was dealing with. At the time of our appointment, I opened his file and read that he had been referred to me."

She exclaimed, "He had been diagnosed with dissociative identity disorder! Don't you know what this means, Katharine? This is the sign!"

I was a bit confused by where she was going with this, so I asked, "What do you mean?"

She gushed, "Hudson passed on Sunday at 4:50 a.m. I went to work the next day and asked for a sign that Hudson was okay and not mad at me. Don't you see? I got that sign!"

Immediately, Brooke's spirit guides began to explain the hidden truth to me: A few weeks back, Brooke had taken Hudson off his medicine and told him he didn't need it. She didn't want him to improve from the disorder. She wanted to continue enjoying the various personalities he had to offer. She also enjoyed being the one to console him.

I must have paused too long like I usually do when listening to the guides because Brooke roared, "Katharine! Are you still there?"

I answered, "Yes, I'm still here. I was listening to your spirit guides explaining things to me. They were telling me that you took Hudson off his medication, which was not good for him. The medication allowed him to be present in his true identity and not shift in and out of other personalities."

I could tell by Brooke's vacillating energy that she didn't care what I was saying and was trying to avoid hearing the truth.

She protested, "Katharine, it doesn't matter! Don't you understand Hudson forgives me anyway? He sent me another person with the same disorder."

Brooke paused for a long moment, huffing and puffing.

When she finally calmed down, she vowed, "I know I can help this new guy, too. This was a sign from God telling me: 'I am sending you another incredible love.'"

"Brooke!" I exclaimed. "That's not what they're showing you. You're being given another chance to do the *right* thing, not so you can repeat bad choices..."

She interrupted, "Bad choices!? That's judgment. What I've done with Hudson—the love we had was special. You don't understand how deep it was. Are you saying it was a wrong choice? Is that your opinion?"

I refuted, "No, Brooke. It's not my opinion. It's the law! It's the oath you took. Hudson came to you for help. He came to you because he couldn't work, function, or hold on to relationships. He needed help, but he couldn't get it from you. He wanted to live a normal life and provide for himself, but your selfish intent got in the way."

I pleaded, "Please, Brooke, do the right thing this time."

I could hear Brooke fighting back the tears. I looked to her spirit guides for guidance and began to receive their message.

I channeled the message and told her, "Brooke, when someone truly loves another that is struggling, they'll do whatever they can to help them heal, feel better, or succeed. You did the opposite of this with Hudson. You selfishly cuddled with him while he lay in broken emotions. You relished in the different personalities and masks he wore. And you took sexual advantage of his estranged personality diversity. You gave into human temptations, although this was a challenge for spiritual growth. You were given the talents and opportunities to help those in emotional deprivation, not take advantage of them."

I stopped channeling at that point because her spirit guides told me that she was finally able to realize the consequences of her actions. She had broken through the selfish barrier that prevented her from empathizing with someone like Hudson. It was now up to her to make ethical choices with other patients.

We had made great progress on the road and were getting very close to our destination. I had spoken to Toni earlier and she asked me to call her when we were fifteen minutes away.

Marilyn looked in the rearview mirror and hollered, "We're about fifteen minutes away. You need to give the detective a call."

I said, "Thanks, Marilyn. I'll call her now."

Toni answered on the second ring, "Hi, Katharine. Are you close?"

I acknowledged, "Yes. We are about fifteen minutes away."

She instructed, "I'm going to text you the address. It's the police station. I want you to meet us there."

"Will do," I answered.

I called out the address to Breezy, and she put it into Google Maps.

Marilyn whooped, "Yay, we're almost there."

The boys cheered, "Yay, yay, yay."

When we arrived at the police station, Toni was waiting at the entrance. She walked us through a small corridor to a larger room with several desks.

We arrived at the desk of an officer who appeared to be helping Toni. We stood before the desk, while Toni sat down. The officer told us to pull up some chairs and relax.

Toni was dressed plainly in a plaid jacket and jeans. The officer that was helping her wore a name tag that read *Timothy Conner*. Across from us sat a clean-cut, red-headed guy being questioned by another officer.

Ramsey was staring at the man. Marilyn traced Ramsey's eyes to see what he was staring at. She brushed it off and pulled Ramsey closer. I looked at the man psychically and saw a dark, murky red energy field around him. There were spirits of several people he had killed lingering around him. They had family spiritual cords connected to the red-headed man. The spirits were asking me for help.

Marilyn addressed the officer assisting Toni.

"Sir, who is that guy?" She pointed to the red-headed fellow.

The officer looked up and declared, "Please, you don't need to call me sir. You can call me Officer Conner. Don't worry about that guy. Now and then, we get these people just coming in for attention. He came in and said he committed murder. I don't have another officer to go and check out his story right now. We're taking down his information, and we'll have someone check it out later tonight."

Officer Conner noticed that Marilyn and the kids seemed a bit terrified and tried to lessen the fear by saying, "He's going to stay here until we check it out, though. Usually, we end up having to get social services to come for psychiatric evaluations."

I looked at the red-headed man and gave him a fake smile. He might have looked harmless if it weren't for the several deceased people lingering around trying to convey that they had just been murdered by him a few hours ago.

I leaned in close to Officer Conner and whispered, "The red-headed guy murdered eight family members a few hours ago."

Officer Conner leaned back in his chair and looked at the guy with a sudden interest. He looked back at me and inquired, "How do you know?"

I turned and looked at the spirits of the dead family standing around the smiling, red-headed man.

I leaned into Officer Conner, "Right now, there are spirits of deceased family members relaying that he murdered them all no more than five hours ago."

Officer Conner called out to the officer talking to the red-headed man and said, "Read him his rights and put him in the cell."

Marilyn looked at Officer Connor and asked, "Don't you want to know how Katharine knew that?"

He quickly responded, "She didn't know that he came in and confessed to murdering his whole family. I only said earlier that he came in saying that he committed *a murder*. She confirmed exactly what he had said. I'm not somebody who believes in this hocus pocus psychic stuff, but Toni explained Katharine's extraordinary psychic abilities to me. And she had validated it with Dr. Vasquez."

He looked at me and said, "You're the only lead we have in finding Sierra. And, since you hopped in a van with little notice and drove here all the way from Texas...well, I'm willing to trust your insights. I just hope we're not too late."

Toni took a call while we all watched the red-headed guy get escorted out in handcuffs. Toni got off the phone and said, "That was the coroner's office. The morgue received a female body that fits Sierra's description."

I psychically knew it was not Sierra's body at the morgue.

Toni stated, "The morgue is right around the block on the backside of this building. We can walk over there."

Officer Connor offered to walk with us to the morgue. On the way, I whispered to Toni, "It's not Sierra."

"How do you know?" she asked.

I explained, "I would have seen her in spirit. She's not in spirit, so I know she's not dead."

"Well, I have to follow this through, explained Toni. "I promised Marisol I would find Sierra. I'm hoping alive, but I must confirm every suspicion."

"I understand," I said.

We walked through the morgue's door and signed in. Breezy waited outside with the boys, and Marilyn walked with me to the back. Toni and Officer Conner led the way. The technician was sitting at a desk, typing on a keyboard when we entered the room. Marilyn and I stood in the center of the room while Officer Conner and Toni talked to the technician.

The technician stood up and walked over to a wall full of small freezer-looking doors. He opened one of the doors and slid out a corpse. The body was covered with a sheet, but I noticed the right toe sticking out at the bottom.

"Wait!" I exclaimed. "That's not Sierra. Sierra has a scar on the top of her right foot, the first toe at the joint. This woman has no scar."

Toni looked at me in disbelief and asked, "You've never seen her in person, so how do you know that?"

She motioned for the technician to pull off the sheet to get a complete look at the body.

Toni looked back at me and confirmed, "You're right. It's not her."

When I turned to exit the room, my eye caught Officer Connor's face. I saw him motion something to Toni. When we got to the waiting area around the front door, Breezy looked at Marilyn for an answer. Marilyn shook her head, no. Breezy sighed with relief, and we all exited the building.

While we were standing on the sidewalk waiting for Toni, I leaned into Marilyn. I whispered, "I can feel the energy of the place that Sierra called me from. It must be close."

Marilyn asked, "Do you think you could guide us there?"

"Yes," I answered. "Sierra told me that she hid the phone in an old rundown building in the middle of an abandoned blueberry farm. I'll need to take some time to walk around the area. I'll feel Sierra's energy and locate the cell phone. When we find it, we'll know the house is only a few miles away. I believe I can find the building by following her spirit guides."

We began walking down the sidewalk back to the van. Toni ran up behind us and exclaimed, "Wait a minute. Not so fast. Where do you think you're going?"

Marilyn answered, "We're going to try to find where Sierra called Katharine from."

She insisted, "If you're going to do that, then I need to follow you."

"Okay, fine," I said.

We all looked at each other in confirmation and departed to our vehicles. We got into the van, and I sat behind Breezy while the boys got in the back. We headed out onto the main road, and I got the immediate feeling Officer Connor wouldn't be too far behind. I asked Marilyn to keep an eye out for him.

I told Marilyn, "Well, he appears to want to help locate Sierra but, I'm getting psychic guidance that he will change his mind and will want us all to leave. Something else seems to be changing his mind."

"Hey Zach," I hollered to the back. "I need you to check on all the deserted blueberry farms in the area and get their locations?"

He answered, "Yep, I'll get right on it."

A few minutes later, Zach said, "Ok, Ramsey and I found a few places and marked them on the iPad."

Okay, great," I acknowledged. "Please give the addresses to Breezy so she can put them in Google Maps. We'll drive to the nearest one first."

When we drove by the first location, my spirit guides said, *no, this one isn't it.* We continued about ten miles further. We noticed a partially dilapidated building at the next stop. All the buildings we saw along the way appeared to be abandoned, just like Sierra had told me. We noticed a separate building further back behind the partial building.

Suddenly, I could feel Sierra's energy.

I hollered, "Stop the van. Pull over to the side and let me out."

Marilyn pulled off to the side and the boys began to get out.

"Hey, you guys stay in the van," I advised. Let me check this out first."

Zach said, "No way, mom. Let us go with you."

I objected, "Just hold on a minute! I'm curious to see if this leads anywhere. I need to walk around and feel if her footsteps were here. I should be able to feel her energetic imprint."

"We want to go with you," Zach insisted.

I consented, "Okay, get out of the van."

I leaned into the window and told Marilyn, "Try to drive slowly behind us as we walk ahead. But whatever you do, please don't pull away. It will completely freak me out."

I looked down the road where Toni's car had stopped. I started to sense that someone else who didn't want us here would be approaching soon. So, I needed to hurry and find what I could.

Breezy had one of the handheld personal alarms that Butchie had bought us, and I told her to set it off if anyone comes near the area. I walked around the building, and my eyes took the direction of a larger structure across the field. My guides urged me toward the building which appeared to be an abandoned migrant workers facility. When we arrived, Zach and Ramsey peered inside what looked like an old canning area. A manual canning press stood in the corner and, a bunch of old broken crates strung all over.

"Wow!" Ramsey exclaimed. "This place is ancient."

Zach nodded in agreement.

As I walked through, I could feel Sierra. I saw her energetic imprint leading to one of the many doors down the hallway.

I followed my spirit guides' frequency to the second door and lightly pushed it open. The building was rotted, and structural parts were missing from the side walls and roof. I stepped into the small space, and there was a wooden cot with small fragments of an old mattress lying on top.

I faintly heard Breezy's personal alarm sounding off. I started to get anxious, but I had to continue looking.

My spirit guides notified me, *the officer is coming*.

I was guided to look under the cot. I started to panic but I knew I had to push myself through. I dropped to my knees, bent towards the ground, and looked under the cot.

A glistening object caught my attention. It appeared to be a plastic bag. I cautiously reached under the cot and instantaneously felt Sierra's energy flow through me. I grabbed ahold of it and pulled it toward my head. As it inched closer and closer, I realized a cell phone was inside.

As I raised and turned, I saw Officer Conner's energy field overlapping the door. I got to my feet and started towards the door, opening the bag to look inside. I recognized two extra batteries with the cell phone, just as Sierra had told me. I smiled and continued toward the entrance.

Suddenly, Marilyn, Breezy, the boys, Officer Connor, and Toni appeared at the door. I looked at Toni and held up the bag.

I proudly affirmed, "This is the bag with Sierra's phone!"

Officer Connor stuck out his hand and declared, "I'll take that. We need to verify that it's her phone."

Toni interjected, "I'd like to take a look at it. If she says it's Sierra's, you can bet it is."

He disputed, "There's no proof that this is Sierra's."

My guides alerted me: *Remember that she saved two numbers in the phone.*

I intervened, "Officer Connor, two numbers are saved in that phone. One is my phone number, and the other is Sierra's sister, Marisol. The numbers are listed under *M* and *K*. Which represents Katharine and Marisol."

He snarled and then opened the bag. He pulled the phone out and pushed the power button to turn it on. When the phone powered up, a blank screen popped up. Toni leaned over his shoulder and tapped the *Contacts* icon. Two contacts were listed: *K* and *M*.

Officer Conner looked disappointed. Toni pushed the *K* under the contacts, and my phone immediately began to ring in my pocket. I pulled out my phone and held it up for everyone to see. As the phone rang and vibrated in my hand, you could see the glowing words displayed on the screen: *Sierra's private phone.*

Toni turned to Officer Connor, "This should be enough proof that there's a problem. The call log shows that the phone has not been used in several weeks."

He shut the phone off and dropped it back in the bag, trying not to make eye contact with us. Looking at the ground, he replied, "What I see is four adults and two children trespassing."

Marilyn and I looked at each other hopelessly. We knew exactly what that meant. Something else was going on, and he was not interested in pursuing this disappearance.

Toni acknowledged, "I understand."

Officer Connor clarified, "Sierra got herself into some trouble. In her line of work, that's the kind of thing that happens. I suggest you all go back to the hotel and leave in the morning. If anything comes up, I will contact Toni."

We all shuffled back to the van with our heads hung low. The thrill of the chase had dissipated, and everyone seemed exhausted. All I wanted to do at this point was get in the van and relax. Apparently, Officer Conner had a different plan.

He motioned to Marilyn and told her to open the back of the van. We looked at each other puzzled as she complied with his request. When the back hatch raised, Zach's backpack tumbled onto the ground.

Officer Conner picked it up and unzipped the main compartment. He looked inside and exclaimed, "Ah ha! What do we have here? Fireworks! There's enough here to light up the whole city."

He set the backpack aside and reached for something else lodged underneath the suitcases and bags. As if he is pulling a rabbit out of a hat, he quickly yanks out Breezy's diorama project.

Officer Conner turned to the group, and, holding up the project, declared, "What in the hell is this sick depiction of a murder?"

Breezy quickly answered, "Hey, that's my project from forensic class. I got an A on that!"

He grunted and then tossed it aside next to the backpack. Next, he pulled out a baseball bat, looked at it inquisitively, and threw it with the other items on the ground.

Lastly, he pulled Breezy's Poison Ivy wig from the Comic-Con costume. He shook his head and looked at me with scrutiny.

"Using disguises?" he queried.

He looked over the rest of the items and tossed a couple of Star Wars lightsabers into the field.

He continued his harassment, "You all look like you're planning something shady. The items in this vehicle all look suspicious. I would hate to have to run you all in for intent to commit a crime."

Toni interjected, "Officer Conner, come on. Give them a break. They're just trying to help like I asked them to. What's changed with you suddenly?"

He abruptly turned to her and stared with dagger eyes. Then, as if sharply breaking a hypnotized trance, he changed his attitude. "Awe, it's all good. I'm just having some fun," he giggled.

He turned back to us and smiled, "Seriously, though. You all should leave the search to Toni and me. I don't want any of you getting hurt. You should leave now and return to Texas, where you belong."

Toni nodded to me and gave a half salute. I could read her psychically saying: *Don't worry, we'll get in contact later.*

I could tell Marilyn was shaking as we all got back into the van. She turned the ignition, put the van in drive, and headed down the road. Nobody made a sound as we drove into the distance.

We got about ten minutes down the road before Marilyn realized she didn't know where to go. She looked into the rearview mirror and asked, "Katharine, what are we going to do?"

Before I could get a word out, Ramsey yelled, "Are we going to jail?"

Zach looked at Ramsey and then turned to the back to look at me. Appearing scared, he asked, "Mom, are we going to be okay?"

"We're going to be fine," I assured him.

My guidance was to return to the hotel, so I told Marilyn to take us there until we could figure things out. I could sense Officer Connor following us, but I didn't say anything because I didn't want the kids to get worried.

We pulled into the hotel parking lot, and everyone quickly jumped out of the van. We were excited to get to our room and decompress. As we were standing at the check-in counter, I noticed Officer Connor's car pull out of the parking lot and onto the main road.

We got to our room and settled onto the beds. We were exhausted as the adrenaline purged from our bodies. There was a silence in the room, and everyone's eyes started to close for an afternoon nap.

We were startled from a loud knock at the door. We all turned to look at each other. The adrenaline started to rise again. I began to panic.

Marilyn got up, looked through the peep hole, and opened the door. Toni walked through the threshold into the main area.

She looked at me shaking her head in disbelief. I psychically knew that she was being called off the case.

She explained, "Officer Conner called my precinct in Chicago and told them what happened earlier. My boss sent me a message ordering me to leave Oregon. If I knew someone to call and get Officer Conner to leave us alone, I would. I don't understand why his attitude about this whole case changed. It appears there's something he's hiding."

We all sat there for a moment, trying to figure out what was causing Officer Conner to act this way. I felt an anxiousness come over me.

My phone disrupted the silence. I looked to see who was calling. It was Butchie.

I answered sluggishly, "Hi, babe."

He replied, "Hello, babe. I wanted to see what you were up to. You sound tired."

I confessed, "It's been an exhausting day already. We found proof of Sierra being here, but the officer, who seemed like he wanted to help, isn't being so helpful. He's encouraging us to leave and let him handle it."

Butchie sputtered, "Why is he trying to get you guys to leave? Oh well, it doesn't matter. You need to do what he wants and just leave. I can't believe you've done all this and gotten this far!"

He paused momentarily and continued, "You know you can't save everybody. You just can't. I know you care about people and love your clients, but God bless, Katharine. You've stepped over the line with this one. You have a *Mystery Machine* full of kids and two adult women trying to solve a disappearance case three states away. All you need now is a Great Dane named *Scooby Doo*! What are you thinking?"

I looked up at everyone, and they stared back knowing I was getting lectured.

I realized that I needed to talk things over with Toni and decide what to do from here. Butchie was worried about me, but I had this overwhelming feeling that I had to do this.

I apologized, "I'm sorry, babe, but I need to call you back later. Detective Toni is here, and I have to talk to her. I love you. Bye."

Marilyn was looking through one of her bags for something. She pulled out a small piece of paper and said, "Why don't you call Mike? Here's his number."

I replied, "I thought about Mike too. Maybe he can help us."

Toni immediately asked, "Who's Mike?"

Marilyn explained, "He's a friend of Katharine's who works for the federal government."

I added, "I've never asked him for anything before but now I really need some help."

Toni urged, "It may be worth a try."

I called Mike and put him on speaker. Toni explained the situation in detail. He took down the information and told us he would call back in thirty minutes.

When he called back, I put him on speaker.

He said, "An FBI agent named Elijah Jensen will be at your hotel in one hour. Did anyone snap a photo of Officer Conner holding that bag you found on the property?"

"Toni replied, "I did."

"Okay, great," he said. "Go ahead and show that to Elijah when he gets there. Let me know how everything turns out."

The phone call ended, and we ordered food while waiting for Elijah Jensen. After we placed the order, I leaned back on the pillows and closed my eyes. I was energetically drained. I could still feel Sierra's energy from the bag I touched earlier.

I ran my thumb across my index finger. I could psychically see Sierra. She was in a dark space. Looking around, I noticed a wine cellar behind her. She was very still, and oddly, she was still where I had seen her weeks ago.

Chapter 11
Spiritual Crossroad

When I brought my focus back into the room, I noticed Breezy was staring at me. I didn't say anything but smiled lightly.

"What was it, Lassie?" she laughed, referring to the Collie from the TV show *Lassie*. "I can always tell when you're looking at something psychically. What did you see?"

Toni was also interested and said, "Did you see something interesting?"

"Yes," I answered. I saw Sierra again. She was in a dark place. It looked like a wine cellar."

"Did it look like she was safe?" Toni asked.

"I didn't get the sense of that, unfortunately. I got the feeling that she was alive but very terrified. She looked filthy and ungroomed. I realized she was in the same place I visualized her a few weeks ago."

Toni queried, "Do you have any idea how we're going to find her?"

I nodded, "Yes, I feel like if we go back near the area where we found the phone, I could follow Sierra's energy imprint to where it ends. If I follow that, we will find Sierra."

Toni suggested, "Perhaps we should drive up the road later. There were only two neighborhoods that I could see. You could get out at the bottom of the hill and walk from there."

Mike called to confirm the room number and let us know Elijah was at the hotel. A few minutes later, we heard a knock at the door. Toni opened the door, greeted Elijah, and then introduced him to the rest of us. He grabbed a chair, positioned it next to the bed where we were all sitting, and took a seat.

He explained, "I am here to ensure Detective Toni gets treated fairly and to help in this investigation."

He glanced at his watch and then continued, "Right about now, Officer Conner and his superiors are receiving an order from the governor of Oregon. The order states that he should stand aside while we conduct this investigation. But they're also being advised to aid us in any way we need.".

Elijah looked up and asked, "What kind of information have you gathered so far on Sierra?"

Toni explained, "We know the location where she had been jogging each day. Katharine found the phone she had hidden there. It was the phone she used to keep in contact with her sister and Katharine until a few weeks ago. From there, we can follow her energy path and find out where she's been staying."

Elijah looked at me and said, "Mike told me a little bit about your abilities and what you've been seeing. I have a little experience with psychics from other cases I've dealt with. I'm looking forward to working with you."

I was secretly fighting off a panic attack. My hands were clammy, and my mouth was dry. I leaned over the bed and stretched my arm out to grab a glass of water on the nightstand. Drinking water always helps relieve my panic.

As I took a sip, I got an energetic flash. I realized the panic feelings weren't coming from me. They were coming from Sierra. I perceived that I was still tuned into her. This could happen during a traumatic event while a spiritual crossroad is present. It was apparent now that Sierra and I were experiencing this crossroad.

Marilyn turned to Breezy and asked, "Do you mind staying here with the boys while we go and check this out?"

The boys looked at Marilyn with sad and disappointed faces.

Breezy replied, "I will if you believe we should stay here, but I think the safest place in this town is with you guys."

I agreed, "I don't trust Officer Conner or anyone else around here. Even from the beginning, it seemed he was trying to stifle this whole thing. I feel like he knows way more than he lets on. They're safer with us."

Elijah interjected, "We need to get on the road soon—every minute counts. Let's go to the area where the energetic imprint was found, and then we'll let Katharine take the lead from there. The rest of us will follow along in the car and van."

I was sitting on the edge of the bed, fighting off a major panic attack and trying to discern the difference between my energy and Sierra's.

Zach put his arm around my shoulder and asked, "Mom, can Ramsey and I walk with you toward the house, or do we have to ride in the van?"

Toni commented, "The boys need to stay in the van for their safety. We don't know what's going on or what's going to happen."

My legs were shaky, and I felt too weak to stand. It felt bizarre, even for me. I sat there for a minute, wondering if I could walk. I noticed my cell phone vibrating on the bed and picked it up. I saw a text message from Ms. Gibson and opened it. She sent a video of baby raccoons eating and playing at her feet while sitting in her recliner. Jeopardy was playing on her TV, as she painted her remaining *nine* toes neon pink.

I turned the phone toward Zach and played the video for him. We both laughed out loud. *Wow!* I thought. *Ms. Gibson lives a very different life than most, but her crazy videos help calm me down.*

My legs were wobbly as I stood up. I started walking toward the door and heard my spirit guides say, *the weakness in your legs is not yours, so center yourself and ground.*

When we arrived at the abandoned blueberry farm, I exited the van by the dilapidated building and walked along the side of the road toward the hill. At this point, I was remote viewing the area through Sierra's eyes from the last time she jogged the street. Two cars and the van followed me along the road.

I wondered where the second car came from since Elijah and Toni rode together.

I psychically realized it was Officer Conner trailing behind in the second car. We were well into the neighborhood when, suddenly, my spirit guides pointed to one of the houses.

As I walked toward the house, my spirit guides said, *that's the house where you'll find Sierra.*

I immediately turned around and walked to Elijah and Toni's car. Elijah rolled down his window and inquired, "What is it? What do you see?"

I replied, "That's the house where Sierra is. The one with the giant lion statues at the front of the walkway."

Elijah and Toni got out of the car and stood beside me. We watched as Officer Conner pulled up behind us, exited his car, and leaned against the hood. It looked like he was keeping his distance and not interfering, but I was still wary about his presence.

Elijah pulled up some photos on his phone and showed them to me. They were pictures of the house we were at but seemed a little older.

He said, "I pulled this address from an online realtor site. It was listed for sale several years ago, but the inside should be relatively the same."

As he sifted through the photos, he stopped and enlarged a picture of a wine cellar.

He showed me the photo and asked, "Is this the wine cellar where you saw Sierra?"

I nodded, "Yes, that's exactly it."

He confirmed, "Ok, that's all I need. We will knock on the door and see where things go from there. You stay beside the car and make sure no one gets out of the van."

I stood beside the car and watched as they walked up to the house and knocked on the door. A man opened the inside glass door but stayed protected behind the iron security gate. I saw his energy field first and recognized it as Sierra's client. The same energy appeared when she first asked me about taking the trip. At that point, I knew without a shadow of a doubt that this was the guy.

I could hear Elijah talking to him, but I couldn't quite make out the words but I think he asked if his name was Stover Prescott. Then, the man stepped outside the heavy iron gate onto the porch. The gate closed heavily on its own without any effort. I noticed a dark orange in his energy field, which meant he was distraught. He didn't let on by his casual demeanor. I could hear them speaking much more precisely now.

Elijah flashed a badge and asked, "Do you know Sierra Delmar?" Stover paused for a moment, glancing outward toward Officer Conner.

Stover looked back at Elijah and said, "What is all this about?"

Elijah calmly stated, "I am an FBI agent Elijah Jenson, and I want to know if Sierra Delmar is presently in this house?"

Stover's energy darkened and started to fluctuate as he answered, "I don't know anybody named Sierra Delmar."

Toni turned and looked at me, hinting for a signal. I confirmed with a nod that Sierra was there.

She stepped forward, identified herself as Detective Chavez, and insisted, "We need to look around. We have an eyewitness who claims that Sierra Delmar is here."

He looked over Toni's shoulder to Officer Conner and stated, "You know I'm going to need to see a search warrant. I'm working on a manuscript now and don't like being disturbed. If you talk to Officer Conner, he can vouch for me. I have visited this community quite often to work on novels. I get much inspiration from these parts of town and bring a lot of money to the local economy."

I knew all along that Officer Conner was obstructing this search, now we knew why. I could feel Sierra's energy closer than ever. I couldn't stand watching the arrogance of Stover's lies.

I suddenly blurted out, "Stop lying! I know she's in there!"

Elijah and Toni turned to look at me in disbelief at what I had just done.

Stover stepped aside to look at me and yelled, "I don't know who you are, but you have no idea what you're talking about!"

I loudly declared, "I know she's in your wine cellar!"

His eyes widened, and a sense of shock came over his face. Elijah quickly pulled out a document and showed it to him. He and Toni brushed past Stover, threw open the iron security gate, and hurried inside.

Stover turned and yelled to Officer Conner, "Why aren't you helping?" And then quickly followed behind.

I remained out front and remote-viewed Elijah jab Stover in the stomach, demanding a key to unlock the wine cellar door. Stover handed over the key to Toni. She grabbed it and pushed it into the keyhole.

My remote viewing was interrupted by Marilyn and the kids rushing over to me from the van. They all grabbed a piece of me and started rambling with questions.

I protested, "Everyone, stop for a minute! Just hold on. I need to see what's going on."

I glanced up as Officer Conner walked past us. He stood by the front door, looking directly back at me, and said, "If you think your well-heeled friend helped you today, think again. This is my town."

We watched him enter the house as Marilyn squeezed my hand in fear.

I turned to Marilyn and assured her, "I'm not so worried since I am doing what the universe had planned. With God for us, who could be against us? Besides, I think Elijah has some things he'll be recommending regarding Officer Conner's harassment."

I paused, took a deep breath, and advised everyone, "Keep quiet for a few minutes while I remote view what's happening."

I saw Toni open the door and lunge toward Sierra, who was chained to the floor, naked, trying to keep warm with a blanket wrapped around her. The brackets around her wrists had been welded to chains that were bolted to the cement floor. They were barely long enough to let her squat on the nearby bucket.

The air smelled like feces and urine, with hardly any ventilation. You could tell the cellar hadn't seen a bottle of wine in years and was being used as a storage room. There were paper plates with dried food stains strung all over the place. Empty plastic water bottles were filling up an empty box in the corner. There were condoms and sex toys piled up in a small half-opened suitcase nearby.

Sierra looked filthy, with stains of dirt, feces, and blood all over her body. She was crying profusely and shaking uncontrollably. I saw Toni unlock the clamps around her wrists and try to help her up. Sierra buckled to her knees and couldn't stand on her own. Elijah was on his phone calling 911 for an ambulance. Stover was nowhere near the wine cellar. I had a flash of him in his office talking to his lawyer.

My remote viewing was suddenly interrupted by loud, persistent sirens in the distance. I realized the ambulance was approaching. I told everyone to move to the sidewalk so they wouldn't impede the incoming ambulance.

I started crying when Toni appeared at the door, waving for the EMS workers to hurry up. Everything turned into a movie scene as the EMS workers unloaded the stretcher from the back of the ambulance and carried it to the front door of the home.

We all waited in anticipation as the EMS workers did their job to prepare Sierra for evacuation. Several minutes later, Elijah broke the vacant front door scene, leading the EMS workers outside. They had Sierra strapped to the top of the stretcher underneath the warmth of several blankets.

I stood off to the side with Marilyn and the kids as they carried Sierra down the steps. Toni walked to the back of the ambulance and motioned for me to come over. I didn't hesitate and walked briskly to the ambulance.

Sierra looked up from the stretcher and reached out to me with her fingers extended. I grabbed ahold of them as tears streamed from my eyes. She winked at me and whimpered, "You're my hero. You've always had my back without judgment. Love you, girl."

Toni abruptly interjected, "I'm going to ride to the hospital with her. I'll call you guys later." The ambulance's back door closed and then pulled away from the curb.

A few minutes later, Elijah came back out of the house. He pulled us to the side and said, "When we walked down into the cellar, Sierra had been chained to the floor. She is experiencing muscle atrophy in her legs and couldn't stand, along with being malnourished. I imagine that's what you kept getting, Katharine."

Marilyn asked, "Is Stover going to be arrested?"

Immediately, my spirit guides said, *no, he's too well-connected.*

Elijah explained, "The FBI would be watching Stover. Still, because of the nature of what Sierra was doing there, countercharges could be brought against her by the state of Oregon. The state holds this type of business illegal. Sierra had decided not to press charges when I briefly spoke to her about Stover. I will check back with her when I visit the hospital. She understands the implications if she were to press charges."

Marilyn's energy indicated that she was very agitated.

She asked, "Katharine, does it bother you that Stover is not going to be arrested for this crime? Or that Sierra is not pressing charges? Doesn't it bother you that nothing will happen to him?"

I replied, "Marilyn, I've psychically read for so many different situations that this outcome doesn't surprise me. I am mainly grateful that we found her alive. I'm grateful that I was able to make this trip. Had we not come, Sierra would have suffered a lot more and this would have all been swept under the rug. This man has a lot of money and can make situations like this disappear. But know this—he can't hide from karma."

I explained, "The universe's plan from the moment I met Sierra was to create a spiritual lesson and experience for us all. We all participated in this lesson: you, me, Breezy, Ramsey, and Zach. Even Butchie had a part. I appreciate all of you so much."

Marilyn looked at me and asked, "Did you know this all along? I mean that we would save her?"

I answered, "No, I didn't. I just knew Sierra wasn't dead. And I knew this trip was more than just for her salvation. It was to see that I could push through the difficult energies. Being around other people's negative energy has always felt crippling, but I found out that I can push through it. Just like when you had me focus on taking calls during the trip. It took my focus off the anxiety of traveling."

Marilyn grabbed and hugged me tight. I could feel her energy shift as we embraced. We both began to cry. I didn't even know why she was crying, but I was crying because I was grateful to have her as a friend.

When we finished hugging, we decided to take the kids out to eat for a fun meal. They certainly had just endured quite the experience, and we all needed to decompress.

There was a local restaurant known for its delicious food and live entertainment that we decided to go to. When we arrived, the kids became excited about the stage in the restaurant's center. It had a forest, a fort, and a two-story castle. The sign above read "Adventures in Sherwood Forest. Performances nightly."

They even had a souvenir shop that sold things you may find in Sherwood Forest like children's bows, arrows, and swords. We all enjoyed the moment, and for the first time, I was not concerned about how far away from home I was.

When we got back to the hotel, I called Butchie. I explained everything that happened and ensured him that we were safe. He seemed relieved that everything turned out the way it did and was happy that we would be returning soon.

Butchie confessed before we ended the call, "You had me worried there for a while, but I really am proud of you. This was a great accomplishment for you, and not just for saving

Sierra. You overcame some pretty tough obstacles. You truly are an angel on earth, and I love you."

Later that night, Toni called and expressed, "When I first heard about you, I didn't understand how you worked or what to expect. I've never been interested in anything other than facts, which I focus on when investigating anything. You changed the way I view paranormal and psychic intuition. The bottom line is that I wanted to thank you. Sierra is doing well and should be released from the hospital in a couple of days. I called Marisol and told her everything that had happened. She was certainly appreciative of what you did for Sierra."

Smiling, I responded, "Thank you, Toni. I know it took a lot for you to say that, and you didn't really like me at first. I knew you didn't quite understand me. I'm grateful Sierra is doing well. May we come by in the morning on our way out to visit?"

Toni quickly responded. "Yes, Sierra would love that. I have you on speaker now. She's been listening and smiling. I hope you can relax tonight. Goodnight."

I shared the phone call with everyone, and then we celebrated a successful trip by ordering room service with popcorn and 7-up to accompany our movie."

The following day, we had a light breakfast and stopped by the hospital to see Sierra. I called Butchie on the way to the hospital. I left a message saying, "We're stopping by the hospital to visit Sierra, and then we'll be on the road if you want to call us later."

I turned to the kids when we reached Sierra's hospital room door and told them that if at any point, they didn't want to stay in the room, they could just come out to the hallway and stay together until I was finished."

I pushed open the door slowly. Sierra was watching the TV and Toni was in a recliner next to the window. It appeared like she was waking up from a nap.

Sierra noticed us all peeping in and smiled. "Come in," she called out.

I returned the smile and moved toward her. I sat in the chair next to the bed. She reached her hand for me, and I held it with mine. Toni stood up and moved next to the bed. Sierra asked Toni to take down the railing on the side of the bed. Toni released the railing and dropped it to the side.

Sierra turned to me and asked, "May I hug you?"

I didn't say anything and just moved in close to hold her. When I put my arms around her, she began sobbing profusely. Through her crying, she said, "I'm so sorry. I know from our conversations that you struggle with anxiety. You told me how hard it is for you to leave the house. And yet you did this for me. I'm grateful for you, Katharine."

She continued, "Stover wasn't planning to let me go. When I get back home, I will receive physical therapy and see Dr. Vasquez again."

Toni politely interjected, "I would not have found you had it not been for Katharine. It was strange that she knew details about you that I didn't know. She knew you were not dead. And she knew you had a scar on top of your right toe."

Sierra laughed as she yanked the sheet off her right foot. "There's the scar," she declared.

I laughed and nodded my head.

Sierra asked, "Will you continue to read for me?"

I looked directly into her eyes and replied, "I genuinely care about you, and those emotions got me on the road. I was able to overcome traveling out of my comfort zone, encountering new spirits, property trauma, and police harassment. I'm looking forward to what the universe wants us to experience next."

Sierra motioned for her cell phone. Toni handed it to her, and she opened some photos to show me.

"Look here," she said. "The retreat where Owen has been staying, has continued to send me daily photos. I am looking forward to being home with him."

We all laughed and admired the photos of Owen.

As we exited the hospital, I realized my cell phone had a backlog of text messages I had not opened. I decided to wait until we got back on the road to look at them.

We loaded up into the van and Marilyn asked, "Is there any place we should stop on the way back?"

Zach excitedly held up a brochure about ghost trails he had picked up from a truck stop on the way to Oregon.

Ramsey yelled out, "Yes, let's go ghost hunting."

I could see Marilyn was waiting for a response from me as she looked in the rearview mirror. I couldn't help but laugh at their desire to go ghost hunting after all we had been through.

I broke the silence, "You know what? Let's stop at a few of those places. I think it'll be fun."

Marilyn announced, "We're probably going to make a lot of people mad, freeing up the spirits from their tourist traps."

We all laughed for the next few minutes and settled in for the long trip ahead.

I decided to sign on to the hotline and take some calls over the next few hours. In the meantime, I answered some text messages and called back clients who wanted to book appointments. I fluffed up the pillows and laid back.

Staring out the window, I noticed the sky appeared brighter than usual. I thought perhaps it was from my newfound freedom. As I contemplated this whole experience, I realized what the real spiritual lesson was: Most of the anxiety I had experienced was not even mine. It was everyone else's. I needed to learn how to separate that energy to be at peace with my own. I knew it wasn't going to be easy, but neither was this trip, and I survived it.

At that moment, I felt pretty good about everything and started to fade off to sleep.

Suddenly, the phone rang. It was a hotline call.

Hmmm, I thought. *Should I take this call or just go to sleep?*

My spirit guides chimed in and said, *if you take this call, be prepared.*

I was sleep-deprived, and perhaps curiosity got the best of me.

I answered, "Hi, this is Katharine. How may I help you?"

A voice burst out, "Hi, Katharine, it's Roxy, and boy, am I glad you're on today..."

About the author

Award winning and bestselling author of How I Found My Superpowers: An Introduction to the Spirit World, the workbook series Self Help Slut®, and It Was Murder. Katharine Branham is a free-flowing psychic medium. She can tap into the spirit world without blinking an eye. She has incredible gifts she learned along her spiritual journey. She explains that anyone can learn to find their own superpowers. Katharine's Superpowers include open channel, remote viewer, clairvoyant, clairaudient, clairsentient, energy healing, and medical intuitive. Katharine grew up in Houston, Texas and currently lives in The Woodlands where she participates in animal rights and rescue. Her life mission is to help humanity return to their natural blueprint and awaken within.

Also by Katharine Branham

Made in United States
Orlando, FL
30 September 2024